IRISH ENCOUNTER

hope Toler Dougherty

Mantle Rock Publishing
www.MantleRockPublishing.com

©2015 Hope Toler Dougherty

Published by Mantle Rock Publishing
2879 Palma Road
Benton, KY 42025
www.mantlerockpublishing.com

Printed in the United States of America

ISBN 978-0-9961734-2-1 Print Book

ISBN 978-0-9961734-1-4 Ebook

Cover by Diane Turpin

Published in association with Jim Hart of Hartline Literary Agency, Pittsburgh, PA

Thank you/Acknowledgements

Kevin—Thank you for introducing me to Ireland in 1993 and for taking all of us in 2000 and again in 2007. We missed 2014, but I'm ready to go back whenever you are. Thank you for your unconditional love, support, and enthusiasm for most everything I do.

Anna, Hattie, Lane, and Quinn—Thank you for praying for me and unabashedly sharing about my writing with your friends. You are spectacular people. I'm so proud of you and so grateful to be your mother.

Momma and Daddy—Thank you for your constant prayers and steadfast belief in my ability to write a book. I love you.

Lisa Carter—You, my friend, are a good writer, a patient teacher, and a faithful roommate with an almost-disturbing dark side— just enough to keep things interesting.

Erynn Reconnu Newman, Charity Tinnan—Our monthly critique sessions helped me grow as a writer and helped make this manuscript better. Thank you.

Peggy Leggett—Thank you for reading one of the early drafts and for your gentle suggestions. I treasure your friendship.

Deb Raney—You read this manuscript in its scraggily infancy, yet you encouraged a scared, uncertain writer with your sweet spirit and kind counsel. Thank you for giving me the confidence to keep writing.

Patti Lacy and Sarah Richardson—Thank you for your editing advice. Patti, I have such special memories of that quick meeting over coffee in St. Louis. Your engaging smile drew me to you, and your encouraging words were a balm to a newbie stressing at her first national conference.

Rachel Stone, Emily Willard, Paula Maurer, and Suzanne Mitchell—Thank you for not laughing at me when I finally admitted I was writing a book, but, more importantly, thank you for praying for me when I was just writing with no agent and no contract—nothing but a dream.

BSF ladies—Thank you for praying for me, for asking about my progress, for being excited for me, for being my friends.

Carolyn Beasley—Thank you for welcoming me onto Heelside Farms. Your insights added authenticity to the scenes with Grainne.

Blue Ridge Mountain Christian Writers Conference and American Christian Fiction Writers—thank you for providing support, teaching, tools, advice, and friends.

Kathy Cretsinger—Thank you for taking a chance on a story set in Ireland.

Jim Hart—Thank you for never giving up on this manuscript. You ignored the no's and kept searching for the yes.

God—Thank you for giving me the ability to write, the desire to write, the opportunity to write, and friends and family who support my writing. Praise God from whom all blessings flow!

Chapter 1

Ellen Shepherd's fingers trembled as she fiddled with the zipper on her small backpack. "I can't wait to see Galway again. It's been so long since we were here." As soon as the words were out of her mouth, an image of her husband, dead now for three years, smiling and popping a piece of brown bread into his mouth, wavered in her mind.

Was she crazy? She didn't want to see Galway without Steve.

"Mom, are you sure you're up to going into town? I should be finished with my exam around noon. Relax this morning, and then I'll come back here for lunch." Olivia, a college junior, sipped coffee out of a mug depicting the Cliffs of Moher. Natural light from the cathedral windows behind her brightened the kitchen despite this morning's low-hanging clouds.

Ellen smiled at her daughter and banished the bittersweet memories that wanted to join forces with the dark clouds overhead. "I appreciate your concern for your poor ol' mom, but I'm not ready for a rocking chair and a warm blanket yet. At least allow me to celebrate my forty-fourth birthday before you cart me away to a retirement center." Ellen drank the last of her orange juice.

Olivia rolled her hazel eyes, the exact color of Ellen's, and bit her toast shimmering with a glaze of blackberry jam. "Mmm. You should plant some blackberry bushes when you get back home. Then next year make some delicious jam like this." She wiggled the remaining half of the triangle at her mom.

"Thanks for adding not one, but two items to my to-do list. They'll have to roost at the bottom for now, though." A pall crept into her chest as she thought about her yarn shop, holding its own but barely, and her farm, the fields lying fallow this year because of her uncle's stroke in March. What would next year bring? She didn't want to think about the answer to that question. She wondered how many of her customers would remain true once the chain crafts store opened in the new shopping complex. If she didn't find a farmer to lease the acres or if her idea to partner with a university as a study farm didn't pan out…

Why in the world had she agreed to come on this crazy trip? She should be at home finding solutions to her problems, not gallivanting half way around the world.

Be strong. Do not be terrified. The Lord your God will be with you wherever you go.

The reminder from her morning devotion loosened her rigid fingers strangling the backpack straps and rescued her from the negative thoughts threatening to ruin her day.

As if reading her mind, Olivia interrupted her thoughts. "Is Uncle Joe doing any better?"

Ellen shrugged. She pictured the old man in the rehab center, sitting in a wheel chair with the right side of his face wrenched downward, his right hand curled into an involuntary fist. She knew his strenuous days of farming were behind him. "He shuffles a few steps at a time with a walker. His speech is still mangled." Her forehead wrinkled with worry about the man who had taken over managing the farm after Steve's death.

"Mom, stop." Olivia held up her hand like a traffic cop. "No sad thoughts today. You're here for an adventure, right?"

Ellen smiled at her daughter. "Yes." She checked the contents of her backpack, zipped it closed, and glanced out the windows at the rose garden that dominated the backyard. "I don't think I could ever tire of this view. Those roses are gorgeous."

"Yeah, they are. You can help dead head them. One responsibility of my sweet living arrangement here at Tohlfair." Olivia dusted toast crumbs off her fingers.

"No problem. Maeve was kind to secure this 'sweet' house for you." Sweet indeed. Maeve, her Irish friend from their home exchange, had arranged the house-sitting assignment for a professor on sabbatical from Galway University. "I hope you sent her a thank you note." She delivered the last line in a sing-song voice to temper the manners check.

"Of course, I did, Mother." She sang back and stacked her plate on top of her mom's. "And when she found out about your visit, she invited us to come for tea this afternoon. Sound good?"

"Sounds wonderful."

"Mom, you yawned five times yesterday during lunch. Are you sure you want—"

"You counted my yawns?" Ellen raised her eyebrows. "And I thought you were counting the cute guys roller blading down the boardwalk at Salthill yesterday. Speaking of cute guys, will we see Tristan today? It's a shame he didn't join us." Her curiosity had been raised by the friend who'd accompanied Olivia to the airport two days earlier but had skipped out on lunch…and church.

When he'd bowed with a flourish and announced in his Scottish brogue, "A gallant gentleman at your service, m'lady," she'd liked him straightaway. Tristan Campbell's loose, walnut brown curls partially hid a silver loop in one ear. His vibrant personality demanded attention, and his sparkling blue eyes promised fun. "He seems like the perfect knight in shining armor." He'd scooped up her bags and carried them to his Peugeot like they weighed about as much as a sack of yarn. "The gap between his front teeth is cute, too."

A cross between a grunt and a snort punctuated Olivia's reply. "Don't go there. Tristan sits across from me in Irish Lit. He was nice to drive me, but we're buddies. That's it." She carried the dishes to the dishwasher. "What'll you do for three hours by yourself?"

"Window shopping, have a cup of tea, more shopping." Ellen replaced the jam in the small refrigerator across from the island with the stove top. "I have to start my travel piece, too."

Olivia jerked straight up from the lower dishwasher rack, her eyes stretched wide. "Your what?"

"My travel article. Remember Sam at *The Dispatch*? He asked me to write a piece about my trip. My adventure, he called it."

"Cool. So he wants something to spice up the engagement pictures and obituaries, huh?"

"Don't forget sports and the community calendar."

Olivia chuckled. "Hey, maybe this is the start of a new career. My mom, ace reporter."

"If the pay is good, I might consider it. Right now, I have plenty on my plate with the shop and figuring out the future of the farm. In fact, that'll be my first priority when I get back." Her eyebrows pulled together as thoughts of her responsibilities resurfaced.

"Mom, stop thinking about home. You're supposed to have fun for the next two weeks. Scott and Laurel and I gave you this trip for a reason. We want to see your sparkle again."

Goose bumps pebbled her arms. Could she enjoy Galway without Steve? Did she even want to?

She shivered and nodded. "I know. Fun—my holy grail for the next fourteen days." Glancing at the clock, she grabbed her backpack. "We've got ten minutes before the City Direct runs, right? So, where are we meeting for lunch?"

കൊകാരൽ

Ellen crossed out the last sentence on her yellow pad. Why couldn't she find the perfect adjectives to describe what she'd seen on the drive from Shannon to Galway two days ago? She'd also counted the myriad shades of greens she'd seen as the car sped by pastures of grazing sheep.

Now she sat at a table in Kane's Café, moderately crowded with people reading newspapers or working on laptops. She twirled her ink pen with her left hand and held a warm cup of tea in the other.

She smiled thinking about the hour or so she could enjoy in this sidewalk café before she met Olivia for lunch. As she took a break from her writing pad, she noticed a little old man at a table near the door studying her. She threw a quick smile in his direction, glanced at her watch, and checked her travel dictionary. Virid—vividly green. Yes, she'd seen virid yesterday. Viridescent—

slightly green or greenish. Everything is at least slightly green in Ireland. Viridian—chrome green—hmmm, probably. Could she work these words into her story or were they too much?

The sound of someone clearing his throat at close range broke her concentration, and the sight of the older gentleman standing in front of her table surprised her. His brown eyes twinkled as he clutched his Irish cap with both hands in front his tweed vest. "Hello. Sure, I'm sorry to intrude." He twisted his cap and shifted his feet. "My name is Seamus Fleming and you, well, you remind me of someone. I just had to come over to say, 'hello.'"

Ellen offered her hand and smiled. "Hello, Mr. Fleming. I'm Ellen Shepherd. Nice to meet you." A reserved person, she hesitated about what to do next. The warnings of Suzie and Frankie, friends from church, reverberated in her mind, "Be wary of strangers. Don't be too nice. You don't want to end up as the next missing person story on the morning news shows."

But Ellen normally read people very well, and she had a good feeling about this stranger. She gestured to the chair across from her. "Would you like to sit down?"

"Oh, thanks a million, dear, and please call me Seamus." Resting his cap on his thigh, he settled on the chair like an eager student on the first day of school.

"Okay, Seamus." Ellen peaked at her watch.

"I told you that you reminded me of someone. It's my wife. You remind me of my dear wife, Fiona. God rest her soul." He crossed himself.

The love in his voice drew her to him. She smiled. "That sounds like a wonderful compliment. Thank you."

"Oh, indeed. She looked like you a bit with her green eyes and chestnut hair swinging above her shoulders. She used to sit and write like you. Every day. Letters and letters to so many people. She was a great encourager." He toyed with the wooden buttons on his vest, and she noticed the heart, hands, and crown that comprised the gold *claddagh* wedding ring on his left hand. "I miss her."

"She sounds like a special person." Leaning toward him, Ellen patted his arm.

"Indeed, very special. The great heartbreak of her life was that we were never able to have any children, but, after a grieving period, she reasoned that God had other plans for us. So she set about to encourage other people."

"Did you adopt children?" The words were out of her mouth before she could stop them, but he didn't seem to mind the personal question.

He shook his head. "No, we prayed about it, but the opportunity never came. We didn't feel God's leading that way, you know. We had several god children, mind you, and enough nieces and nephews and now grandnieces and grandnephews to keep us busy and happy." He paused and then continued with effort, "She's been gone for almost five years, my Fiona, and I still miss her dearly. I do at that." His gaze dropped to his lap.

"Well, I'm glad I made you think of her today." She stole another glance at her watch and realized the start of Olivia's exam neared.

"Sure, I'm keeping you from something. I'm sorry. I just wanted to say, 'hello,' and here I am running on and on, intruding on your time and all." The chair squeaked as he pushed away from the table.

"No, no. You're fine. I just—I promised my daughter I'd pray for her at 10:30 when her exam starts. She's in class at NUI. It's almost time."

"Oh, and you're a believer, too, then?" His eyes shined with pleasure. "Just like my Fiona."

She nodded. "Yes, I am."

He stood up this time and said, "Well, I'm glad to have met you, Ellen Shepherd. Thanks a million, dear, for spending time with an old man. You've made my day." He beamed a charming grin over the table.

"I'm glad you came over, too, Seamus. I'm happy to have met you." Shaking his hand again, she smiled into his crinkly face. He turned and exited the café, whistling as he settled his cap back on top of his wispy hair.

Ellen picked up her pen, rolled it between her fingers, and

doodled in the margin of her paper. At 10:30, she rested the pen and closed her eyes. She prayed for wisdom for Olivia, for total recall of all she'd studied, and for a calm spirit to complete the test successfully. Thanking God for the chance encounter with Seamus Fleming, she also asked for a blessing for the sweet man. Before she finished, she asked to be sensitive to anyone else He might bring into her life.

After the prayer, she opened her eyes, noticing for the first time another man at a table to the left of hers. He lounged, watching her, and their eyes met for a second before she broke the connection and resumed writing.

"Do you really believe that works?"

She glanced toward the table where the words came from. The stranger continued staring.

Her heartbeat accelerated. He was talking to her? "I'm sorry, what?"

"Praying. Praying for your daughter's exam. Do you honestly believe that works?" Leaning back in his chair with his head tilted to one side, he clasped his hands just above his battered, leather belt. Fatigue emanated from him like Pigpen's perpetual dust cloud.

"You were eavesdropping." She laid her pen down on the table.

"I wasn't eavesdropping." He shrugged his broad shoulders. "You two were just talking so loud I couldn't help but hear what you were saying."

"We were not talking loudly. We were having a private conversation at my table." Her usually cool temper warmed to simmering.

"So do you?" He persisted.

"What?"

"Believe in prayer."

"Of course, I believe in prayer. I wouldn't pray if I didn't believe." Her voice sounded a little prim to her own ears. She softened her tone. "Don't you believe?"

Ignoring her question, he rose from his table instead. Grabbing his mug of coffee, he moved over to the chair that Seamus had occupied only minutes earlier. She watched wide-eyed as he placed the mug onto her table, pulled back the chair, and sank down in front of her.

Chapter 2

He settled into the chair, extending his long legs to the side of the table. "Why?"

She knitted her eyebrows. "Why do I believe in prayer?"

"Yes. Why?" His nonchalant pose belied the sharp interest she saw in his eyes.

She returned his stare. With his two or three days' growth of beard covering his face and his black hair long enough to curl over his collar, he presented a scruffy, shaggy figure in his crumpled, khaki clothes. His arrogant air ruffled her serene disposition.

He waited for her answer.

She licked her lips. She couldn't recall having to explain her feelings about prayer before. "Because I see evidence of answered prayer all over the Bible and because I experience God's answers pretty much every day. That's why." She folded up an inch of the top page of her pad.

"That's sweet." A tiny smile hinted that her answer amused him.

"It's not sweet. It's the truth." She frowned back at his amusement and folded another inch.

"The truth for you maybe."

"Oh, my stars. Truth is truth. Truth is absolute." She couldn't believe her quiet morning of writing had turned into a debate with a homeless-looking stranger.

"So you want to discuss philosophy?"

"No No, I do not. I loathe philosophy." She crimped another

section of paper and realized she'd created a fan on her pad.

He scratched his chin. "Why?"

"I had a horrible college professor who ruined it for me. So, no, thanks. No philosophy." Pressing her forearm against the pad to smooth out the folds, she grabbed her pen hoping he'd take the hint and leave.

"Fine. We don't have to discuss philosophy. What else do you believe in?" Leaning back in the chair, he folded his tan arms over his chest, crossing his legs at the ankles.

She chewed her lip. She didn't want to discuss anything with this man. She wanted him to go back to his own table and leave her alone, but then she remembered her prayer. *Seriously, God? Is this annoying guy the answer to that quick little prayer a while ago?* She straightened in her chair and let out a breath, preparing for battle.

"Well, I believe in divine appointments." She leaned her head to the side. "Maybe you're one for me today." She threw those words out like a chess move, challenging him to voice his disagreement.

"You believe God brought me over here?" His eyebrows disappeared behind the locks of jumbled hair that fell over his brow. Skepticism winked at her from his eyes.

"I don't know for sure. What I do know is that you boldly eavesdropped—"

"Boldly?" More amusement replaced the skepticism.

"Yes. You boldly eavesdropped on my private conversation, you interrupted my writing time, and you sat down at my table without being invited. That's what I know."

He rubbed the handle of the mug with his thumb. "Why does it bother you so much that I heard your conversation?"

Good question. Why did it? She and Seamus hadn't talked about anything inappropriate. They'd simply shared a few kind words. This man sitting across the table irritated her and, though she'd never admit it to him, intimidated her, too. Her normal circle of social contacts—prayer shawl ministry, aquarobics class, school planning committee—none of these groups included brooding, button-pushing, edgy men.

She poured more tea into her cup, hoping the warmth would soothe her. "Your eavesdropping doesn't bother me because I didn't say anything I'm ashamed of. I didn't give away any deep, dark secrets."

His quick grin and snort suggested he couldn't believe she might have any deep, dark secrets, aggravating her even more.

"It just irritates me that you listened, and now you're throwing my words back in my face. For Pete's sake, it's impertinent of you."

"Impertinent? Now that's a word I don't hear every day. Are you an English teacher or a librarian?" His slight smile should have softened the remark, but a mischievous spark lit his gaze, fanning her exasperation.

She forced herself to take in a slow breath for ten beats then trickle it out again before answering. "Although both occupations are admirable, I'm neither one. But you, sir, are annoying."

"And impertinent. Don't forget impertinent, right?" A cheeky grin accompanied the teasing note in his voice.

How could she end this conversation? No one had teased her in forever, and she wasn't sure she liked it—especially from this stranger. She shook her head. "I don't know you. I'm just observing."

"But you've already begun to form an opinion of me." He yawned behind his large palm.

At least he has some manners

"What else do you think about me?"

She rubbed her index finger across her bottom lip and studied him. Should she really reveal her honest thoughts? He resembled a vagrant with his dusty, wrinkled clothes, his shaggy hair, and banged up boots, but he acted like he owned the café, not exactly winsome attributes. She didn't want to hurt his feelings, but maybe if she answered his question with as much honesty as she could, he'd slink back to his own table, leaving her to write in peace again.

She sent up a quick prayer. *Okay, God. If I'm really supposed to talk to this man, help me. Please.* She inhaled. "Fine." She huffed an exhale. "You look like you just quit a safari expedition that, that... Well, your clothes are…" Shaking her head, she swallowed the adjectives that formed on her tongue. She couldn't say them. She could not describe his clothes as she saw them—dirt-streaked, wrinkled, grungy—no matter how much she wanted him to leave her alone.

Her gaze flickered to his dusty cuffs.

He glanced at his clothes and laughed. "Oh man. I guess I do look a little suspect. Sorry. Had to catch a plane in a hurry." He tugged at the hem of his shirt. A few wrinkles disappeared. "This is kind of fun…I think. What's next?"

"You really want me to keep going?" The prospect of hurting him wrinkled her brow.

He shrugged. "Why not?"

"Okay. Your word choice and accent tell me you're American. In fact, every now and then, a twangy word betrays you, and says, 'southern.' So I think either you grew up in the South or you've lived there." She sighed before continuing.

"So let's see. If you grew up in the South, you probably have some knowledge of Christianity. The South is supposed to be the Bible Belt, right?" She sipped her tea. "Maybe you went to church with your family, but if you didn't, you could've attended a Bible summer camp with a friend and that's how you found out about God."

She dropped her gaze, thinking about him as a young boy. "Now, though, you seem quite opposed to prayer. I'm wondering if—" She trailed off, considering reasons for his negative attitude.

"Did you believe at one time, and then something happened? Something—bad maybe?" Her eyes followed her fingers tracing the rim of her teacup. "If that's right, then maybe you used to believe, but now you choose not to believe." Meeting his stare with wide-open eyes, she waited for him to answer, shocked a bit at her presumption of him.

He'd remained still during the last half of her monologue except the teasing grin had deserted his face. His jaw tightened. His gray eyes narrowed, turning icy. She sensed she'd stumbled onto something true.

"Geez, Louise. I'm sorry. I didn't mean to make you angry.

I just…I just supposed things." She hadn't deliberately chosen words to antagonize him, but now that she'd clearly struck a painful chord with him, perhaps he'd move back to his table and leave her alone. Hoping that he'd accept her apology, she waited for him to speak.

He blinked twice before he shrugged again and gave what sounded like a forced laugh. "'Oh, my stars. For Pete's sake. Geez, Louise.' What is this—high school—in Mayberry?"

Her simmering blood boiled for the second time. This man infuriated her. She'd tried to be obedient, to talk with him if God wanted her to, but his insufferable attitude grated on her every nerve. He'd worn out his manufactured welcome.

"You're insulting my word choice again. And that's one of my favorite shows, by the way, so don't knock it." She squeezed the pen in her fist.

"Sorry to ruffle your feathers. I like Andy and Barney, too, by the way. So—some common ground."

Common ground indeed. She didn't want common ground. She wanted him to let her finish her tea in peace. An idea to turn the tables on him popped into her mind. She bit the inside of her cheek to suppress a smile.

"Okay, if we're in high school, then what's this?" She spread her open palms on the table. "A date?"

"What?" His drooping eyelids widened.

Yes. Caught him off guard. A flush of satisfaction bolstered her confidence at the surprise registering on his face.

Still trying to provoke him to leave, she smiled as sweet as her old babysitter had taught her to. "Uh-huh. A date. You're a man. I'm a woman. We're talking. We're at a café." She nodded. "A date." She rested her chin on her clasped hands, anticipating a quick "Ciao, baby" thrown over his retreating shoulder.

He didn't move.

He watched her for a couple of beats and nodded, stretching a slow grin across his tan face. His earlier, mocking smile disappeared, and a new one took its place. This smile, a real one, crinkled the corners of his eyes and added a sparkle she hadn't noticed before. A tingle, familiar but long-forgotten, tickled the bottom of her stomach.

He could be handsome with those eyes—probably was handsome underneath the shaggy hair, the stubble, the attitude. Oh, that tingle. She hadn't felt a tingle like that since...since a long time, and she didn't want to feel it now. She straightened her spine and leaned back in her chair.

"Hmm. I guess this might look like a date." He scratched his cheek.

Drat this man. Fine, then. She could keep playing, too. She raised her chin. "Except that I don't usually date men whose name I don't know. So what's yours?"

He leaned forward, extending his hand. The warmth of his touch surprised her. Prickling sensations skipped through her insides. The firm strength surrounding her fingers coaxed dormant memories making her wonder what it'd be like to have his arms around her.

Jerking her head back, she dismissed that crazy thought. What was she thinking? She'd met a stranger and shook his hand. End of story. Her Earl Gray must be too strong.

She realized he'd spoken, grateful for the interruption of her runaway thoughts. "I'm sorry. What did you say?"

"My name is Payne."

A tinkling laugh escaped before she could stop it.

His eyes narrowed. "What's so funny?"

She yanked at her hand, but he wouldn't let go. "Payne? That's really your name? It sounds more like a character trait of yours." She mentally high-fived herself for that joke. She normally didn't think fast enough for witty zingers. "Is that your first or your last name?"

"Enjoying yourself?" He stretched closer. "My. Name. Is. Payne. Anderson." He spoke slowly as if he were explaining a difficult concept to a child. "I'd hoped you might be original and not succumb to the well-worn joke about my name."

This time she grinned. "I can't help it. It's too easy. Your mother named you well, didn't she? You've certainly been a bit of a *pain* to me this morning. Are you always a *pain* to people you've just met?" She giggled.

A reluctant smile accompanied his exaggerated groan. "Okay, that'll be a Euro for the lame name joke, Ellen Shepherd." He released his hold and opened his palm for the money he requested.

She clinched her rescued hand in her lap, glad to have it back. "Hey. You *were* eavesdropping."

"Are we going to keep beating that dead horse?" He rubbed his hand across his eyes

She glanced at her watch. "Yikes. It's almost 11:30."

He smiled a tired smile. "You have to be somewhere?"

"Yes, I do." She stuffed her writing pad into her black nylon backpack, pushed her chair from the table, and stood. "I'm meeting my daughter for lunch after her exam. Mr. Anderson, it was definitely," she paused, "interesting meeting you." She held out her hand, and he clasped it as he rose.

He inclined his head toward her. "Likewise."

Ellen tilted her head back to meet his intense, gray eyes. He loomed over her. Six foot? At least. She broke away from his steady gaze and noticed her hand still captured in his. "Well, goodbye."

He wouldn't release her hand. "Is that all? You're not going to offer to pray for me? Isn't that what you people usually do?" His mouth wavered between a smirk and a smile.

She raised an eyebrow. "'You people?' You're making fun of me now, right?" He didn't deny her accusation, and something flickered across his face. Sincerity? No, of course not. Payne didn't believe and didn't want to. He wanted to annoy her, to challenge her, but...what if...?

"Do you want me to pray for you?"

He ignored her question. Silence hovered over their table though tea cups clattered and conversations swirled around them.

She narrowed her eyes. "You know, I think I will pray for you. Keep your eyes open for the blessings," and tugged hard on her hand so that he'd let go.

She rushed to the door, grabbed the knob, and surprised herself by glancing back at him. Another shock waited for her.

He stood where she left him, staring after her.

ഇരുഇരു

With a nagging disappointment that she'd ended their conversation, Payne watched her glide out of the café. He resisted a strong urge to run after her that rattled him. He hadn't initiated a conversation with another woman in as long as he could remember. Why did he start today? With her?

He covered a yawn with the palm of his hand. Sleep deprivation. That's it. He'd been on a plane or a bus or in a car for almost forty-eight hours straight. Grabbing his mug, he stretched his back and returned to his original chair. A streak of dust along the cuff of his pants caught his attention, reminding him of jogging over the gritty tarmac to catch the last plane out of Entebbe two days ago.

Wrinkled shirt, grimy pants—he rubbed his hand over his scratchy chin. He must resemble a derelict. He chuckled, surprised she'd even bothered to talk with him.

He didn't give her much of a chance not to. What was he thinking, planting himself at her table like that?

That was the problem. He hadn't thought before he spoke to her. He simply acted. Actually, he couldn't think anymore. Exhaustion seeped out of every joint and robbed his concentration. He blew out a long, slow breath and squeezed the back of his neck.

He blamed this encounter on his chocolate fixation. He might have chosen another café if not for the free pieces of fudge offered at the front door. Maybe he should buy a sampler box for the weekend.

He scanned the scene outside the window for Charlie and Kate, his ride to what he hoped would be a long, hot shower and a big, soft bed. Waiting at the café for his friends to finish errands seemed like a good idea an hour and a half ago, but now he just wanted to sleep. For a solid twelve hours. Maybe more.

He rested his head on his open palm and swirled the remaining now-cold coffee. His thoughts floated back to his encounter with Ellen and to his question. Why did he strike up a conversation with her? A stranger.

A woman.

He glanced back at her table, now occupied by a family with a small child eating bits of a scone. He envisioned her talking with the old man. Smiling and listening intently, she'd appeared graceful and kind like she really cared about the man's story.

That's it. She'd seemed almost too good to be true. He'd barged in on her to provoke her a little, to push her to reveal her true self. And she did show a tougher side when they talked about truth and again when she described her impressions of him. So maybe she wasn't the Goody Two Shoes he'd presumed her to be.

He'd asked her to pray for him to get a final rise out of her, but that tactic backfired when she agreed without much more than a question. Remembering her soft green eyes and the way her hand felt in his, he almost wanted to believe in prayer again. He also wanted to believe that somehow in this international city with the small town feel he'd see her one more time.

Chapter 3

After a lunch of potato and leek soup at Lynch's Pub on Shop Street, Ellen and Olivia drove out to Eamon and Maeve Kelly's cottage, their former home exchange partners. Scanning the road, Ellen related the meeting with Seamus.

Olivia tilted her head and patted her heart. "That story is so sweet, Mom." She reached for the radio, changing stations from classical to a pop rock ballad. "But didn't you feel weird with him just walking up to your table out of the clear blue? Didn't you wonder why?"

"No and no. I was perfectly safe. He was the perfect gentleman. He said I reminded him of his wife, Fiona, so maybe seeing her in me made him feel comfortable striking up a conversation."

Ellen enjoyed sharing about Seamus with Olivia, but she kept the clash with Payne to herself. Seamus treated Ellen with kindness and respect. Payne lived up to his name, irritating her with every word out of his mouth. Thoughts of him still vexed her. Why ruin the upcoming reunion with old friends? What good would it do to tell Olivia about her encounter with Payne? She'd probably be upset that a stranger had bothered her mother and worry about Ellen the next time she ventured into the city alone.

True, he had annoyed her, but she remembered his smile when she teased him about his name. Why did that memory send warm flutters through her midsection even now?

✵✵✵✷✷

Ellen clanked the Claddagh door knocker on Clybaun Road. Memories of the three weeks she and her family had lived in this house while the Kellys lived in hers swirled in her mind—trying to figure out the unfamiliar washing machine settings, the children riding bikes in the driveway, playing Uno in the den.

Scenes like these from her other life, her life with Steve, could pop up at will without ambushing her now. She counted them as gifts from God. Grateful that He had brought her to this new place of peace, she lifted a silent prayer of thanksgiving that she wasn't crawling down that dark path of fresh grief anymore.

Footsteps tapped on the parquet floor she remembered sweeping with a red-handled broom. The front door whooshed open, and Maeve Kelly stood grinning on the threshold.

Except for a few strands of silver in her auburn hair she'd twisted into a bun, Maeve looked the same as she had thirteen years ago. She shrieked and pulled Ellen into a tight, bear hug. "Yes, it's good to see my dear friends from North Carolina. This is so much better than an email or a Christmas card. Come in, come in. The water is almost boiling for the tea, and I just now put the biscuits on a plate."

They visited in the cherry-themed kitchen munching home-made shortbread biscuits and sampling chocolate fudge Ellen had brought as a gift. Maeve swallowed a bite of the rich candy. "Kane's fudge—the best in the city. My sweet tooth is grateful to you."

So. Choosing the café with the fudge display had been a good decision. She had begun to doubt that move when her quiet morning had turned into a debate with a skeptic named Payne.

Maeve poured the tea and asked, "So how are you liking Professor O'Callahan's nice house, Olivia?"

Before Olivia could open her mouth, Ellen jumped in with her two cents. "Well, I can tell you that I love it. The books, the wall of windows in the kitchen, the rose garden. It's wonderful. I wish I could stay longer than two weeks."

Olivia laughed at her mother. "It's a great place. Thank you again for connecting us. House-sitting has been a God-send."

"I was thrilled to do it. He's a good man, he is, though we

don't see him very much. Maybe once or twice a month at our church coffees."

When Ellen stood to leave in late afternoon, Maeve protested. "Sure, you'll be staying for supper. Eamon will be home soon, and we've a lovely jelly roll for dessert."

ഔഔഏരെ

After breakfast the next morning, Ellen rode the City Direct to Eyre Square accompanied by a blue mood that had settled on her shoulders. Catching up with Maeve and Eamon had been bittersweet. A lonely ache accompanied her through the ride home and all night, diminishing with her morning quiet time but leaving her in a reflective spirit.

Stepping off the bus, she determined to be positive and not wallow in the past, promising herself to create some new memories today. Looking forward to fresh possibilities, she floated up Quay Street with an unaccustomed lightness in her heart that reminded her of happiness.

Ellen browsed through two gift shops and a woolen market and then stepped inside a pottery shop that beckoned to her. She smiled at the intricate shapes of the display pieces, remembering the misshapen bowls and cups she'd created in a long ago pottery class. The blisters on her pinkies from the friction of the pottery wheel and her exhausted hands and forearms had convinced her to leave throwing pots to more talented people. She supported the art but didn't try to create more of it.

She meandered all the way to the back of the shop, stopping in front of a display of pitchers and vases. Not really a collector, she did, however, own several handmade pitchers. The smooth, round shape of pitchers and the imagery they evoked comforted her. They reminded her of God's blessings pouring out over her.

Picking up a particularly beautiful one, she admired the striking colors—blues, purples, and a bit of scarlet. She considered buying it, but the temptations of other treasures waiting for her in other shops restrained her from committing to a purchase so early in her vacation.

Setting the pitcher back onto the display shelf, she turned to her left to move up the aisle again and bumped right into what felt like a brick wall. Two strong hands grabbed her arms to steady her. "Oh, I'm sorr—" Her words evaporated into a familiar tanned face.

"Did you pray for me this morning?" Payne's teasing grin greeted her from only inches away.

"Payne?" She pulled her eyes away from his, glancing up and down as she leaned back. Failing to hide the question in her eyes, she compared his appearance yesterday with this new and improved version of Payne.

"The one and only." He shrugged, keeping his attention on her. "I cleaned up good, huh?"

Ellen sucked in a calming breath and let it soothe the panic that had seized her when she'd felt strange arms around her. He cleans up good, all right. Faded jeans complimented a periwinkle blue polo shirt. He'd shaved, and a few thin gray streaks peppered the black hair at his temples. His hair, fresh from a trim, still looked damp, but a few dried locks brushed his forehead.

Her gaze landed on his wide grin and skipped over his high cheekbones to find his laughing eyes locked onto hers. Snapping hers closed, the scent of his woodsy aftershave and sandalwood soap, a potent mix, provoked her sense of smell. His close proximity sucked away the air in her personal space, making breathing difficult.

What is wrong with you, Ellen? You're a grown woman, not some high school—. She pushed against his chest. "Oh, let me go, will you?"

"Okay. Okay. Sorry." Holding up both palms, he backed away from her. "You ran into me so hard I thought you might fall."

"I couldn't help it. You were standing right beside me. Why?" She pulled at the edges of her sage green cardigan, wishing her jumbled emotions would smooth as easily. "What were you doing? Spying on me?"

He shook his head. "No, I wasn't spying on you. I came out of the barber shop across the street and saw you walk in here. I wondered if you prayed for me." He dipped his head toward her. "So did you?"

She frowned. "Did I what?" For the life of her, she couldn't remember his original question.

"Pray for me."

"Pray for you?"

"That's what I asked you." His mouth twitched.

She combed trembling fingers through her hair. Stop thinking about him. Think of the answer he wants. Her heartbeat, so hard and fast, seemed strong enough to ruffle her blouse. *God, please don't let him see how flustered I am.*

She held her breath, then slowly blew it out and licked her lips. She caught his gaze lingering on her mouth.

He bent his head. "Did you pray for me?" He whispered the question this time.

She nodded. His nearness, his intense eyes, his aftershave— the whole package—rendered her mute.

He smiled. "Thank you." Straightening, he asked, "What did you pray?"

Just like that he broke the spell.

Irritating. That's what he is. Yeah. Irritating and handsome. She caught her breath. Handsome? Where did that come from? He's irritating. Irritating and too close.

Aggravated with the crazy conversation in her brain and determined to push her jumbled thoughts aside, she said, "I prayed for your soul."

"My soul?" His jaw dropped.

"Hmm. That's my standard prayer for someone I don't know and I'm not sure about his salvation." She jerked away from him and moved back toward the front door, her immediate goal. In the last five minutes, the shop had shrunk to the size of a walk-in closet. She needed fresh air and more space.

He stayed on her heels. "You prayed a 'standard prayer' for me? Nothing special? Did you pray anything else?"

She glanced over her shoulder. The young storekeeper's attention focused on the cell phone in his hand.

Did Payne sound disappointed? No. Definitely not. Stick

with his irritating qualities. "Do you realize how conceited you sound? You're not content with just a prayer. You want something special."

Reaching around her, he grabbed the handle and opened the door for her. The brisk air cooled her flushed cheeks and settled her racing heart.

"If you must know, I prayed for you to draw near to God." Skirting a chair on the sidewalk, she turned to him and stopped. *How do I get rid of him?*

He tapped his index finger against his temple. "'Draw near to God, and He will draw near to you.' That's in James, isn't it?"

The heat returned in her face as he studied her, waiting for her response.

She arched an eyebrow. "So you can quote Scripture. See, I knew you probably had some church background, but quoting Scripture? Now that's a horse of a different color." She kept her words light, avoiding sarcasm with effort.

He stuck his hands in his pockets. "And what color would that be? Would that be a bay, an Appaloosa or maybe a black Stallion?" He smiled and shrugged. "Don't be too impressed. Satan can quote Scripture, too, remember?"

"Is that a warning?" She pulled her backpack strap up higher on her shoulder, gripping it like a life-line.

"Well, you did call me a *pain* yesterday. Maybe it's just a slippery slope," he shrugged again and smiled. Her mouth mimicked his in spite of herself.

"Hey, are you meeting your daughter for lunch?" His gray eyes shined, full of hope. "No—"

"Good."

"But I—"

"But what? Are you meeting someone else?" A vulnerable look darkened his eyes before he blinked it away.

"Well, no. I planned to do my own thing today. Just, you know, do whatever comes up." *Getting rid of him might be harder than she expected.*

"Great. What about having lunch with me? What if that's what comes up?" Cocking his head to the left, he rested his hands on his slim hips.

She pulled her backpack off her shoulder holding it in front of her like a shield. "Well, I, uhmm." Lunch? With him? More time alone with this man who teases at every turn?

Ellen remembered his "you people" comment from yesterday. Couldn't be more obvious that he's on an opposing team. She should stand firm, say, "No, thank you," and walk away.

"Come on." He ducked his head toward her. "We're two Americans in an international city, just having lunch together—my treat. It'll be my apology for interrupting you yesterday and my thank you for your prayer today. I'll even try not to annoy you." One corner of his mouth tipped up.

He could try not to annoy her with words, but his presence played havoc with her insides. Her lungs lost breath. Her heart tapped a warning in her chest.

She remembered the last time she felt like this—with Steve. She bypassed the numbness she felt during the past three years without Steve, skirted over the anger and grief of the first few months of widowhood, and ignored the disbelief of the diagnosis announcement. Instead, she conjured images of the early weeks with him. The pounding hearts and quick breathing, hidden kisses from curious roommates, calling the dorm director to unlock the door after curfew, needing to study for final exams but reluctant to give up precious minutes together.

She could see Steve in her mind as easily as when she'd seen him for the first time walking into calculus with one of his buddies. His curly blond hair springing over his forehead, he'd almost filled the height of the doorframe in his Izod shirt, Madras plaid shorts, and Sperry Docksiders before choosing a seat at the back of the classroom. His smile said he loved people, and people loved him back.

She closed her eyes against the memories. She'd worked hard at finding an even keel again. She didn't want the roller coaster ride of crazy emotions. She didn't have the energy to feel these zings and flutters. Not the energy or the desire. She'd had the excitement. Once was enough.

She wanted quiet now, a low-key adventure in a foreign

country with her daughter, not with a disturbing, handsome man.

A gentle touch on her forearm brought her back to the present. "Hey. Earth to Ellen. Whadda ya say? Lunch? With me?"

His smile, exuding dangerous charm, trumped the mantra repeating in her mind, "He's dangerous. Choose quiet," and made resisting him impossible.

While one half of her reason silently screamed, "*NO*," the other half melted under his magnetic appeal. And that half triumphed she knew because her head bobbed, "*Yes.*"

Chapter 4

Payne beamed at her and inclined his head in an exaggerated nod. "Thank you. Do you have a preference of where to have lunch?"

She combed her fingers through her hair. "I have to meet Olivia later this afternoon, so maybe some place near the college."

"No problem. Which way?"

She pointed to her left. "This way."

They strolled down Newcastle Street toward the college, and he positioned himself on the traffic side, remembering his father's lessons on a gentleman's manners. He hadn't had much opportunity to walk with a woman in the past few years—in a couple of decades if he had to confess. He'd avoided contact with women outside of work, in fact. Any long-ago pointers on interacting with a lady dredged up from the dusty caverns of his memory would be welcome while he spent time with this interesting woman.

While they waited at a crosswalk for the light to change, a breeze caught the hem of her skirt and swirled it against his pants leg. That same breeze wafted a hint of lilies-of-the-valley, his grandmother's favorite flower, to his nose, the wonderful scent compelling him to squeeze her elbow as he guided her across the street.

She stiffened at his touch, and he caught her sideways glance at her arm, but she didn't shake off his hand. Grateful, he accepted that reluctant tolerance as a positive sign.

Payne had surprised himself by inviting her to lunch. He

certainly didn't wake up this morning thinking about lunch with Ellen. True, an image of her had flitted through his musings while he shaved, but his original agenda hadn't included her. He'd planned to get a haircut and then drink plenty of sweet, black coffee while he read *The Irish Times*.

When he'd seen her studying the front window display of the pottery shop, all thoughts of paper and coffee fled. He couldn't resist following her inside like a lovesick schoolboy. Or a kid running after an ice cream truck.

Totally against his normal character, the urge to talk with her again had propelled him through the store until he'd found her admiring pottery on a table at the back. In the fog of her heady, floral scent, he hadn't realized how close he stood to her until she'd turned and plowed into him.

He smiled at that memory and dropped his hold on her elbow before he squeezed it again.

They stopped in front of Uncle Paddy's, a bistro near the college. Payne gestured to the building and then to the campus across the street. "How about this one? You won't have to walk far to meet up with your daughter. We could sit out here if you're not too chilly."

She smiled, nodding her agreement, and accepted the chair he held for her.

xxxx

Ellen liked the location of the bistro. From their outside table, she could see the main building of the university. Interesting shops flanked both sides of the street, and she anticipated browsing through them before meeting Olivia later in the afternoon.

She also liked Payne's quick compliance when she suggested they eat near the school. His behavior today forced her to rethink her original opinion of him. His gentlemanly manners—walking between her and the street, guiding her through the cobblestone crosswalk, pointing out interesting sites as they meandered through the city, holding the chair for her—showed a sharp contrast to the vagrant she'd imagined him to be yesterday.

His thoughtful conduct combined with his cleaned-up, shiny self presented a potent package that charmed Ellen in spite of herself.

Although only a few patrons dined in the café, a long time passed before a waitress appeared to take their order. They waited even longer to receive their food. Payne assumed the role of host, directing the conversation.

"So let me get this straight. You let a family you never met before stay in your real house, not a vacation home somewhere else?"

Ellen had answered the question many times before... and dealt with the same concern herself when she first heard about house swapping. "Exactly. We don't have a second home anyway." She spread her hands on the striped tablecloth. "It's really about trust. We trusted that the family would take care of our house, and we took care of theirs."

Resting his chin on his fist, he smiled. "Sounds good in theory."

"It works well in practice, too. Listen. This kind of vacation isn't for everybody, but we loved it."

He leaned back in his chair. "Would you do it again?"

"Absolutely."

Their soup arrived, and Payne asked her to say grace.

She centered the soup bowl in front of her. "After all that talk yesterday, you want me to say grace now?"

He unfolded his napkin. "I don't want to be responsible for your backsliding."

"Don't worry. I'll just say a silent prayer."

"Oh, go ahead. You won't embarrass me. I figured you'd be one of those people who normally pray out loud in restaurants."

Ellen let out a sigh and smoothed her thumb along the spoon handle. Why did he insist upon this him-versus-her approach with his 'those people' comments?

"When I'm out with friends, we pray. When I'm out by myself, I say grace to myself."

A whisper of a smile played around his lips. "You're not by yourself now."

Was she with a friend? "Why do you insist on a verbal

prayer? So you can critique my words? Make fun of me? Start another philosophical discussion?"

Genuine surprise highlighted his features. "No. Of course not. I want you to bless our food. I thought you'd be happy to pray with a reprobate like me."

You'd think.

Praying out loud had never been one of her strong suits. Ever since Miss Irma Lee Worley had shocked the straps loose on her Mary Janes with a request for a prayer at the end of Sunday School when she was all of eight years old, she'd avoided public prayer when she could. On that long ago morning, she'd squeezed her eyes shut, opened her mouth, and out came, "Now I lay me down to sleep." Billy Weaver had guffawed on the floor until Miss Irma Lee had requested a prayer from him.

Now, no matter what the circumstances, that scene played in her mind before every public, "Dear God."

She licked her lips. "Do you really want me to?"

He nodded.

"Fine. I'll say a blessing." Ellen bowed her head. Something pressed on her hand. Her eyes flew open.

Payne had taken hold of her hand.

"Isn't this how you do it?"

More heat rose in her face. His hand was warm and strong. Felt comforting and… felt right.

"Hold hands during a prayer, I mean."

Yes. My family holds hands before a meal, but…"

"Then let's do it right. Now, please pray. I'm hungry." He bowed his head, closing the conversation.

She mumbled something about God's goodness and the food and finished with a quick, "Amen."

He squeezed her hand and the warmth was gone.

"Good. Short and to the point. I like it. Don't have to wait for the fried chicken and mashed potatoes." He cut the small loaf of warm, brown bread in front of him with a serrated knife.

"Southern food! You *are* from the South."

He grinned. "True. I grew up in Virginia, and I've had to wait through many a prayer before I could sink my teeth into a chicken leg." After offering a slice to her, he cut one for himself and dunked a piece into his carrot soup. "Why didn't you want to pray out loud?" He tossed the piece of bread into his mouth.

"Not really in my skill set. And I can't tell if you're making fun of me or not."

He held her eyes with a steady gaze and swallowed. "I'm not."

They lingered over their food. He explained that he was working in Africa and admitted that he'd just arrived in Ireland when they met. "I'd been traveling for about two days with hardly any sleep, but it's better to stay awake a while before crashing. I adjust to a new time zone faster... with less jet lag, too."

"So those were safari clothes yesterday, and you tried to stay awake by picking a fight with a stranger in a café." She smiled at him as though she'd just given the correct answer in a board game.

He shook his head. "Huh-uh. I stayed awake by talking with a beautiful woman." He leaned his forearms against the table.

She blinked twice. Was he flirting with her? She wasn't sure. A warm tingle rose from the bottom of her stomach, grabbing the breath from her lungs and stealing her smile. She concentrated on breathing and searched her brain for something to say. "Ah, now I find out that you're a flatterer, too."

"Wrong. I don't flatter. I say what I mean. Always." His eyes refused to let go.

She couldn't think of a comeback. She felt sixteen years old again, all flushed and tongue-tied. She wiped her clammy hands with her napkin.

"You are beautiful, Ellen. That's a compliment." He pushed his empty dish to the side. "I believe now you're supposed to say, 'thank you.'"

Her whispered "thank you" seemed to satisfy him, but it did nothing to calm the zings curling her toes.

"You're welcome." He leaned back in his chair. "Hey, here comes our wayward waitress. How about dessert? You up for it?" He studied the list posted in colored chalk near the doorway.

"No, really." She held up her hand as if to stop the calories from coming. "I don't usually eat dessert at lunch."

"Do you usually have lunch with someone you just met?" A corner of his mouth tipped up.

"No, but—"

"Exactly. Do something different. Come on. We can share, and then maybe you won't feel so guilty about a midday treat." His shining eyes willed her to agree.

"Share? But you just left Africa. You might have been bitten by a tsetse fly or something worse." She wrinkled her nose, hoping to return to their teasing.

"If I had been bitten by a tsetse fly, I might still be lying under a mosquito net in Uganda. But I've had all my shots, so I'm safe. How about the Death by Chocolate? Sounds go."

"It sounds like something you'd get back home, not in Galway." She bit her bottom lip. She wouldn't admit it to him, but he was right. She was on vacation in a foreign country, trying new things. Why not have dessert for lunch? "Oh, for Pete's sake. Okay. I'm game."

Chapter 5

Ellen laughed at Payne's delight when the waitress served a chocolate tower in a goblet that could have doubled as a goldfish bowl. He dug in his fork, dismantling the layers of chocolate shortbread, coffee ice cream, and hot fudge sauce. She scooped up slivered almonds and mini chocolate chips sprinkled in the fudge at the bottom of the glass.

"You like chocolate, huh?"

"This is fantastic." He dredged a corner of shortbread through the fudge. "Can't get anything like this in my camp in Uganda."

"Uganda?"

"Yea. I'm doing some research. Environmental stuff."

Between bites, he regaled her with stories about his work in Africa. Laughing at one of his silly jokes, she heard a sharp, "Mom!" Glancing toward the voice, she saw Olivia crossing the street toward her with such purposeful strides that she resembled a momma bear on a mission. Tristan and another friend followed in her wake.

"Olivia!" Ellen grabbed the watch on her wrist. Her mouth popped open. "Oh, no. It's almost 3:30!" She looked at Payne. Had he realized how long they'd been talking over lunch? How could she have forgotten to meet Olivia?

Ellen dropped her crumpled napkin.

Olivia stomped to the table, gulping air like a long-distance swimmer.

"Sweetie, I'm so sorry. I didn't realize the time."

Her daughter's stare ping ponged between Ellen and Payne, a mixture of hurt, confusion, and anger evident in her eyes. Her brows hung together. "Is this who you met yesterday? I thought you said he was a little old man."

"No, no. This isn't Seamus." The taste of chocolate had turned bitter in her mouth. She gestured across the table. "This is Payne Anderson. But I did meet him yesterday. After Seamus left."

Olivia's lips pushed into a pout. "You didn't mention meeting someone else."

"You didn't mention me?" Payne sounded hurt, but his eyes teased her.

Ellen glanced at him, wishing he'd be quiet. She focused on her daughter again and cloaked her words with a calmness she didn't feel. "No, Olivia, I didn't mention every little detail about my day to you." She disapproved of the petulant sound in Olivia's voice, but she still felt guilty about forgetting their appointment. What had gotten into Olivia? She knew better than to behave this way.

The pretty red head standing next to Olivia stuck out her hand, "Hello, Mrs. Shepherd. I'm Susanna."

"Hello, Susanna." Ellen clasped her hand and then smiled at Tristan. "Hello, Tristan. It's nice to see you again."

Tristan leaned forward to grasp her hand, too. Payne stood to greet Susanna.

"I'm Payne Anderson." He offered his hand to Olivia who waited a couple of beats before accepting it. However, she didn't return his smile.

"Olivia. This is Payne. As I said, we met yesterday after Seamus. Then we ran into each other this morning in a little pottery shop." Without looking at him, she sensed Payne's smile at her explanation of running into him. "We decided to have lunch on the spur of the moment. That's it." She raked her hair away from her face and waited for Olivia to digest the information.

Olivia crossed her arms over her chest, digging in her heels. "So you decided to have lunch and share a dessert with someone you met barely twenty-four hours ago?"

Embarrassment and anger fueled the heat that rose in Ellen's chest. If her guilt allowed it, she could quickly lose her patience. "Yes, that's pretty much it, Olivia." She pressed her hands
together in her lap. "We decided to have lunch here across the
street from the college. I'm glad you found us. Sorry I forgot the
time."

Olivia flattened her mouth into a stubborn line, refusing to
acknowledge the apology. Hoping to re-establish her authority
as the mother, Ellen pushed her chair away from the table and
stood like everyone else.

She blew out a cleansing breath. "Listen, this morning, we
said we'd plan the rest of the day when we got together. So what's
up for this afternoon?"

Olivia remained silent but divided her stares between Payne
and her mother.

"Well, there's a massive music concert out at the park on
Oughterard Road tonight." Tristan smoothed into the conversation—and the unease. "It's part of the arts festival. Traditional
bands galore if you like Irish music." He trilled the *r* in *Irish* with
a grand flourish and grinned when everyone—except Olivia—
laughed.

"We ought to grab some take away food and then head on
over. Claim a spot. The park always gets crammed." His face
brightened. "Hey, Payne, want to come with us?"

Ellen's heart dropped to her feet. What if he agreed? She
needed time to herself to process the three-hour lunch, the confrontation with Olivia, and, most of all, how much she enjoyed
being with Payne.

Payne returned to his chair. "Thanks for the invitation,
Tristan, but I already have plans. Sounds like fun, though."

Ellen smiled her relief and turned to Olivia. "If you want
to go inside and order, I'll catch up with you in a minute, okay?"

Olivia glanced one last time at Payne before reluctantly
following her friends inside the cafe. Ellen sank into her chair,
grateful for a break after the tension.

Payne watched the trio disappear through the door. "Is your
daughter normally this friendly to men you have lunch with?"

"I don't normally have—" She clamped her lips together. "Olivia has a right to be angry, for Heaven's sake. I forgot to meet her, remember?" She shook her head in disbelief.

"Yes, and you apologized."

"Look. I know she was rude, and I'm not going to excuse it, but she's had a rough time since—" Icy fingertips cooled her forehead.

"Since what?" Payne prompted.

She avoided his eyes and studied a carving of a Celtic cross hanging by the front door. "Since my husband died. We've all had a hard time. It's been almost three years, but it was a hard blow. Anyway." She sighed and glanced back at him. "Thank you for lunch, Payne. I enjoyed it."

"Until the end, at least." His smile softened his words.

"Yes, well. I need to catch up with them." She planted her hands on the edge of the table.

He reached over to grasp her wrist, preventing her from rising but released it when she glanced at his hand. "Are you having lunch with Olivia tomorrow?"

"Yes." She held her breath, waiting for his next words.

"Okay, then have breakfast with me." As if he anticipated a negative answer, he hurried to present his case. "Come on. We can't end our conversation like this."

She didn't want to end the conversation at all. She wanted to sit here and make him laugh again. She wanted him to hold her hand again. She wanted him to come to the concert tonight.

She knew Olivia would have more questions about this lunch. If she met Payne again, Olivia's questions would multiply. Probably intensify, too. "I don't know—"

"Please?" He tilted his head, raised his eyebrows. "Pretty please?"

His hopeful, encouraging expression mesmerized her. Her racing heart felt light and bouncy. She couldn't control the grin spreading across her face. What was happening to her? How could a simple invitation to breakfast flutter her stomach? "All right. Breakfast sounds good. Where should I meet you?"

"How about in Kane's, our café from yesterday. Is 9:00 too

early?"

Our café. Her stomach flipped again.

She grabbed her backpack. "No. Nine's good."

"Great, then." He smiled. "Till tomorrow."

Chapter 6

Ellen wanted to relax on the blanket and allow the music to take her away. Two days ago, she would have loved every minute of being here with her daughter and her friends, listening to the lively Irish music.

That was before she met Payne.

After spending several hours with him, she couldn't concentrate on the fiddles and whistles, much less the lyrics. She periodically scanned the people around her, hoping to see him, all the while knowing he had other plans. That fact didn't keep her from looking, though.

She dreaded the end of the concert and Olivia's inevitable questions. Quick as well as observant, Olivia noted every detail. She'd seen the shared dessert plate and made sure to mention it.

Ellen winced recalling the scene. Olivia had been shocked at seeing her mother sharing a dessert with a strange man, but that didn't excuse her rudeness.

Sharing a dessert? How intimate. What had possessed her? Was she losing her mind? If she didn't watch herself, she might lose a whole lot more.

Payne had affected her. She knew how his focused gaze warmed her insides. She knew how his touch raised goose bumps along the back of her neck. His attention had revived feelings dormant since she buried her husband, and she didn't know what to do about them.

After only two meetings with Payne, he'd stirred her. She felt the pull of his attraction when he smiled at her and looked into her eyes. She felt her heart catch when he teased her and made her laugh. She felt the electricity crackle between them when he held her hand with his strong, warm grip and wouldn't let go.

She'd have to guard her heart and do it well. She'd stop letting him hold her hand. She'd keep him at arm's length.

Really. She would.

She'd have to stop losing herself in those gray eyes. She'd have to look at his nose or his forehead, anywhere but those eyes.

Resisting him might be difficult, but she could do it.

I am woman. Hear me roar.

She'd enjoy this time with Payne for as long as it lasted.

Then she'd board a plane and go back home and back to being Ellen Shepherd, grown woman, mother, widow.

God, please help me to navigate through this new territory. Guard my heart, too.

ഇഇ∞ര

Since Olivia had an early class the next day, they left the concert before the end and arrived back at the house just before eleven. Tired and hoping to avoid a discussion, Ellen headed for her bedroom.

"Wait, Mom. We have to talk." Standing in the middle of the family room with her hands on her hips, she could be the poster child for obstinate determination.

"About what?" Opting for nonchalance, Ellen willed Olivia to do the same. Unfortunately, her daughter had an agenda to follow.

Olivia cocked her head. "You know what. That Payne man. Who is he and why didn't you mention that you'd met him yesterday? You told me about Seamus." She lifted her shoulders. "Why didn't you mention Payne?"

"I didn't think it was important." Ellen tensed. Shepherds don't lie. "I mean, we had an argument or, I don't know, a conversation about religion. Well, it wasn't so much about religion as it was about prayer." She searched for the best words to explain the conversation. "He saw me close my eyes to pray at the start of your exam, and he asked me if I really believed in prayer. That's all."

Struggling not to let her anger spill out, she pressed her lips together and waited for Olivia's next question.

Olivia's eyes softened. She'd believed in prayer since she was a little girl. "You remembered to pray for me?"

"Of course I did." Ellen smiled at her daughter. "We talked for a few minutes and that's it."

Olivia seemed to consider her mother's comments. She shifted her feet. Then all softness evaporated, and she jumped back into interrogation mode. "Going from talking a few minutes to lunch and dessert is a great big jump, if you ask me."

"I don't think anybody did ask you about it, Olivia." Why wouldn't she just let this go? "I told you. We just happened to meet again. Nothing was planned." A new line of questioning for Olivia. To calm her frustration, Ellen moved about the room, straightening magazine piles and pillows.

Olivia followed so closely she almost bumped into Ellen when she stopped at the coffee table. "It wasn't planned? What about now? Do you have plans now? You took forever saying goodbye to him this afternoon. Did you make plans to see him again?"

"Olivia." Her voice dropped with a warning tone. Really, her daughter should think about switching her major to criminal justice. She'd be a brilliant prosecutor.

"You *are* going to see him again! But we're supposed to have lunch tomorrow, Mom." Olivia whined like five-year-old overdue for a nap.

"You and I are having lunch just like we planned, but—"

Olivia crossed her arms in front of her. "When are you seeing him again?" If Olivia had stomped her foot, she would've completed the picture of an overtired child.

Ellen held a pillow for support. "We're going to meet for breakfast tomorrow. I think he wants to talk about prayer again."

Another lie. She needed to go to bed. Exhaustion was tweaking her personality.

Olivia narrowed her eyes. "It didn't look like you were talking about prayer when I saw the two of you laughing over that plate of chocolate this afternoon. What else were you talking about?"

Ellen had had enough of the twenty questions. She shook her head. "You don't look or sound very attractive right now, Olivia. I haven't done anything morally wrong or anything I'm ashamed of. I've apologized several times for not meeting you after class today. It's up to you to accept it or not."

She dropped the pillow on the couch and faced her daughter. "Yes, I'm meeting Payne for breakfast tomorrow and that's all. I thought you wanted me to have an adventure in Ireland. At least that's what you said. So. I'm going to breakfast with him. Whether you like it or not, I'm a grown woman who makes my decisions based on what I think God is leading me to do."

"You think God is leading you to date this man?" Olivia's eyes widened and filled with something that looked like hurt or maybe fear, resembling more the little girl she used to be than the twenty-one-year-old young woman who stood before her now.

"That's not what I said, Sweetie." Ellen drew a calming breath.

"Because it's not like it used to be, Mother." Olivia folded her arms across her chest. "The world has changed a lot since you and Daddy dated."

"I know that." Ellen ignored the not-so-subtle dig about her age.

"People date for a while now, sometimes they even have a baby together, and then—just like that, they're with somebody else."

"Yes, Sweetie, I know." Were they seriously having this conversation?

"And do you know that most adults in relationships are usually lovers, Mother?"

"Well, I don't—"

"It's true. Are you really ready to date again, Mom?"

"Olivia, I've talked with this man twice. That's it. I'm not looking for a relationship, but if I were, I'd want someone who believes like I do. I'm not sure he does." Ellen massaged her temples.

"Look. Yesterday when I prayed for you, I also thanked God for Seamus. He was such a sweet little man. Then, I asked God to bring someone else He wanted me to meet into my path. Not five minutes later, Payne started asking me about prayer. You tell me if that was a God thing or not." She waited for more questions.

Olivia remained silent, but her eyes had softened again.

Ellen covered a yawn. "I'm tired. I'm going to bed, and so should you. Making that eight o'clock class will be rough." She reached for Olivia, hugging her tightly. She whispered into her ear, "I love you, Sweetie. See you bright and early, okay?"

As stubborn as always, Olivia accepted the hug but didn't return it. Ellen sighed. Would she have to face round two tomorrow? What was she letting herself in for?

‬‬ ‬‬‬‬‬ ‬‬‬‬‬‬‬‬‬

She'd talked with Payne twice before, but this time seemed different. The first two had been surprises, spur of the moment, serendipitous.

They'd planned this get-together.

An intentional meeting.

A date?

Her feet slowed on Cross Street. Kane's Café neared with every step. Panicky butterflies not only filled her stomach but also fluttered up around her lungs making her breathing less an involuntary action and more of a labored effort.

She needed a plan of action.

First, pray again. Then, greet Payne with "hello," not a handshake. Keep him at a distance. Focus on the food. Maybe order Irish oatmeal. Listen to his stories. Say "goodbye." Enjoy the rest of the day with Olivia.

Someone jostled against her shoulder and fell into step beside her, intruding into her planning session. "Good morning, Ellen. You're not having second thoughts, are you?"

Gasping, she turned, meeting Payne's smiling face. "Payne." Of course. "Second thoughts?" Oh, this man. He stood too close. Close enough that she caught a whiff of soap and cloves.

The scent sped up her heart and deleted the plans in her brain. She struggled to replace those plans with a silent pep talk. Calm down. Keep walking. You can enjoy breakfast with this man.

Wishing she could believe the words swirling through her mind, she forced herself to concentrate on the conversation instead of his nearness.

He jiggled her elbow. "Second thoughts about having breakfast with me."

"And why should I have second thoughts about having breakfast with you?" She tried to think of a polite way to extricate her arm from his warm clasp, but nothing came to mind.

Did she really want to shake off his hand?

"I don't know. Maybe Olivia raked you over the coals last night about the strange man you had lunch with. I was worried you might not be up for breakfast this morning." He grinned.

She arched an eyebrow and cut her eyes to him. "I can hold my own with Olivia, thank you very much."

He chuckled. "Just teasing. I assure you I don't doubt you can handle Olivia."

They arrived at Kane's, and Payne pointed to an open outside table. "Let's sit out here, want to?" He pulled a chair out for her. "It's a beautiful morning. Have to enjoy good Irish weather when you can get it."

Settling herself into the chair, she scanned the sky. He was right about the unpredictable climate. Although the sun was shining now, darker clouds peeked over the edge of the horizon. The weather would probably change before lunchtime.

A waitress appeared at their table before they could shake out their napkins.

Payne laughed. He leaned toward her to whisper, "I guess we don't have to worry about a three-hour meal like yesterday, huh?"

She smiled, a glow spreading through her at their shared joke.

After the waitress left, Payne asked, "So. How was the concert?"

"It was fine." She nodded. "I enjoyed it." Specific details refused to stand out because her attention had been concerned with thoughts of him, but her impression had been positive.

"What was your favorite band?"

Her stomach dropped like a student's who'd been caught day dreaming in class. She bit her lip. "Well, it's hard to pick a favorite." She racked her brain for details, then straightened. "I don't remember the name, but one band was made up of five brothers and one sister. They were good. Each one played at least two different instruments. It's cool that the family is so musically talented."

She relaxed feeling the wooden slats against her back, satisfied that she could contribute to their conversation.

"Yeah. I liked them, too." A slow grin reached his crinkling eyes as he watched her processing his words.

Her eyes widened. "You were there? But I didn't see—" She pressed her lips closed before the words betrayed her. "I thought you said you had plans."

"True. I did have plans. I just didn't say what they were. We arrived late and just stayed for an hour or so. We sat at the back near the road." He paused. "You didn't see me?" The broad grin engulfed his whole face. "So, you were looking for me?"

Hoping to withstand the attraction of his smile, she pulled her eyes away from his handsome face and frowned. "I didn't say I looked for you. Why do you deliberately try to annoy me?"

"Because it's so much fun." He stirred a generous amount of sugar into his coffee and sipped, watching her reaction.

Back to teasing. Good. She could handle teasing. If he continued to irritate her, then maybe she'd have no danger of succumbing to his charm. Better to be annoyed with him than attracted to him, unable to breathe like when he'd held her in the pottery shop yesterday. Her mind settled until a new thought entered. Who is "we?"

Chapter 7

Ellen enjoyed listening to Payne describe his favorite parts of the concert. The details he noticed revealed that music occupied an important place in his background. "You know a lot about music," she said. "Do you play an instrument?"

"My mother insisted on piano lessons which gave me a good start at learning notes and just basic stuff about music, but then I escaped those torture sessions and switched to trumpet in my junior high band."

"Aha. Arrogant, irritating, and a band nerd." She smiled, counting on her fingers.

His gaze followed her gesture. "Look at those long fingers. You probably play something." He narrowed his eyes. "You're a band nerd, too, aren't you?"

She laughed. "Guilty. I play the piano, and, yes, I played the clarinet in the marching band. My high school was so small, though, that during football season, I had to play saxophone since the real sax players played the game."

The waitress returned with their food, oatmeal for her and the tradition Irish breakfast for him complete with eggs, sausages, and black and white pudding.

Ellen cupped the warm bowl in front of her. "Do you play anything else?"

He thanked the waitress before answering. "As long as I played the trumpet during marching season, my director let me play the bass guitar in the jazz band. And I've fooled around with a banjo for a few years." He held out his open hands. "How about another quick grace, please?"

From music to grace in less than a second. She should be happy that someone who, two days ago, doubted the power of prayer had asked for it for again. She should be grateful, of course, but an image of a laughing Billy Weaver flared as usual.

"Isn't it your turn this time?" She knew he wasn't ready to pray, but she needed a second to ban the humiliating scene from her brain.

He shook his head, his eyes twinkling. "You pray so well. Like I said yesterday, I don't want to be responsible for your backsliding."

"Don't worry about me, Payne. Think about your own relationship with God instead." She'd pray that he would because her first impression of him had dimmed. She'd discovered his interest in music, his kindness, his humor. She'd discovered she liked him.

ഇരുത്തു

"So you're visiting your daughter in Galway even though she's in school most of the time?"

"Maybe that seems strange, but Olivia and I spend a lot of time together between her classes. I wanted to make sure she's settled. She'll be in Galway through next semester. July is a relatively slow month at my shop, and I have an assistant running it for me."

"A dress shop?" He sipped his coffee.

A dress shop? Where'd he get that idea? Time to have some fun.

"No, I run an auto parts store." She laughed at his surprise as he sputtered coffee.

"Sorry, but you deserved that for assuming I own a dress shop."

"A thousand pardons, ma'am for being sexist. It's just—I've noticed you've worn a dress or a skirt for the three days I've known you. And, well…" He shrugged. "Okay. My thought processes don't make sense. The better question would have been— what kind of shop?"

52

"A yarn shop."

"You crochet?"

Surprise popped open her mouth. "Yes, I do, but most people usually think yarn work equals knitting. Why'd you mention crochet right off the bat?"

"Haven't you realized yet that I'm not most people?" His tone dropped with the teasing remark.

Rolling her eyes, she shook her head.

"My grandmother taught all of us to crochet—including the boys. I even crocheted a scarf once." He announced his accomplishment with straightened shoulders and a proud tilt to his head.

"Oh, my stars. You're kidding me." She couldn't hide the admiration from her voice.

"No, I'm not. I promise." He crossed his heart with his hand.

So, he knew how to crochet. One more good quality to add to his positive traits.

"Are you impressed with my skills?"

His reading-her-mind skill she'd add to his negative traits. "I'd have to see the actual scarf before making a final judgment, of course, but mentioning crochet over knitting has just moved you from wholly irritating up to maybe just slightly annoying."

"That's positive, I guess." He smiled and picked up his coffee cup again.

She smiled back. "Anyway, while I'm here, I'm also looking for more yarn suppliers. Olivia doesn't have class tomorrow, so we're shopping for yarn. I've made a list of stores and sheep farms that I hope will yield some great new contacts."

She threaded her fingers together and leaned forward. "I can't wait to see what we find. I've read about some fabulous new dyeing techniques, too." She pictured the lovely website images. "I've spent hours on line. You wouldn't believe what's available. The colors are fabulous. The textures …I can't wait to run my hands over them."

She wiggled her fingers, then stopped, realizing that his ready smile had disappeared, replaced with a thoughtful expression. He fiddled with his napkin.

The waitress appeared and collected their dishes, signaling the end of breakfast. Ellen sensed that Payne's attitude had changed from teasing and inquisitive to quiet and reflective. Payne studied his coffee cup with the intensity of a scientist observing a slide through a microscope.

What thoughts absorbed his attention? Had she gushed too much about yarn? Surely women business owners didn't make him uncomfortable. Did he think her silly for being excited about new colors and textures? Honestly. Her livelihood depended on searching for new yarn and new patterns. She needed to be current on all the innovations in the craft, or her customers would shop somewhere else.

He didn't make a move to end the breakfast, but he'd already taken care of the bill when the waitress had brought the food. He'd won the battle of who pays with, "I asked you, so I get to pay."

The silence hovering over the table changed from companionable to uncomfortable. The lightness in her heart evaporated with the increasing quiet.

Deciding to end the awkwardness, she pushed back her chair. "Ahmm… I have to run some errands before I meet Olivia, so I'll say, 'goodbye.'" She stood, and he met her beside the table. Offering her hand, she smiled. "Thank you for breakfast, Payne. I enjoyed talking with you again."

He took her hand, his gray eyes reflecting determination mixed with a hint of surprise. Instead of releasing the handshake, he held on and stepped closer. He settled his hand on her shoulder, his thumb resting on her collar bone. He leaned forward.

Her heart skipped. She watched him come toward her, fascinated by the darkening of his gray eyes, by the anticipation of a kiss.

His kiss.

A second before his mouth touched her cheek, she turned slightly, and warm lips brushed hers. She felt the jolt of his momentary surprise as she stretched toward him offering her mouth to his.

He drew her closer, his lips moving over hers, hesitant at

first, then firm and tender. Her free hand slid up his arm, gripped his shoulder, and she yielded to his spicy fragrance. Sparks shattered way down deep, waking up slumbering sensations. Her brain stopped processing thoughts except for one. Being with Payne felt perfect, like coming home.

His fingertips trailed along her spine, and she shivered at his touch.

Young voices passing by on the sidewalk crashed into her muddled mind. Someone giggled. Someone else cried, "Get a room!" and the others roared at the joke.

Ellen stiffened. Heat flashed through her body, climbed up her neck, and colored her cheeks. She shoved out of his hold and caught a glimpse of his bewildered face which she guessed mirrored her own dazed feelings.

She stepped back and covered her mouth with trembling fingers.

"Uncle Payne!" A voice from down the street shouted a greeting.

She glanced toward the sound. A twenty-something young man strode toward them with a stunning blond woman by his side. Had they seen the embrace? Ellen couldn't be sure, but she refused to hang around to find out. She had to get away from Payne. Now. She saw her chance to escape idling at the bus stop half a block away.

"Thanks again, Payne. Bye." She grabbed her backpack, dashing away from him and the humiliating scene.

"Wait a minute, Ellen."

She could hear frustration in his voice as he shouted after her.

"I've really got to go. Sorry." She called to him over her shoulder. Willing the City Direct at the corner not to leave, she sprinted to catch it. Hopping on board, she trained her eyes on the driver to avoid looking back.

She thanked God she didn't hear Payne following her.

෴෴ඖ෴

Payne wanted to pursue her but had to abandon the idea when his godson, Michael, pulled up beside him. Both of them stared after the red bus, but only Michael spoke.

"Who was that?"

"You don't know her." Payne ran his hand through his hair, frustrated with Ellen's getaway. Frustrated with Michael's timing.

"And that's why I asked who she is." Michael grinned and clapped Payne on his back.

Payne drew in a long, slow breath, held it for a beat before exhaling. "Her name is Ellen. I met her a few days ago. She's here visiting her daughter." He pulled his eyes from the shrinking bus to give his reluctant attention to Michael and his companion. He clenched his jaw, struggling to summon common courtesy.

Michael's hair ruffled in the breeze, and he smoothed it down with his palm. "I want you to meet Jane's mother, Mary O'Callahan." He gestured to Payne. "Mary, this is Payne Anderson, my godfather."

Payne nodded a greeting to Mary, noticing her arched eyebrow. Had she seen that kiss?

Michael rested his hands on his hips. "We're working on a surprise for Jane. You've been fitted, right? You're ready for this weekend, right?"

Payne thought of the sharp creases of the tuxedo he'd tried on yesterday. Crisp, neat, elegant—exact opposite of what he felt now. "Yes. It's all good. I'm here, and I'm ready. Your wedding to Jane will be perfect, Michael. Listen, I'm sorry, but I need to run." Payne backed away. "Nice to meet you, Mary."

"Sure, but don't forget, breakfast and pictures Friday morning. Rehearsal dinner starts at seven Friday night. Bring a date if you want." Michael grinned and wiggled his eyebrows, a true replica of his father.

Great idea if he'd thought to ask where she was staying or for her phone number or anything that might help track her down. He clinched his jaw at the hopeless situation.

Payne noticed a bench advertising *Cinderella* at the Children's Theatre. A faded memory of Prince Charming staring after a fleeing Cinderella taunted him. He shut his eyes against the childhood image similar to his own predicament. A pleasant time ending too soon. At least the prince had a shoe to work with. Payne had nothing.

No, not exactly. He did have one idea. She mentioned meeting Olivia at the college before going to lunch. He didn't have to give up yet. Head for Galway University first, then all the cafes near campus. This plan might stand on shaky legs, but for him, never seeing Ellen again wasn't an option he wanted to consider.

Chapter 8

Ellen had never been so relieved to board a bus in her life. She dropped into an empty seat and crammed herself against the side of the bus. What in the world had she been thinking? Clearly, she'd lost her mind. Why had she turned into his kiss? And then responded to it? She cringed and pressed her hot cheek against the cool window.

In the seat in front of her, a young dark child chattered to his mother, her head wrapped in a scarf patterned with geometric designs. Any other time, Ellen would have enjoyed the child's animated conversation. She would have grimaced at the pungent fumes of the bus's exhaust pipes. She would have nodded at the white haired lady who joined her in the seat, but today her mind concentrated on one thing and one thing only—that kiss.

Squeezing her eyes shut didn't keep the scene from replaying in her mind. She saw Payne lean toward her and remembered feeling disappointed that he hadn't asked her what her plans were, that he hadn't asked her to meet him for another meal. Realizing their breakfast would be the last time she'd ever see him, sharp disappointment had pricked her insides. Was the kiss about wanting him to remember her as much as she knew she'd remember him?

The reason didn't matter. She'd kissed Payne, had practically thrown herself at him. If she'd ever been more embarrassed, she'd blocked it from memory. Maybe with time she'd forget this humiliation, too.

Not likely.

The only saving grace in this whole fiasco is that she'd never see Payne Anderson again.

ರರರರ

Payne arrived at the front of the college and settled on an empty bench near the front walkway. Ellen had mentioned running errands before meeting Olivia for lunch. He should have plenty of time to catch her before she found her daughter. Leaning back against the tree behind the bench, he reflected on the morning's events.

The beginning of breakfast had been fun. Good food. Good conversation. Lots of bantering and learning a little more about each other.

When she'd described the yarns and shared the hopes she had for this trip, he'd been fascinated. The way her hands emphasized points she wanted to make, the way her eyes lit up with the anticipation of new colors, the way she smiled her enthusiasm—everything enchanted him. Yes, Ellen Shepherd had definitely caught his attention.

He checked his watch and scanned the front lawn. No Ellen. Yet.

How did she feel about him? She'd accepted his invitations to lunch yesterday and breakfast today. She'd laughed at his jokes.

She'd kissed him.

That's right. She'd kissed him.

He'd been aiming for a chaste goodbye kiss on the cheek. She was the one who made sure lips touched lips.

And touch they did.

But now what? Was their time together over?

Her descriptions of combing the Irish countryside searching for the Holy Grail of yarns sounded like fun. His racket ball buddies might laugh at him, but he wanted to be part of the search team, especially if she led it.

But she hadn't invited him. Was all that talk about yarn stores and sheep farms her gentle way of telling him she didn't have time to see him again?

Well, he didn't have a lot of time either. He'd be tied up with Michael's wedding, and then he'd fly back to Uganda.

Maybe today's breakfast ended their acquaintance after all.

Maybe that's why he'd suddenly decided to kiss her when she'd stuck out her hand for goodbye.

Maybe he'd meant that kiss to be an exclamation point to their time together.

Maybe he'd wanted to see what kind of rise he'd get out of her.

He remembered aiming for her cheek near the corner of her mouth, but then, the unexpected. Just before contact, she'd turned her head, and BAM.

Caught off guard at first by her willing, soft lips, he'd quickly yielded to the delightful surprise. His intended brotherly kiss had become something much more interesting, stunning him with its effect on him.

He never anticipated that that little kiss would have become—what?

Who knows?

He couldn't figure out his reaction to that kiss, or his reaction to Ellen. Since arriving in Ireland, he'd become a different version of himself that he didn't recognize. Initiating a conversation with a woman? Asking her to lunch and breakfast? Kissing her?

He'd kissed a woman before; in fact, he'd kissed many women before his self-imposed bachelorhood, but he'd never been rocked to the core like when Ellen's lips touched his. The astonishment in her eyes when she'd pulled away attested that the kiss had dumbfounded her as well.

He shifted on the concrete bench and stretched his back. Where could she be? He flexed his fingers, expecting to see bruises where her death grip had crushed his hand.

How dare she kiss him like that and then run away leaving him to make polite conversation with Michael and his future mother-in-law? Ellen Shepherd had a lot of explaining to do, and he looked forward to asking the questions. Leaning back against the tree, he closed his eyes.

He remembered the feel of her touch and smiled.

ℰℰℐℭℛℛ

Her lips still tingling, Ellen had been on the bus for several minutes until she realized she was headed away from the college. She exited the bus at the next stop and walked back to Quinn Lane toward University Road. Maybe the walk would help release her jittery energy. She tried to empty her mind of all thoughts of Payne so that she could concentrate on her daughter. If she didn't compose herself, Olivia might discover the secret that Ellen vowed to keep. What in the world would Olivia think if she found out about that kiss?

Ellen didn't want to know. As much as Olivia had pushed for Ellen to come to Ireland for an adventure, her reaction to the first meeting with Payne had been less than positive. Adding a kiss to the picture of the shared dessert in Olivia's mind might send her daughter spinning into an over-protective tizzy.

She crossed University Road at the entrance of the college.

Payne sat on a stone bench, his head resting against a tree with his eyes closed. Heart pounding with the shock of seeing him again, she stumbled and veered to the left. She had to avoid his line of vision if he opened his eyes.

Where was Olivia's classroom? She scrambled for the number in her brain that seemed to have shut down.

When she pushed open the heavy side door, she spied a stairwell. Stairs. Her brain kicked in. Second Floor. Room two twenty-two. As her feet touched each step to the second floor, she repeated the mantra, "Calm down. Breathe. Calm down. Breathe."

She stopped on the landing and leaned her forehead against the cool, metal door. She had seen him first. A good thing. He didn't know she was in the building. Another good thing. Her brain worked, and her breathing had slowed to normal. Almost. She straightened and smoothed back her hair.

But why was he here?

The kiss?

62

The teenagers' voices swirled in her ears again. She squeezed her eyes to escape the humiliation. He'd teased her about her word choices and about praying, too. He'd probably love the chance to tease her about that kiss. She imagined his grin, and her heart rate jumped again. She jerked the door open and peered into the quiet corridor. Spying a crooked, abandoned chair in the hallway, she stepped over the threshold.

Ellen disregarded the warped seat and gave her trembling legs rest, grateful for the sanctuary she'd found. Reaching into her backpack, she retrieved the cotton sweater she'd begun crocheting on the plane. That flight seemed an age ago.

Hands trembling with adrenalin and anxiety, she split the yarn with her hook on almost every stitch. Frustration forced her to stop pretending to crochet. Instead, she clutched the yarn with both hands. Simply holding the soft, familiar fiber soothed her tangled emotions. She closed her eyes against everything but her prayer. *Oh, dear God, this comedy of errors with Payne is crazy. Is he the adventure You had in mind for me in Ireland? You are so pushing me out of my safe, little box. Please, please, please help me.*

♠♠♣♣

"Hey, Mom? Are you asleep?"

Ellen's eyes flew open. Olivia loomed over her. Deep into her calming exercise, she hadn't responded to the far away sounds of the door opening or the handful of students streaming out of the room. Silent prayers and soft yarn had slowed her heart rate and steadied her breathing, but they hadn't erased Payne's smile from the forefront of her brain.

"Hey, back. I finished my morning early and decided to relax while I waited for you." She stuffed the hook into the rolled skein of yarn and folded the beginnings of the sweater into her backpack. 'Do you mind if we just go to the house and grab a sandwich today? I don't feel like eating out again."

"No problem. How'd breakfast go?" An innocent question on the surface, but Ellen caught the raised eyebrow that accompanied it.

63

She didn't want to face Olivia's inquisition yet. "Fine. I had oatmeal."

Olivia made an unladylike grunt. "Mom. Tell me about that guy."

Linking arms with Olivia, she glided down the hallway. "Payne's fine, too. He had scrambled eggs and black pudding." She tightened her grip on her daughter, determined to redirect their route. She couldn't see him. Not now. "Hey," her voice quavered. "Let's go out this way. I want to check out those beautiful fuchsia borders, okay?"

With a few steps pointed in a different direction, they strolled away from the man waiting in the front of the college, the man who had the power to turn her world topsy turvy.

⁂

Payne waited for at least fifteen minutes after the last student sauntered by him before admitting he'd missed her. He searched up and down nearby streets, enduring inquisitive stares as he scoured the lunch crowd at outdoor cafes. He knew discovering her paralleled finding a needle in a haystack, but he meant to discuss that kiss with Ellen.

Acknowledging defeat, he tunneled his fingers through his hair and blew out a long breath. Hungry and thirsty, he had nothing to show for almost two hours of his time. The haystack had prevailed.

He could have avoided this fruitless search if he'd asked for her phone number. Sounded easy, but the thought had never occurred to him. His conversation skills with the opposite sex were rustier than he thought.

He had a few days left in Galway. He'd keep his eyes open. Maybe he'd check out a few yarn stores himself. He didn't give up easily. He wanted to ask Ellen about the kiss and maybe…have another one.

Chapter 9

Early the next morning, Ellen drove a rented Volvo south towards the little town of Gort. She noticed her white knuckles contrasting with the black steering wheel and loosened her grip. She hoped to circle around County Clare, visiting two farms and three yarn stores, if time and weather permitted, and return to Galway by early evening.

Driving on the right side of the car and the left side of the road required all of her concentration. No gazing at the passing green fields of peat and the thatched roof cottages. This car, a standard model, required her to change gears with her left hand and steer with her right.

Intersections stirred up dread in Ellen. She had to think through each turn to end up in the correct lane. Left turns weren't too bad, but right turns always panicked her a little. At least the gas, clutch, and brake pedals stood in the same order as they did in cars at home. She didn't have to think about what to do with her feet.

Olivia adjusted her seat belt strap. "So, Mom. You never did tell me about your breakfast yesterday. Every time I brought it up, you conveniently changed the subject."

"I changed the subject? Why would I do that?" Ellen glanced over at her daughter who made a face at her. "I enjoyed it. Hey, he told me he knows how to crochet. At least he used to, and he made a scarf once. His grandmother taught him. Pretty cool, huh?" The memory tipped the corners of her mouth.

"How do you know he's telling the truth?" Olivia shifted in

her seat, staring out the window instead of Ellen. "Maybe he's just telling a good yarn to the lady who owns the yarn shop. Ha."

Ellen rolled her eyes at Olivia's pitiful attempt at humor. "Because he brought up crocheting first. When I mentioned the shop, he asked me if I crochet. Crochet, Olivia, not knitting. And anyway, why would he lie about crocheting, for Heaven's sake?"

"Who knows?" Olivia rasped the words. "People lie about all kinds of things."

Ellen risked a sideways peek. Olivia stared out the window.

After falling quickly for a boy she met during her freshman year of college, Olivia discovered that he whispered the same pretty words to one of her suite mates. Coming so near to her father's death, the betrayal of two friends smacked an already fragile girl.

"You're right." Ellen softened her voice. "Some people do lie, unfortunately. But Payne didn't have a reason to lie about crocheting." She leaned forward to scan the road ahead. "I think we're getting close to the turnoff. Check the map again, please."

A purple and green wooden sign for Brambleberry Farm appeared on the right. Ellen turned down a gravel path and drove between two high hedges to an opening that revealed a modest house, a two-story purple barn with shelters on both sides, and acres and acres of grazing sheep. With loud, sharp barks signaling the arrival of guests, a Springer Spaniel quivered in the driveway.

As Ellen and Olivia stepped out of the silver Volvo, a woman in her mid-forties with close-cropped strawberry blonde curls exited the barn door, heading toward them. Those reddish curls reminded her of the neighbor child she babysat during the early years of her marriage. Longing for that time gripped her, but she pushed the thought away.

"Hush, Sam." The woman fluttered a hand toward the dog. "Be gone with you now." Dangly earrings of lapis beads swung back and forth as she shook her head at the dog.

Her knitted cardigan partially concealed a rose-colored cotton shirt and brushed the waistband of her brown capris. A leather cord threaded through a skinny, long tube of silver encircled her ankle just above mud-covered purple gardening clogs.

Her blue eyes smiling, she waved to them. "Well, you found us, did you? I'm Grainne. Welcome to Brambleberry Farm."

Ellen extended her hand and returned the smile, instinctively anticipating a long kinship with this engaging sheep farmer.

After quick pleasantries, Grainne guided them into her barn. Wondering at first about the necessity of such a tour, Ellen soon fell under the enchantment of Grainne's soft brogue. An enthusiastic host and a natural teacher, she led them by the now quiet individual stalls which Grainne called *jugs* in the sheep maternity ward located in the first floor of the barn.

Grainne leaned against a railing. "Controlled chaos was what we had here last spring when thirty-four ewes gave birth." She grimaced. "It was brutal around here for two weeks at least. We were up the bigger part of every night makin' sure that everything went right and well. We got several twins, we did."

Ellen couldn't imagine chaos describing anything Grainne undertook from the looks of the immaculate building. Neat, hand-lettered labels identified bottles of what Ellen assumed were medicine and other necessary sheep-raising supplies. The bottles stood in orderly rows stacked on shelves filling part of the wall opposite the jugs. More jugs lined another wall.

Would the researcher in Payne find this barn interesting? Would he be impressed with Grainne's well-organized system? It didn't matter. He'd never see it, and she'd probably never see… Ellen corralled her thoughts and concentrated on the tour.

If the maternity ward had been chaotic in the spring, the summer brought the opposite view—quiet sounds and clean straw. The earthy barn odors, more pleasant than pungent, welcomed them. Two calico cats slept in the corner of one jug while a black and white kitten pounced on an insect in another.

Wooden stairs creaked as the women ascended to the second floor. At the top, they entered a wonderland for yarn crafters. Cubbies full of skeins of wool extended from one wall to a double window across from the door. Two stoves and a refrigerator dominated the right wall. Two double sinks completed the makeup of the back wall.

Several boxes of roving, rolag, and fiber rested near an enormous spinning wheel holding court in the closest left corner. Ellen drew in a sharp breath. "What a cool spinning wheel."

Grainne grinned. "That big daddy belonged to my great grandmother. I don't really spin with him anymore. I just keep him because I love him. I send most of my wool to a company up in Donegal, but I do spin a little wool for myself." She pointed to a smaller wheel made of cherry wood. "I use this beauty for that."

Ellen knelt by the small wheel and caressed its rich dark wood.

Grainne joined her and touched her shoulder. "Sit down and try her out. Spin some, why don't you?"

The wheel already had a strand of wool threaded around the spindle. Ellen plopped on the stool. Grainne positioned one of Ellen's hands on the tuft of wool, the other holding the thread nearest the spindle.

Ellen bit her lip, wrinkling her brow. She wanted to please her new friend. "I took a short spinning course a few years ago, but I wasn't very good at it. My head knows what to do, but my fingers get confused."

Grainne laughed, knelt beside the wheel, and offered gentle tips as Ellen pumped the pedal to spin the wheel with her foot. "You're doin' grand, Ellen. Don't think too much. Just let your fingers do the work."

Her confidence grew under Grainne's instruction. Careful teaching made the skill seem less tedious and more fun. As she watched her fingers guiding the thread that wrapped around the spindle, she remembered Payne's hands holding hers, ready for prayer. She needed prayer, too. Prayer to resist thoughts of him that interrupted every activity.

Leaving Ellen to practice, Grainne crossed the room to the old spinning wheel. "You can have a go, too, Olivia, if you want."

"Thank you, but I'll pass. I can crochet a pretty serviceable beanie when I try, but Mom's the crafty one in the family." Olivia slid into the rocking chair draped with two wool afghans near the window.

Grainne selected two skeins from a basket near the large

wheel and brought them to Ellen. "These are part of my new experiment. I'm combining silk with the wool now. We raise Finns, and those sheep give the softest wool you can find, but the silk softens the texture even more. Lightens the weight a bit, too."

Removing her foot from the pedal, Ellen took the skeins. She burrowed her fingers into the downy softness of the fiber. Tension from driving on the wrong side of the road, from dealing with thoughts of Payne every few minutes dissolved as she stroked the silk and wool blend. "It feels like clouds."

Olivia, resting her head on the back of the chair, burst out laughing at her mom's enthusiasm. "Mom. Seriously?"

Ellen waved a skein in the air. "Come feel for yourself. Prepare to apologize for laughing at me, Missy."

ഇഇ෫෫

By noon, Ellen and Grainne chatted like old friends. Grainne asked them to stay for lunch, and they enjoyed a meal of scones and Tipperary cheese, strawberries, and spinach soup. Her entire family—her husband, Liam, two sons, and three daughters—joined them under the rose-covered pergola in the back yard for the meal. The fruity smell of the yellow roses combined with the buttery aroma of the scones, creating a heady invitation for lunch.

Warming to Ellen and Olivia, Grainne's sons bounced Irish humor back and forth across the table until their dad called them to a halt. Grainne protested, but Liam was firm with his sons. "Don't mollycoddle them, Grainne. They've been as useful as a bucket of steam this morning, and they need to be settlin' down."

Although his words sounded gruff, twinkly eyes revealed teasing rather than scolding. The older sisters, familiar with their dad's jokes, rewarded him with giggles and smiles.

Toward the end of the meal, the breeze changed, turning cooler and bringing dark clouds. Rain crashed the party before they could gather the dishes. This rain, displaying more than a little Irish mist, grew in force and blew in sheets of continuous drops from across the meadow.

69

Turning toward Grainne, Ellen said her reluctant goodbyes. Grainne squeezed her hand. "Thanks a million for the order. I'll get it to you as soon as I finish dyeing the next lot." Ellen scrunched her shoulders and laughed, anticipating boxes of the silk and wool yarn in five different colors arriving in her shop.

Huddling under an oversized, charcoal colored umbrella, Liam accompanied the visitors through the pouring rain to their car. The rest of the family, the young ones wiggling on the front porch, waved as Ellen turned the car around to head back down the driveway. Sam barked his farewell from the open barn door.

Chilled from the raindrops, Ellen turned on the heater. Rivulets of water ran down the windshield. "With this deluge, I think Duffy Farm is out of the question, but we could probably still visit the yarn shops, if you're up to it. The one called *What's Knew with Ewe?* Is in Ennis, only about twenty minutes south. Does that sound good, Sweetie?"

"Sure." Olivia leaned back against the headrest. "Grainne was really nice. I like her whole family."

Ellen nodded. "I had fun this morning. I'm glad you did, too." Back on the main road, she shifted into high gear.

Olivia stared out her window for several miles, seemingly lost in her own thoughts. Was she thinking about treasured times with her own dad? The morning had been bittersweet for Ellen, watching the interactions between Grainne and Liam.

"I mean, yeah, it was fun, but…at the same time, it kinda made me sad. Made me think about Dad a little bit."

"Me, too, Sweetie." Ellen reached over and patted Olivia's knee.

"So you think about Dad?"

"Of course, I do."

With a heavy sigh, she turned away from the window. "Well then. What's the deal with that Payne man? Do you like him?"

Ellen jerked her head in Olivia's direction. "Good grief. Where did that come from?" Ellen's heart rate, already accelerated from driving on the left side of the road *and* in the rain, rammed into overdrive.

"Mom, just answer me…please." She folded her arms across

her chest. "What's going on with him?"

"Olivia, I've talked with him exactly three times." Ellen stalled for time, hoping to think of how to answer her daughter's question.

"Mom, I'm waiting." Olivia, not relenting, tapped her wet sandal against the floor.

"Fine." Ellen grimaced. "Yes, I enjoyed meeting him. Spending time with him was fun. I haven't enjoyed talking with a man like that in a long time." She didn't want to admit to herself, much less Olivia, how much she'd enjoyed it. She'd been trying to squelch the feeling of missing Payne all morning as thoughts of him dogged her at every turn during her tour of Grainne's barn. How could she miss someone she had met only days ago?

"What about those guys Ms. Nancy and Ms. Frankie tried to set you up with? You talked with them, didn't you?"

Ellen groaned. "Oh, Olivia."

On three separate occasions, Nancy and Frankie from church had held dinner parties and had conveniently forgotten to tell her that they had invited "someone I'd love for you to meet." One of the prospects had two subjects of conversation, his boat and his dog, but at least he had talked. The other gentleman might have said more than "hello" and "goodbye," but if he did, she couldn't remember.

By the third invitation, Ellen had caught on and made sure she always had plans when those friends called. "Nancy and Frankie meant well, but our taste in men doesn't exactly line up."

Olivia frowned. "Does your taste in men line up with that Payne man?"

Concentrating on the road, Ellen kept her eyes glued straight ahead, avoiding her daughter's stare. Thankfully, the rain had subsided. "Will you stop? It's over and done with. We didn't make plans after yesterday. I don't know how to contact him, and he doesn't have my phone number either, so that's it. A—what's it called? I can't remember. Oh, yes. A shipboard romance—although we weren't on—"

Olivia's eyes popped with shock. "A romance. Is that what you'd call it?"

Ellen's hands squeezed the steering wheel. "Wait. That's not the way I meant it. I just meant…" What did she mean? She didn't understand it herself. Part of her still missed Steve, but Payne intrigued her. And now…"We knew each other for three days, and now it's finished. That's all." Willing the conversation to be over, Ellen relaxed her shoulders and loosened her grip in the steering wheel.

Olivia's jaw slackened. "That's all? You sat and talked with him from lunch till mid-afternoon and didn't exchange phone numbers? That's hard to believe, Mom." She shifted in her seat, changing tactics. "What does he do for a living?"

"He's working on an environmental project in Africa right now." Ellen mentally patted herself on the back for knowing that much.

"Environmental project. Africa. Very specific, Mom. You do know that Africa is a whole continent, right?"

"Sarcasm doesn't become you, Olivia." Ellen's eyes narrowed as she continued to focus on the road.

"You said he's working in Africa now. Does that mean he lives somewhere else normally?"

"I don't know."

"What's he doing in Galway?"

"I don't know that either." Reality tapped on her brain. She didn't know much of anything about him.

Olivia shook her head, exasperated. "Then what in the heck did you talk about, Mom?"

"Obviously nothing of great importance. See what I mean? Neither of us must have been too interested in the other because we didn't get any normal information." Ouch. A painful thought.

Now that she considered the idea of knowing personal facts about him, she realized she did want to know more about Payne, but asking those kinds of questions simply hadn't occurred to her. She'd been too busy enjoying the natural flow of their conversations to think about addresses and phone numbers.

She wished she had now.

"Okay. We're coming into Ennis. I've got to concentrate on traffic." No more questions about Payne. It's over—whatever she called it. "What street should we be looking for?"

Olivia examined the sheet with Ellen's handwritten address-es. "Parnell Street. But you have a note beside it that says it's a pedestrian street. We'll have to park somewhere else."

"Right. Look on the map, please, and find a street that's close, okay?"

Olivia scanned a street map of Ennis. "Abbey and O'Connell are close, but they're listed as one way. Be careful. You don't want to end up going the wrong way on the wrong side of the road, you know."

"Yes, I absolutely do know. So help me out. Thank goodness the rain's stopped. Oh, look at that gorgeous church." The gray stone building showcased beautiful stained glass windows. "And there's O'Connell. Let's see if there's a parking place for us."

She carefully turned onto the street and prayed a quick thank you after spotting an open space a few yards down the block. Not trusting the reprieve in the fickle Irish weather, she grabbed her mini umbrella from the backseat. "According to the map, *What's New With Ewe?* sits right in the middle of Towne Centre. Let's get going before the next cloudburst."

As they strolled toward Parnell Street, a tall, slender man exited a book shop at the corner and turned toward them. Ellen's stomach flipped. Was it Payne? A second look, however, confirmed what she already knew. Payne was not in Ennis.

Ellen ignored the emotion—whether disappointment or relief—that coursed through her, determined to focus on other thoughts. For all she knew, Payne could have already returned to Africa, but she had several days left to enjoy in Ireland.

As soon as they stepped onto the Towne Centre, the yarn shop beckoned to them. The scalloped edge of its pink and yellow striped awning flapped in the breeze remaining from the storm. Ellen smiled. "If the inside is anything like the outside, I'm going to love this place."

"That awning kind of screams, 'Here I am. Come on in,' don't you think?" Olivia giggled, and linked arms with her mother to be closer, her testy mood vanishing like the Irish mist.

Chapter 10

The cheery theme continued inside the shop. Alluring scents of cinnamon and vanilla invited them in. Vivaldi's *Four Seasons* played softly in the background.

A group of women sat in overstuffed, mismatched chairs beside the bay window chatting and knitting socks on circular needles. At the squeaking of the door, the knitters glanced up, welcome smiles warming their faces, their needles flying. A plump woman wearing a light blue cardigan over a floral blouse greeted them. "Hallo. If you need anything, simply let us know, will ya?"

Ellen introduced Olivia and herself. "I'd hoped to meet with the owner if that's possible." She raised her eyebrows and caught her bottom lip with her teeth.

The spokeswoman rested her needles in her lap. "Oh my, I'm so sorry. Mary O'Brian's gone down to Timoleague in County Cork to see her ailing older brother. His horse jumped a ditch and left him behind on the first side with a broken leg. He's not married, that one, and needs some help, ya know. She had to leave her shop in our hands and her four wee ones with her very capable and very handsome husband, Angus. You can see her tomorrow, though. She'll be back then."

Chatty Cathy, whose words had gushed out in one gigantic breath, sucked in air like a swimmer at the end of a hard race. Two of her friends tut tutted and shook their heads, but she either ignored them or didn't notice their reaction to her broadcasting the details of Mary O'Brian's private life.

Ellen shook off her disappointment at the owner's absence.

"No problem. I'll take a look around today, if that's okay, because I can't come back tomorrow."

Chatty Cathy resumed her knitting. "Enjoy then, Dear. We'll be up here in the window if you need anything."

Turning away from the sound of clicking needles, Ellen surveyed her surroundings. If the outside awnings had promised a quirky shop, the inside delivered. She spotted Olivia perched on a chartreuse bench near an old library card catalog box, flipping through a knitting magazine.

Ellen moved toward an interesting display. Mary O'Brian had a knack for unexpected presentation, incorporating yarn with accessories. Instead of the usual wire racks, collections of knitting patterns nestled in distressed, wooden crates. Crochet hooks, knitting needles, and buttons peaked out of the open card catalog drawers. Decorative hat boxes of bulky yarn took up residence underneath.

She studied knitted garments displayed on fabric-covered hangers and draped over tables and chairs, admiring the intricate stitches and patterns. Discovering some new yarns, she selected a few skeins she liked well enough to buy. She looked forward to researching the yarn companies listed on the wrappers with Olivia's laptop when they returned to the house.

"Thanks a million." Chatty Cathy rang up her purchases, placing the skeins in a bright pink and yellow polka dot bag. "Mary O'Brian will be so sorry she missed the both of ya'. Enjoy your knitting and the rest of your holiday."

Outside the shop, the rain had dwindled to a cool light sprinkling, but rolling, dark clouds threatened a possible wash out for the remainder of the day. Returning to their car, they headed west for the next shop on her list. Unfortunately, that one turned out to be an alcove in a post office/candy/ice cream/stationery store. Cubbies banished to a back corner offered a few yarn choices but nothing exciting.

On their way out, Ellen spied the ice cream counter. No matter the location or time of day, ice cream called to her, an irresistible temptation. "Want a cone? My treat."

"You don't have to ask me twice." Olivia sidled up to the bar, wiggling her shoulders.

The teenaged cashier, with jet black hair covering one eye and a silver hoop imbedded in the eyebrow of the other, stuck a mini Flake candy bar into the side of the swirled soft serve. "Mmmmm. Ice cream *and* chocolate. If I didn't already love Ireland, this combination would definitely tip the balance."

Olivia bit the ice cream end of the Flake bar and nodded. "I know, right?"

Ellen dabbed at the corner of her mouth with a brown napkin made of recycled paper. "This cone's as big as my head. Maybe it should be my dinner." She glanced at her watch. "Are you ready to turn back now?" She wanted to get started on the drive back to Galway.

"Yeah. That sounds good. We can pop some popcorn and have some fruit if we get hungry later. Thanks for the ice cream, Mom."

As they retraced their path to the car, Ellen enjoyed reducing the ice cream to a more manageable size. By the time they reached their destination, she'd diminished the swirled concoction by half. "I think I'll be able to drive now that I've whittled it down some."

Holding the cone with her right thumb and forefinger and gripping the steering wheel with her other three fingers, Ellen shifted the gear stick into reverse with her left. She glided out of the parking space with relative ease, but going forward with traffic and an ice cream cone demanded concentration and skill. "On second thought, I'm not sure driving with a cone in hand is a great idea, especially when everything's backward. Don't try this yourself."

"Don't worry. I'm not planning to drive at all over here." Olivia ran her tongue around the sugar cone and swallowed. "I'm proud of you, though."

They moved slowly through the street filled with cars as well as pedestrians. Ellen leaned forward, eyes darting back and forth on the alert for traffic mishaps. Maybe she could learn to enjoy Irish driving.

She relaxed her fingers on the steering wheel as Payne

stepped from the sidewalk and walked through the intersection ahead. She gasped and slammed her foot on the brake but forgot to depress the clutch at the same time. The car choked off, jolting the women against their seatbelts. Ellen's cone jumped out of her hand and landed in her lap.

The man, who, of course, wasn't Payne, disappeared down the sidewalk, oblivious to the traffic snarl.

Ellen groaned and squeezed the steering wheel. She glanced in the rearview mirror at a driver blasting his horn.

"It's okay, Mom. You crank the car and get going. I'll scoop up your ice cream." Olivia grabbed the cone from her mother's lap.

"Just hold it for a minute, please, and I'll park the car so I can clean the mess." Somehow she had to get control of her imagination. She had to stop seeing Payne in every man who crossed her path.

Olivia turned the cone, inspecting it. "Do you still want it, or do you want to throw it away?"

"I don't want to gross you out or anything, but, yes, I want it. If you're sure you don't see any lint from the spinning lesson clinging to the ice cream." Ellen wiped off most of the melted dairy mess on her skirt. She laughed. "I guess I'm doing laundry tonight."

ಬಬಚಚ

Draping the last few garments on the drying rack, she found the floral skirt she'd worn the day Payne had surprised her in the pottery shop. She fingered the soft cotton fabric. Pictures of him blinked in her mind before she could prevent them.

If she were honest, she didn't want to stop those images. She liked thinking about Payne. She liked remembering how his gray eyes crinkled when he smiled. She liked hearing him laugh. She liked the feel of his calloused palm in her hand, and she liked that kiss, too.

She needed to stop letting her mind walk down that road of memories. She'd told Olivia—the thing with Payne was over.

Her mind knew the words were true, but her heart hoped for something more.

Unfortunately, this diversion, this adventure with a strange man in a foreign country had run its course before it'd really begun. She almost wished that he had seen her at the college yesterday.

Grimacing, she shook her head. Not a good idea. Payne would have had a field day over that kiss. Her heart constricted with that thought, and she flattened her hand against her chest.

She should stop wishing and dreaming. Enjoy the memories and look forward to a realistic tomorrow.

Enjoying the memories. That plan seemed safe but boring.

And empty.

ഇൽഇ൩ഇ൩

Although Payne knew Ellen's plans for Thursday were to shop for yarn outside of Galway, he rode the City Direct bus into Eyre Square anyway, holding on to a slim hope that she might have changed her plans. He searched the pottery shop, the café they'd met in, and Uncle Paddy's Bistro. Realizing his hunt resembled a wild goose chase, he surrendered to the obvious and ordered a cup of coffee and a scone in place of the breakfast he'd skipped before starting his search.

As hopeless as the quest seemed, he'd had to come and look, thoughts of Ellen tormenting most of his hours. Why and how had she become so important to him? Important to him?

That thought jerked his hand, sloshing drops of coffee over the edge of his mug. He stuck the smarting index finger into his mouth.

Was she important to him? No, not really. But he liked himself when he spent time with her. Instead of his usual dark feelings, he sensed lightness and something akin to happiness rolling around inside his chest.

No, she wasn't important exactly. He refused to allow any woman to become necessary to his well-being. She interested him, that's all. Her old fashioned word choices amused him. Her quick wit and sweet spirit attracted him. And that kiss... That kiss definitely got his blood pumping.

Unfortunately, for him—she was a believer. Someone who actually prayed and expected God to hear. Probably surrounded by other believers, too. And she didn't need to be dragged down by an ex-believer. Someone like Payne who'd realized a long time ago that God may have created the world, but He didn't concern Himself with the everyday details of His creation now.

If He did care about His creation and listen to prayers, then wouldn't He have heard Payne's cries for help to save and heal his little boy?

A flickering image of his smiling son floated before his eyes. Sharp pain sliced through his insides. Leaning on his elbows, Payne covered his face with his hands. He shook his head against the memories, but sure enough, as soon as he thought about Jamie and his chocolate-covered curls, a picture of his wife's face, altered by rage after their last fight, forced its way into his mind.

Why? Why couldn't he let these pictures go? Why didn't God protect his little boy? Why had He let that accident happen?

My ways are not your ways, drummed in his mind.

Payne snorted. 'My ways aren't your ways.' An easy answer. Humans are supposed to be made in God's image, right?

Draw near to Me, Payne.

He gritted his teeth to obliterate the unwanted pictures and silent words. Where did these thoughts come from? He hadn't let these images surface in over ten years. And the accident that had claimed two lives had happened fifteen years ago. Why think about all these painful memories now?

He shook his head and took a deep breath. He'd go back to Charlie's rented house and spend the rest of the day hanging out with his college roommate's family. Then he'd do the wedding thing for his godson this weekend, and he'd stop thinking about Ellen Shepherd.

In a few days, he'd be back in Uganda finishing up his project, and she'd be— She'd be where? Rusty at talking with interesting women, he hadn't found out where she lived in the States. He hadn't learned much of anything that would help him find her now—not her phone number or how to find her in Galway. Besides the yarn shop and her daughter, he didn't know any other important details about her.

Good. That should make forgetting her easier. But something inside him didn't want to forget her. She'd made him laugh, which hadn't been an easy feat to accomplish in the past few years, and she'd kissed him like— Like what? Like she'd wanted to be with him.

Like she'd wanted to kiss him.

Like she'd enjoyed kissing him.

Yes, she had enjoyed kissing him. He knew it, and with another chance maybe he could prove she liked that kiss.

That interesting confrontation would have to remain a fantasy, however, because, more than likely, he'd never see her again.

So he'd have to work hard to push her out of his mind. He'd done it before with Jamie and Cynthia. He could do it again. He'd will himself to stop thinking about Ellen, too.

Chapter 11

Friday morning greeted Ellen with a cool breeze and overcast skies. Staying in the house all morning might have been an appealing possibility, but she didn't want to take the coward's path again. Olivia might expect her to sleep in this morning especially after the busy day yesterday, but Ellen didn't want fear of seeing Payne again and enduring his inevitable teasing about their kiss to dictate her vacation plans.

She wanted to prove to herself that she could be brave. She ignored the tiny part of her that hoped to see him again.

She hesitated in front of Gilley's Café, the site of their first conversation. Instead of entering, Ellen moved farther down the street to Morgan's. Choosing a table near the front window, she ordered a pot of tea. Having her morning tea in Gilley's evoked images of a sitting duck. If Payne did look for her today, she didn't want to be found at their café. Payne would probably tease her about that, too.

Assuming he was still thinking about that kiss. And that he wanted to find her. And that he was still in Galway. She should drink her tea and stop thinking about Payne.

Good advice if only she could follow it. Wrapping her hand around the steaming mug, she waited for the heat to relax her. She sipped the Irish Breakfast Blend and doodled in the margins of her travel notes for *The Dispatch*. Distracted by her thoughts of Payne, the whirring of the cappuccino machine, and cheerful Irish accents, she wrote awkward and disjointed sentences. Every time the front door jingled opened, she looked up hoping to see

Payne smiling at her with his teasing grin.

Realizing that good writing refused to cooperate with her pen, she decided to pray to settle herself. She'd continued to pray for Payne since the first time he'd asked her to. He had probably been goading her, but she'd promised to pray for him and felt a sort of an obligation to keep it up.

Ellen didn't feel guilty thinking about Payne when she prayed for him unlike when thoughts of him and his smile and his tan arms and that kiss invaded her mind. She continued to pray for him to draw near to God and for abundant blessings on him. She wanted him to be happy, but she had a hunch he nursed a lot of sadness.

Although he had some knowledge of God, Payne had seemed closed off to God, even a little antagonistic at first. She suspected he harbored a painful secret because of his reaction to her description of him during their initial conversation, but he'd turned the tables and teased her about her word choice. He didn't want to discuss something in his background, and he'd skirted the off-limits topic like a master politician.

Father, please help him sort through whatever he's hiding. Lead him back to You.

She lingered over three cups of tea before admitting he wasn't looking for her. Leaving Morgan's, Ellen strolled back to the pottery shop intending to buy the pitcher she'd admired earlier in the week.

Her heart felt lighter at the prospect of owning the striking pitcher.

When she arrived at the display at the end of the aisle, however, a blue and green honey pot sat in place of the pitcher. She searched the table and the shelves above but couldn't find the pitcher. "Excuse me." She caught the attention of the short, plump shopkeeper. "I'm looking for a pitcher from this collection that I saw a few days ago, but I can't find it now—"

"Oh, Darlin'," the shopkeeper adjusted the neck strap of her green apron. "That potter is one of our most popular artists. Our inventory turnover is quick as a wink. I'm afraid if you don't see your lovely pitcher sitting out, it's gone for good. Sorry, dear."

She wasn't meant to have it. No big deal. She shrugged off her disappointment and headed out to discover other treasurers.

ഇഇൽരൽ

Early Friday afternoon, Ellen and Olivia traveled out of the city on the N59 Road and checked in at Mary's Bed and Breakfast in Clifden. Olivia dove onto the bed and stretched her legs. "So what do we do first? Take a nap?"

"Don't you wish? I've got a list of places I want to see." Ellen rummaged through her overnight case until she found her brush. The bristles felt good on her scalp. "One shop is right here in Clifden, just a block over from us, I think. We could pop in there before dinner. Sound good?" She reapplied her lipstick.

"It sounds like what we're doing. I hope I get a sweater out of all this yarn shopping." Olivia rolled back over onto her stomach. "A short, cute pullover from Grainne's yarn. With a boat-neck neckline. With cool buttons at the sleeves. You can surprise me with the color. But not blue. I've got three blue sweaters already." She giggled and waved her bare feet in the air.

"I'm sure I'll get on that right away, Your Majesty." Ellen curtsied to her daughter. "You've designed the sweater already in your mind. Why don't you crochet it yourself?"

"Because you do it so much better, Mom." Olivia batted her eyes and grinned at Ellen, and Ellen couldn't help but smile back.

The first shop, located in downtown Clifden, held no surprises for Ellen. As inviting and beautifully decorated as the shop was, she knew all of the yarn companies and stocked a few of the yarns in her own store. They ate dinner in Mannion's Pub and then finished Friday back at their bed and breakfast.

Spoiled by Grainne's outgoing manner and enthusiasm, they were taken aback by the cool, unfriendly manner of the sheep farmer who owned the wool business they toured Saturday morning. With his lanky frame and craggy features, he reminded Ellen of Abraham Lincoln but lacked the president's charm. He trudged several paces ahead of them, leading toward the barn.

Olivia whispered, "Mom, he's a sourpuss. Even his animals

85

know it. Look at 'em." She pointed to the handful of sheep gawking at them from the paddock beside the barn. Sad eyes followed their movements from the other side of the fence.

"Ladies." The farmer spun around so fast, both women startled and took steps backward. "Hurry along now and stop slinjing, if you please. I've got a full day's work ahead and no one to do it but me."

Stung by his chastising attitude, Ellen decided to make an immediate break, not willing to suffer through any more time in his negative presence. "Mr. Dunne, thank you so much for your…umm… for seeing us this morning, but we don't want to take up any more of your time. We can see you're such a busy man. We need to get on down the road now."

He blinked and blinked again. "You haven't seen the wool yet. T'will take but a quick minute." He turned, continuing to the barn.

Ellen exchanged a glance with Olivia and shrugged. As much as she wanted to stand her ground and leave, the lure of the yarn tugged at her to follow her host.

Moments later, she sent up thank you prayers that she'd obeyed the siren call.

The yarn he showed her resembled nothing she'd ever seen before. A beautiful rainbow of fiber filled cardboard boxes, ready to ship. She caressed the vibrant colors of daffodil, pomegranate, amethyst, moss green, and periwinkle.

"These colors are beautiful." She peeked at him, expecting a reprimand. Instead, she noticed a twitch at the corners of his mouth. Compliments work on even the most cantankerous people.

"They're not too bad. I've been trying some new dyeing strategies." He hooked his thumbs in his belt.

Ellen nodded and tilted her head. "I'd love to hear about your new dyeing processes."

As quick as the nice Mr. Browne had shown himself, the aloof one returned with narrowed eyes and a stubborn set of his jaw. "Nope. Nope. Still workin' on my ideas. Will you be buyin' anything today then?"

೫೨೦೦೮೨

Olivia laughed as they headed for the next yarn shop near Kylemore Abbey. "Did you see his face when you said we were going to leave—before we even saw any yarn? Classic. I wish I had a picture."

"Yes, well. I was tired of him running roughshod over us. Talk about rude. And what is 'slinjing' anyway?"

"Who knows, but, Mom, I've seen you swallow a lot of comebacks trying to be good. I'm proud of you for pushing back a little today." Olivia reached over and patted Ellen on the shoulder. "Good job."

"Thanks, Sweetie, but I'm glad I gave in at the end. I'd have hated to miss those sumptuous colors. How does he come up with those shades?" Ellen downshifted as they neared their next turnoff.

"We'll never know. Mr. Meany doesn't share info."

"True. Here's the road for Taggart's Wool. Wonder what we'll find here?"

At the yarn shop, however, a hand-lettered sign greeted them with "Closed for the Afternoon" hung over the front door. On a whim, Ellen suggested traveling on to Kylemore Abbey just a few miles down the road, and Olivia agreed. "The Abbey was one of my favorite places last time we were in Ireland. I thought it was so romantic that the owner built this castle as a gift for his wife."

"Yeah. Quite a wedding present."

They decided against touring the Abbey itself again. They couldn't resist, however, the Abbey's Walled Garden. Wearing their rain gear in case the overcast sky made good on its promise, they strolled through the Flower Garden by the Herbaceous Border, enjoying the beautiful, bright blooms of the Cuckoo Flower and the geraniums that contrasted with the foliage the color of green found only in Ireland.

Later, they visited the Tea House beside the garden. As they nibbled on apricot scones and sipped dainty cups of Earl Gray, their eyes feasted on breathtaking views of the Connemara National Park

Olivia broke off a piece of scone. "I love Ireland. It's so beautiful. I feel like I'm in a post card picture. Look." She nodded toward the tallest mountain called Diamond Hill.

"I know. Sometimes I have to pinch myself to make sure it's all real."

Olivia grabbed her wrist. "I'm so glad you came, Mom." She bit her lip. "And I'm sorry I've been a little bratty about Payne."

Ellen lifted an eyebrow. "A little?"

"Fine. A lot bratty. It's just... I don't know. It's weird, I guess, to think about you and someone besides Daddy." A hint of pain flickered in Olivia's eyes.

Ellen laid her hand overtop Olivia's still encircling Ellen's wrist. "I know, Sweetie, and that's why I gave you some slack when you slipped over into rude mode." She smiled. "The whole thing with Payne kind of blindsided me, too. It was fun while it lasted, but you don't have to worry about him anymore."

ℰℰℭℛ

Although the Irish mist had descended on them throughout the day, by the time they arrived back in Galway, the sun peeked through the remaining clouds. Driving through Eyre Square, they passed a wedding party coming out of the Galway Central Church, the one they had visited last Sunday. "Oh, look at that beautiful gown." Olivia pointed toward the bride.

Glancing at the group of groomsmen, Ellen spied Payne and gasped.

"What is it, Mom?"

Ellen swallowed her shock. "Nothing. It's—it's just that dress. It's really gorgeous, huh?"

She blinked to refocus her contacts and grabbed a second look. Yes, one of the groomsmen was Payne.

She'd seen Payne transformed from a dusty derelict in safari clothes to a handsome tourist in khakis and button downs, but she'd never seen him in a tux. Breathtaking.

Payne was still in Galway

He stood beside a young man—the one from the street who'd called out, "Uncle Payne." The one who'd probably seen the humiliating kiss. That young man wrapped his arm around the bride and smiled at a photographer.

Ellen shot a glance at the street in front of her then snatched another sight of the wedding party. A blond woman, the same one who'd accompanied the groom the other day, floated down the front steps of the church, stopping to touch Payne's sleeve. He bent toward the blond woman as she spoke to him.

Risking one last peek out the side window, Ellen glimpsed him nod and flash a beaming smile. She repositioned herself in the seat and focused on her driving.

The groom was Payne's nephew, but who was the blonde? Flustered, Ellen scrubbed the gears as she shifted into second, preparing for a turn. Her insides flashed hot and cold. Payne's attention had centered on the blonde, spectacular in an ice blue cocktail-length dress.

At the next stop sign, Ellen flexed her clammy hands. "Still want to go to the Galleon for dinner, or would you rather go home and get something?" She willed her daughter to choose eating at home. She didn't want to chance running into Payne tonight. Not escorting the blonde. Not in that tux.

"I don't really feel like cooking, Mom, or doing dishes either. You have to be tired, too, from all the driving. Let's grab a quick salad. Then we can head back to the house, watch a movie, or go to bed early, okay?"

Ellen's shoulders sagged. "Sure, Sweetie. I just don't want to be out too long tonight." Her calves protested as she changed the gears once more.

The picture of the blonde on Payne's arm flickered in her mind, refusing to give way to other images. A growing green pall ringed with disappointment invaded her chest and clamored for a bedroom retreat. Cocooning there sounded like an attractive plan for the remainder of her stay in Ireland.

Yes, it'd be a perfect plan for cowards and losers. Exactly what she didn't want to model for her daughter.

She sat up tall in the driver's seat. "All right. Which way to the Galleon?"

෨෨෨ଊଊ

Payne woke up early with a renewed determination to find Ellen. As usual when he visited Charlie, his college roommate, and his wife, Kate, they invited him to attend church during breakfast, but this morning, instead of politely but firmly refusing the invitation, he agreed. If surprised by his answer, they hid it well except for the quick glance Payne caught between them.

"But, hey. I don't have a tie. The only one I brought with me has that soup stain from the rehearsal dinner when the waitress dropped the ladle on my plate."

Charlie grinned at his old roommate. "One of my fondest memories of that night. The look on your face and hers, too—priceless."

"Stop, Charlie" Kate's eyes chastised her husband. "Don't worry, Payne. He's not wearing a tie this morning either. Causal is good. Listen. There's supposed to be some sort of free music concert down around Erye Square this afternoon. Might be fun to check out after lunch. Sound good?"

Payne swallowed the last of his coffee. "Sounds like a plan."

When Michael had asked him to be one of his groomsmen, Payne contemplated declining because he'd have to enter a church, and he hadn't crossed the threshold of one since the funerals.

Not wanting to disappoint his godson, he forced himself to accept the request. Pleasantly surprised that the inside of a church hadn't been as excruciating as he had anticipated, he'd relaxed and enjoyed watching Michael and Jane's joy on their special day.

When the three old friends walked into Galway Central Church, he punched Charlie's shoulder. "How about we sit here, okay?" Payne pointed toward a back pew and surveyed the sanctuary for Ellen.

Charlie grinned. "Thinking you might need to cut and run,

90

ol' buddy?"

Kate elbowed him so hard in his ribs that Charlie grabbed his side and grimaced. "This pew is fine. Ignore him Payne."

Payne patted her back. "I usually do." He didn't want Charlie to realize how on target his question had been. Attending a church wedding was one thing. Sitting through a sermon was quite another.

The first few minutes breezed by like a meeting between old friends. Thankfully, the welcome, a general one, didn't require the visitors to stand up and shake hands with the amiable locals. Payne forced his fingers to release the fists curling at his sides. So far so good. He could do this church thing.

The minister invited the congregation to sing the first hymn. Payne wiped his hands on his khaki pants and flipped the pages to one of his favorite hymns, *Come Thou Fount of Every Blessing*. He scanned the pews once more while the pianist played the introduction but didn't see Ellen.

As the people around him sang, he found himself listening to the message of the words for the first time. "Streams of mercy, never ceasing," "redeeming love," "Jesus sought me when a stranger, Wand'ring from the fold of God," "Prone to wander, Lord, I feel it, Prone to leave the God I love." He didn't remember hearing the lyrics before. They reached over the heads of the other congregants and grabbed his hardened heart.

Emotion thumped in the middle of his chest. His lungs floundered. His windpipe felt constricted. He had to force air through them. Rigid fingers gripped the green edges of the hymnal.

He considered leaving but the awkwardness made him hesitate. He eyed the aisle, but a young couple appeared and joined them on their pew, pushing him in and away from his getaway path. Now penned in, he checked his watch. Just forty-five minutes to go. He rubbed his hand across his chin, still smooth from his morning shave. He surrendered. He could endure the service. If he didn't, Charlie would have a field day.

Before he could process his reaction to the first hymn, the minister introduced the second hymn, *Great is Thy Faithfulness*.

With the first chords, Payne returned the hymnal to the rack and shoved his hands into his pockets. He didn't need to see the words. He knew it by heart.

That hymn played prominently in the soundtrack of his childhood. His grandmother sang it almost every day as she peeled potatoes, washed dishes, or ironed his grandfather's work shirts. These lyrics washed over him as sweetly as the ones from the first song. "Pardon for sin and a peace that endureth," "Strength for today and bright hope for tomorrow, Blessings all mine, with ten thousand beside."

"Bright hope for tomorrow." He wished he could have bright hope for tomorrow instead of the unending grind of living in his anger and guilt and pain. Ellen had lived through pain with the loss of her husband, but she didn't act as if she were locked up inside.

How did she do it? He knew that she'd say the answer was God.

Both of the hymns mentioned blessings. What had Ellen said to him the day he had asked her to pray for him? Something about blessings. *Watch out for blessings.*

Did she still pray for him? Did she pray for blessings for him? *Dear God, I hope she is. Please, let her be.*

The soft sounds of the old familiar melodies wooed Payne. Lost in his musings, he continued standing at the close of the hymn as church members found their places on the cushioned pews. Kate's tug on his sleeve interrupted his musings in time to catch Charlie's grin and hear the minister's invitation to open Bibles.

"Please turn to James 4:8. It's found near the back of the New Testament."

Payne heard pages flipping across the sanctuary. Beside him, Kate held her travel Bible out so that both he and Charlie could see the words.

"James is a powerful book, and I challenge you to go home and read all five chapters if you've never taken the time. Today, however, we're going to concentrate on one wee little verse."

Only one verse? Was he being serious? How could he base

an entire sermon on one verse?

Clear and strong, the minister's voice read the verse, "Draw near to God, and He will draw near to you."

At first, Payne refused to believe he'd heard the words correctly. The minister repeated the verse for good measure, "Draw near to God, and He will draw near to you."

No. No way would the preacher use the same verse Ellen threw at him the other day. He pinched his elbow to wake up from this bad dream.

Ignoring the drumming in his chest, he turned in the pew to bolt out of the suffocating church. The movement attracted Charlie and Kate's attention, and she touched his forearm with a question in her eyes.

Noticing the two pairs of knees blocking his way to freedom and the fact that the minister had already begun his sermon, Payne surrendered his escape plan. He patted Kate's hand and pushed his spine against the pew. Trapped, he had to sit and listen to what God wanted him to hear whether he liked it or not.

෨෨෨෬෬

"Mom, are you sure you don't want anything? Olivia pulled several Euros out of her wallet and stuffed them into her shorts' pocket.

"I'm sure. Go get your iced coffee and hurry back before the music starts."

"I will. Keep your eyes open for Tristan and Susanna. I told them we'd be near the statue." Olivia pecked her mom on the cheek and left to purchase the coffee.

Ellen relaxed in a canvas camping chair crocheting, glancing up every few stitches to watch the diverse crowd grow in anticipation of the concert. As she'd done in the church service this morning, she also scanned faces for Payne's gray eyes.

She had to stop thinking about Payne Anderson. If he came to Ireland for that wedding, he's probably already left for Africa. Maybe with that blonde. She should think about the good music coming up and the gorgeous day instead.

Yes, the weather deserved some good thoughts. The sunshine, a rare sighting in the past few days, brightened her spirits and caused her to push up the sleeves of her cotton sweater. They'd come to Eyre Square after church and a quick lunch to hear more bands play for the arts festival. From the looks of the growing crowd, most of County Galway intended to do the same.

She pulled a loop through the first stitch in a new row and smiled at the progress she was making.

"Nice yarn. Did you find that on Thursday?"

She gasped. Payne. She squeezed the half-finished sweater in her lap.

"Hello, Ellen. I'm glad I finally found you. I have a question for you." He stood with his hands at his belt, a cat-got-the-canary grin on his face.

"Finally found me?" Her pounding heart telegraphed what she knew was coming.

"Yeah. I was looking for you. I wanted to ask you about that kiss the other day." He dropped, uninvited, into Olivia's chair.

After three days of wondering about Payne, seeing him at every turn, he sat beside her ready for the tease fest. She resisted the desire to shrink at his grin. She opted for an offensive approach, instead. "Yeah, I was wondering about that kiss, too. What was that all about?" She crossed her arms, hoping she looked assertive instead of uncomfortable.

He laughed and stretched out his legs, cargo shorts revealing muscular calves. "You tell me. You were the one who started it."

"Are you kidding me?" He was impossible. "You were the one who pulled me over and leaned down and—"

He pointed at her, his eyes dancing. "And you were the one who turned your head and moved your lips toward a kiss that was supposed to be a little peck on the cheek."

This man added a new level to insufferable.

She twisted the metal hook clutched in her fingers. If it had been made of plastic, it would have snapped in her death grip. Heat rose in her cheeks. Blushing at forty-three years old? Really?

"So you're just going to sit there? You're not going to defend yourself and say that you didn't mean it or you lost your head for a minute?" Payne raised his eyebrows, a mischievous smile plastered across his handsome face.

"I'm not going to dignify your outrageous accusation with—"

"Outrageous accusation? All right." He shrugged. "Don't admit out loud that you turned that kiss up a notch or two. But I think you know that I liked it, and I'm positive you liked it as much as I did." He swiped his hand across his chin. "I've thought of little else for the past three days, and I have a few Euros I'd be willing to lose that you've replayed that kiss in your mind more times than you can count, too."

Chapter 12

"Oh!" The exchange she'd been dreading. How could she ever live this down? "You are beyond arrogant."

"Okay. I accept that charge, but," he paused, leaned over toward her with a smile. "You didn't deny it."

"Mom!" Olivia marched toward them with her iced coffee. Thank goodness for daughters who rescue their mothers.

"You didn't tell me you'd invited Payne today."

Thank goodness for even impolite daughters.

Ellen brushed her hair back from her face and shook her head. "I didn't invite him, Olivia. I didn't know how to contact him, remember?"

Payne waved to Olivia. "I'm here with some friends. I spotted your mother on my way to the river and came over to say, 'hello.'"

In the corner of her eye, Ellen saw Payne turn toward her.

"Our breakfast ended pretty quickly the other day."

Ellen refused to meet his eyes as the heat warmed her cheeks again.

Olivia scrunched her brow. "You two keep having these accidental meetings, don't you?" Could Olivia be thinking about their conversation from the other night? The fact that neither of them believed in coincidences?

Payne stood. "I wanted to take a look at the river. Would you two like to walk with me?"

Olivia took a long sip of her coffee and swallowed. "No, thank you. I'll stay here with our stuff. Tristan and Susanna should be here in a few minutes. You go ahead, Mom, and I'll wait for them."

Ellen glanced at her daughter. This version sounded more like the Olivia Ellen was used to. Was her ice-cold attitude toward Payne thawing a bit?

Olivia tipped her head toward the river. "Really. It's good."

Ellen studied Olivia's eyes. Soft and round, they looked anxious, but not angry. "Are you sure?"

Olivia nodded.

"Will you come with me, Ellen?" A kind, hopeful expression crossed his face, not a teasing, I-can't-wait-to-make-fun-of-you smile.

Ellen's heart pounded. Being alone with Payne probably meant more questions about the kiss, but she couldn't refuse his invitation. "Yes, but I won't be gone long, Olivia." She zipped up her backpack with the yarn inside and didn't take the hand he offered to help her rise. She didn't want his touch to throw her even more off balance than his surprise appearance already had. She stood without his help and moved toward the river.

As they stepped around outstretched legs and watched for flying Frisbees, Payne didn't grab her hand. Instead, he placed his hand on the small of her back, gentle pressure to guide her. His touch, firm and steady through the fabric of her blouse, sapped her concentration, leaving her distracted, struggling to maneuver through the maze of sandals and tennis shoes.

When they arrived at the wall overlooking the Corribe River, Payne dropped his hand from her back. They leaned against the stone wall facing the river for several minutes until he gave a short laugh. "I thought of all kinds of things to say to you if I ever saw you again, and now here you are, and I can't think of a thing I wanted to say." Sighing, he rubbed the back of his neck.

Ellen let out the breath she had been holding since he started to speak. "I was hoping you'd said all you wanted to say back there. It was quite enough, believe me."

His laugh, strong and delighted this time, rang out over the river. He grinned at her. "See, you make me laugh. I like that. It's been a long time."

She smiled back at him but couldn't speak. So happy to see

him and be near him, she bit her lip to keep herself from crying.

"Hey. I know something you might find funny. I went to church this morning." He cocked his head, waiting for her reaction.

She blinked. "You went to church?"

"Yeah. Hard to believe, but there I was." He reached down and grabbed a pebble near his foot. "Hadn't been inside a church in years, well, except for my godson's wedding yesterday, but that doesn't really count." He tossed the pebble into the river. "Guess what else?"

She heard the plop of water but kept her eyes focused on his face, waiting for him to continue.

"The minister preached a really interesting sermon this morning. Try and guess the topic."

"I don't know."

"James 4:8."

"James 4:8?" She knew that verse had some significance, but she couldn't remember for the life of her why it should be important.

He nodded. "You know the verse, Ellen. 'Draw near to God, and He will draw near to you.'"

She caught her breath. "Seriously?"

"Seriously."

"Oh, Payne." The hairs on the back of her neck and on her arms zinged to attention. This petition had been her continual prayer for him, and now he'd heard it from someone else. She hoped he'd listened to the minister.

She wanted to ask about the sermon, if it spoke to him, and how he felt about it, but she decided to let him offer that information in his own time. Another question occurred to her. "I don't think it's funny that you went to church, Payne, but if you haven't been to church in years, what prompted you to go today?"

Mischief lit his eyes. "I was looking for you." Leaning toward her, he tapped his index finger near her collarbone. "So add that hour to the almost two hours I spent after breakfast on Wednesday and the one I spent Thursday morning, and that makes about four hours I've spent this week looking for you."

Eyes rounded in disbelief, her hand flew to her wide open mouth. "You spent almost two hours looking for me after our breakfast?"

"Yeah. I sat in front of the college thinking I'd catch you when you met Olivia for lunch."

When she'd thought Payne might have looked for her, she'd envisioned him checking a couple of cafes on his way to a cup of tea. She never dreamed he'd have spent so much time looking for her. She hadn't thought beyond hiding from him that day. "I'm so sorry that you wasted all that time. I never thought…"

He'd been honest with her. She had to be honest with him, too.

Payne shook his head. "Don't be sorry. It's not your fault I chose to look for someone I barely knew. I chose to waste all that time when I could have been taking a nap or helping my old college roommate lose golf balls or shopping or—"

"I saw…" She swallowed. Was he teasing? Didn't matter. She had to tell him. She had to confess fast and be done with it.

"I saw you in front of the college and entered the side door so you wouldn't see me. I didn't want to hear you tease me about that kiss, so I, ah, I just left you sitting on that bench. I'm so sorry you wasted all that time, Payne." She couldn't look at him. Facing the river, she closed her eyes and waited for him to speak.

"You little coward."

She turned back to him intending to refute his accusation, but he smiled at her, and she couldn't speak a word. She simply nodded, agreeing with his accurate description. She had been a coward. Caused him to waste four hours.

"I'm sorry about Wednesday, but…" She took a breath for courage. "But, I'm glad you found me today."

His eyes widened slightly, and he pulled her toward him, wrapping his arms around her. She surrendered to his embrace and rested her cheek against his chest. Kissing the top of her head, he whispered, "I am, too."

A shiver rolled through her body, popping goose bumps up and down her arms.

He stepped back a half step but kept one arm anchored at

her waist. Lifting her chin, he bent down brushing her lips with a soft, warm kiss. His brief touch turned into a smile.

Before she could smile in return, his mouth came down again. More than a brief testing-of-the-water, this time his kiss questioned and promised at the same time.

He caressed her cheek, stroked her ear lobe, and settled on the back of her neck. She rose on her tiptoes drawing closer to him and threaded her fingers through the thick hair at his collar. His arms tightened around her.

She could feel herself sinking into a warm, misty place she'd ached for without knowing it. She wanted to yield to his velvety caresses, but an annoying whisper chanted, "Stop, Ellen. Stop, Ellen. Stop, Ellen." As much as she wanted to ignore that voice, she couldn't. Dragging her mouth away from his, she rested her forehead in the warm crook of his neck, felt his racing heartbeat underneath her palm. His rapid breathing matched hers.

He hugged her like he didn't want to let go and kissed the top of her head again. Releasing her with lingering fingers trailing across her back, he turned and leaned against the stone wall. She pressed her tingling body against the ancient stones for support, relieved that her wobbly legs didn't have to hold her upright.

He reached over and placed one of her hands between both of his. They stood side by side, silent, watching the ducks on the river for several minutes. With his fingertips, he traced her fingers and lightly stroked her wrist. "When do you go back home?"

His quiet words jolted her back to reality. She crushed her bottom lip between her teeth. For the past three days, she'd thought the fairy tale with Payne already over. Today's surprise had given her hope of spending more time with him. She didn't want to think about the end for a while. "You do get down to brass tacks, don't you?" She hoped her remark sounded witty.

"Ellen." He squeezed her hand. "When?"

"Saturday. When do you leave?"

He sighed. "Tuesday morning, bright and early. I'm driving down to Shannon with Charlie, my college roommate and his wife, Kate. Our planes leave within an hour or so of each other. We also arrived at the airport about the same time last Monday. They'd dropped me downtown while they finished some last minute wedding plans." A teasing grin tugged at the corners of his mouth. "That's when I met you."

Grateful for serendipitous occasions like meeting in an Irish café and for how his eyes twinkled at her now, she couldn't think of a snappy comeback. His circles on her wrist didn't help either.

Shaking his head, he rubbed his brow. "Anyway, I really should have left today, because I need to get back to my project, but I hadn't seen Charlie in a good while. And he had this notion of the two of us playing golf all over three Irish counties."

"Oh." A cold knot formed in the pit of her stomach, but she refused to acknowledge it or let it grow. She'd always taught her children to look for the positive in any situation, but finding the positive in this disappointment required more creativity than she could muster.

"Well. Unless you have to spend the whole day tomorrow packing, or you have a golf date, maybe we could have lunch again." Her eyes wide with hope.

He shook his head.

Disappointment.

"I want to spend more time with you than just lunch." Hallelujah.

"Our lunches are pretty long, remember?" Her joke fell flat. She knew something special slipped away from her with every tick of her wrist watch.

A familiar voice reached her over the din of the music and shouts of others throwing Frisbees and kicking soccer balls.

"Look, there they are. Hey, Mom, we found you."

Ellen turned to face her daughter. Smiling by her side and holding an iced coffee, too, Susanna waved with her free hand. Both girls appeared tentative at interrupting the couple.

Olivia nodded to the sky. "It looks like it's going to pour any minute now. We've heard a few rumbles of thunder, too."

Thunder? Ellen scanned the sky surprised to see angry clouds drifting overhead. Being with Payne obscured all notice of her surroundings.

"We thought it'd be fun to go back to the house and just

hang out there. We could watch a movie, or Tristan suggested playing Apples to Apples. He's miffed that he lost so badly last time and wants another try. Then we could grill out for dinner if the weather clears. If not, we could just make something else. What do you think?" She turned her attention to Payne and took a breath. "You could come, too, if you don't have other plans."

Both Payne and Ellen gaped at Olivia.

"What?" Color rose in her cheeks. She squared her shoulders. "Would you like to come with us, Payne?" Her mouth managed a hint of a smile.

His gaze swung to Ellen and then back to Olivia. Smiling, he accepted. "Yes, I would. Thank you for asking me, Olivia. Your mother and I were just discussing seeing each other again." Turning to Ellen, he asked, "Is this plan okay with you?"

"It sounds fun to me." Silly happy with the prospect of spending more time with this interesting man, she calmed her doubled heart rate with slow breaths.

They crisscrossed back through the thinning crowd to find Tristan, Payne's light grasp warming Ellen's upper arm. "I'll catch up with Charlie and his wife and tell them what I'm doing. They're probably leaving, too, and I can borrow one of their cars. If you give me your address, I can use the GPS to find your house."

When they found Tristan, he already had the chairs packed up. The trees swayed with the growing breeze, and Ellen pushed down her sleeves. She tore a sheet from her yellow pad for the information he needed to find them.

Sticking the folded paper in his pocket, he locked his eyes with hers. "It'll take me a little while to get all of this settled, but I'll see you in maybe an hour or so. Sound good?"

She nodded. He held her gaze for a moment longer and then winked. "See you soon." He backed away from her.

She managed to squeeze out, "okay," over the lump forming in her throat. Trying not to be disappointed that he hadn't kissed her goodbye, she reasoned he'd noticed Olivia watching them. Instead of slighting her with no quick goodbye kiss, maybe he'd saved her from more questions from her daughter.

But he hadn't asked her to go with him to meet his college

roommate either. Wouldn't it have been easier if she'd gone with him to help find the house?

Quit borrowing trouble. She'd see him again soon. They were having dinner together.

Thrilled that he'd accepted Olivia's invitation, she smiled in gratitude that her daughter included him. But what had gotten into Olivia? Inviting Payne? What kind of new tactic was she trying?

Chapter 13

Hurrying back to his old friend, Payne braced himself for the inevitable teasing. He found Charlie and Kate scanning the crowd for him. "Thank goodness." Charlie slapped him on his back. "We thought we'd have to have your name announced over the loud speaker. Did you get lost?"

"No, I'm ah, I'm going to—" He let out a hard breath. "Look, remember the woman I had lunch with last week?"

"The one you blew off our golf match for? The one you spent, what was it, five or six hours with over lunch that day? You found her in this crowd?" Arms akimbo, Charlie raised a skeptical eyebrow.

"It wasn't a five-hour lunch. And we played a late round, so what are you complaining about? And, yes, I found her." Payne struggled to keep the irritation out of his voice. He wasn't accustomed to explaining his plans.

"Listen, boys," Kate played referee. "It's beginning to sprinkle. Let's take this conversation to the car, okay?"

"Good idea." Payne grabbed the food basket. "Do you mind if I borrow one of the cars tonight? Ellen's daughter invited me to dinner. They're somewhere south of the city."

"Well, I don't know." Charlie rubbed his chin. "Maybe we're gonna need the cars. What if we just drop you off now?" Mischief lit his face. "Hey, that's a great idea, then we can come in and meet this mystery lady." Charlie warmed to his idea. "Kate, we don't have anything planned for tonight. Maybe we can wangle a dinner out of the deal, too. Sounds good, huh, babe?"

"We planned to go out for dinner, Charlie. Remember? Give

me the keys, and I'll open the door."

Charlie tossed her the keys. "I'll have to take a rain check, darlin'. As much as I love you, going out to dinner can't compete with meeting the woman who's caught the confirmed bachelor's eye." He turned to Payne who searched for the seatbelt in the back seat. "I've got to meet her. She must be something special. You never did tell me what she looks like. Is she tall? Is she short? Does she kiss good?"

A muscle worked in Payne's clinched jaw. "Are you enjoying yourself?"

"Indeed I am, my friend. Indeed I am."

Kate tore paper towels from a roll. "Charlie, stop. We are not going to crash a dinner party."

Usually, Payne gave as much as he got, but today he didn't feel like sparring with Charlie. He only wanted to get back to Ellen as fast as he could. Their time was running out, and he didn't want to spend the last few hours listening to Charlie's insufferable attempts at humor.

"Okay, fine. I'll call a taxi. That's probably a better idea anyway." He wiped his wet face with a paper towel Kate handed him. Charlie eased into traffic.

Kate fastened her seatbelt and half-turned to face Payne. "Of course you can use one of the cars. Take this one. It's nicer than the one we rented for Michael. Drive it back to the airport Tuesday, too. Tonight will be good practice for you, and that means I won't have to drive on the left side of the road."

Her exaggerated sigh of relief made Payne laugh. He'd liked her since the first time he and Charlie had met her in the bookstore at the University of Virginia. Charlie had loved her from that point and had spent most of their senior year trying to make her love him back. "Thank you, Kate. You're a kind woman. What are you doing with that bozo?" Payne jerked his thumb toward her husband.

"She's just lucky, I guess." Charlie reached back and thumped his knee. "Now, what about my questions? You didn't answer a single one."

"Not going to either. Give it a rest, Charlie. I was invited to dinner, and I'm going. End of story." Payne clamped down his jaw, willing Charlie quit his comedy routine.

Kate switched on the radio, and the jazzy guitar sounds of an old Earl Klugh song filled the car. "Payne, tell me more about your project in Uganda. Do you think the new ways of irrigation will take?"

The men conceded the new topic, and Payne explained more details about his African project.

ಣಣಣ಄಄

Ellen forced herself not to check the kitchen clock or her wrist every five minutes, but her will power deserted her around four thirty. What was taking him so long? Was he lost? Had he changed his mind? Was the blond woman to blame for his prolonged absence?

Pushing these negative thoughts out of her mind proved as difficult as not looking at the time.

Her wise, inner voice worked to calm her. *He said he was coming. He even said it would take a while. He wants to be here. Trust him.*

The negative thoughts fought to resurface.

She remembered to do what she should have done an hour earlier. *Father, I'm being ridiculous. I believe You helped him find me in that huge crowd this afternoon. I believe You have a reason for us to be together. Help me to focus on Your plan and not on my inability to breathe. You're the Prince of Peace. I need peace, please.* Fortified, she returned to the chaotic kitchen where four pairs of hands chopped vegetables.

Since the rain had parked on top of Galway, the twenty-somethings had decided to prepare a chopped salad instead of grilling. In the produce department of Joyce's Grocery, they ran into Samuel, an exchange student from Nigeria, and invited him to dinner. They chose Tipperary and Blarney cheeses along with several loaves of warm bread to round out their meal and begged Ellen to make brownies for dessert.

While Olivia led the others in chopping the vegetables, Ellen prepared the brownies. For the ten minutes it took to mix the ingredients, she kept her eyes off the clock. Closing the oven door, she peeked at the clock again. Five minutes till five.

⌘⌘⌘⌘

Getting back to the house took longer than he had anticipated because of the traffic. Not wanting to show up empty-handed, he'd bought some chips, cookies, and ice cream, staples for college kids. On an impulse, he grabbed a bouquet of flowers, too. By the time he found Ellen and Olivia's house, it was almost five o'clock.

As he raised his finger to ring the doorbell, a picture of himself in front of Lizzy Cooper's door flashed in his mind. He'd worn his first tux and clutched a wrist corsage in a clear plastic box. That scene happened thirty years ago, but his heart and lungs remembered their act then and performed an encore now.

He rolled his head from shoulder to shoulder. He wasn't sixteen anymore and nervous before the prom. He could go inside and have fun. He could enjoy the little time he had left with her.

Payne wiped his hand on his pants leg and pressed the buzzer before he could lose his nerve.

⌘⌘⌘⌘

Ellen grabbed plates and utensils to set the table. As she slid a folded napkin beside a plate, the doorbell rang. Her stomach flipped, and all of her breath seemed to whoosh out of her lungs. For a moment, she stood squeezing the back of a dining chair. Absurd questions kept her rooted to the floor. Should she answer the door? Everyone else was covered in vegetable clippings. If she opened the door, would he think her too eager? If she didn't, would he think her indifferent?

"Mom, are you going to let him in?" Olivia made the decision for her.

"Of course, I am." She baby stepped to the door, forcing herself to breathe.

When she opened the door, she laughed out loud. An enormous bouquet of beautiful flowers hid Payne's face.

He lowered it. "Are the flowers too much? Dorky, right?"

"Absolutely not. I love flowers. They're gorgeous. Thank you."

As she reached for the bouquet, her hands closed on top of his. Distracted by his touch, she remained at the threshold, blocking his entry. He met her eyes and glanced into the foyer. She laughed at his subtle hint, pulling him into the house.

He shifted the grocery bags into both hands. "I brought a few things. Junk food mainly and ice cream."

"Wonderful." She turned to the kitchen. "Hey, everybody, we can have ice cream with the brownies." Happy shouts filled the house. Ellen wanted to shout with joy herself.

With all the vegetables chopped, Olivia shooed the boys out of the kitchen so that she could assemble the salad. Susanna grabbed the bags from Payne, ooohing and ahhing over the flowers. "Gorgeous flowers. The perfect thing for a Sunday evening."

Ellen silently agreed with her. Sunday evenings had always been a melancholy time for her. She suspected tonight would have been a major melancholy event if Payne hadn't accepted Olivia's invitation to dinner. Happy to have him here, she'd leave the blue thoughts for later. She'd concentrate on having fun tonight instead.

Tristan introduced Payne to Samuel as they took seats in the family room. Ellen found a vase and filled it with water while Olivia and Susanna sliced the bread and arranged the cheese on a plate.

Ellen brought the bouquet out into the dining area, placing the vase on a side table so they wouldn't have to talk around the flowers during dinner.

She joined the men in the family room. Payne and Samuel lounged on the couch discussing Africa, so she chose the chair opposite Payne. Tristan kneeled on the floor selecting music from the huge pile of CDs. Payne caught her gaze, holding it for a couple of beats before a slow smile stretched across his face. She grinned in return, an Irish jig dancing in her heart.

The current song had been playing for several minutes when Payne asked, "What's the name of this band? I don't think I've ever heard it before."

"It's called Leeland. It's a Christian rock band from Texas. They have some awesome songs, man." Tristan handed him the CD case.

Payne studied the case.

"This one's probably my favorite. It's all about tears of the saints, you know, for the lost people in the world. The saints are crying for them to come back home to God. Awesome, man."

Ellen slipped out of the family room, and left Payne with the haunting strings and beautiful lyrics. *Father, thank You for that song. Please let it be a blessing to him.*

When they were seated at the round table, Olivia asked Tristan to say grace. As everyone grabbed hands, Ellen caught Payne's quick glance and returned his grin. The silent joke between them lightened her heart.

Ellen passed the bread basket and noted the nationalities sharing the table: three Americans; Tristan, the Scotsman; Susanna, the native Irish from Manor Kilbride in County Wicklow, and Samuel, the Nigerian. She loved meals like this one with different kinds of people sharing good food and good conversation. She was especially glad that one of those people sharing this meal was Payne.

Olivia broke her reverie with a question directed to him. "So, Payne. Tell us about yourself."

His surprise flashed briefly in his gray eyes, but he recovered, smiling to Olivia before answering. "Well, I work at Maryland State University."

"Work at Maryland State." Olivia scooted her chair closer to the table and propped her chin on the palm of her hand. "Does that mean you teach? Do you have a Ph.D.? Or are you in administration or maintenance or something else?"

"Yes, I have a Ph.D. I sometimes teach a class or two, but mainly I do research, and lately I've been spending more time with environmental projects." He leaned back in his chair and smiled at Olivia.

"What kind of environmental projects?"

"We're trying to find more efficient ways to collect and distribute water in developing countries in Africa. I'm also interested in wind energy and renewable resources."

"A tree hugger!" Tristan laughed, reaching across the table to bump fists with Payne.

Payne grinned. "Somebody's got to do it."

Ellen raised an eyebrow at Olivia. She'd been the environmental policewoman at home ever since studying pollution in third grade. She scoured the trash for recyclables and chastised the family whenever she found a plastic or aluminum or glass item in a wrong bin. She made sure the computers were completely turned off at night, and when she was fifteen, cut off the tops of plastic milk jugs so that everyone could catch the gallon of water usually wasted before the shower ran hot. The saved water, stored in the laundry room, went into the next load of clothes. She even asked for a rain barrel and a composter for Christmas one year.

Ignoring her mother, Olivia rose from her chair. "Anyone ready for brownies and ice cream?"

"Absolutely."

"For sure. Thought you'd never ask."

"Bring'em on."

Susanna hopped up to help her, and the conversation turned to soccer or football, depending on who was talking. Tristan, still excited over how well his Scottish team had played in the world soccer cup playoffs earlier in the summer, led the discussion with waving arms and stomping feet.

The brownies, tasty with extra chocolate chips and walnuts, became a delicious indulgence with a scoop of ice cream melting on top. Ellen stopped with one. Olivia and Susanna shared a second brownie. Payne and the boys finished off the rest of the dish.

"It's a good thing we had a light dinner, or did you eat all those brownies because we had a light dinner?"

Samuel rubbed his stomach. "The brownies were great. I just couldn't stop."

Payne glanced at Ellen, "You were smart to stop with one. I

should have, too. Now I'm stuffed."

Ellen moved to the window. "We could take a walk if it's stopped raining." She pulled back the curtain to gauge the weather, but the overcast sky made seeing raindrops difficult.

Tristan stretched his arms above his head. "I'm afraid I'd have to roll along the sidewalk. I feel like I'm going to explode."

"Mom, why don't you two take a walk? We'll clear the dishes. Right, people?" Olivia gathered the brownie dish and serving spatula.

"Sure."

"Of course."

"The faster we clean up, the faster I can lie down on the sofa." Tristan stacked the plates.

Ellen hated washing dishes and didn't give the young people a chance to change their minds. "Come on." She touched Payne's forearm. "I'm getting a jacket. Would you like one?"

Payne declined the jacket but grabbed an umbrella. The rain had turned to light sprinkles. He put his arm around her shoulder, pulling her under the umbrella. "I think this might be the best part of dinner." He grinned.

"I'm sorry, but your actions are more believable than your words. I think you liked dessert the best. Three brownies?"

"Two and a half actually, and I can't believe you counted."

"I didn't mean to. I had fun watching Tristan and Samuel race to the end of the dish. Thank goodness no one got in their way. I was halfway afraid someone might get stabbed in the hand with a fork." She remembered the boys scraping the crumbs from the pan.

"You get along really well with that age group. They like you a lot."

"Twenty-somethings are fun. They have a lot of enthusiasm, and they're not as annoying as they were in middle school and early high school. I've had a lot of practice at different ages like Girl Scout leader, Boy Scout den mother, soccer mom, youth group chaperone."

"Wait. Boy Scout mom?" He stopped, turning to look at her.

"Oh." Ellen bit her lip, realizing she'd never mentioned her twins to Payne. "Besides Olivia, I have two more children, Scott and Laurel. They're twins. Eighteen months younger than Olivia." She rushed the words out of her mouth, expecting his shock at the new information.

She laughed a little self-consciously when he remained silent. "Are you too surprised to speak? Three children, that's a lot to take in. Believe me, I know."

He rubbed his chin and took a step forward. "No, I'm just trying to imagine you with three babies. It must have been—."

"Chaos. Pure and simple. But we had a lot of help from our families and our church for those first few crazy months. We survived. To be so close in age, they get along very well. They're great friends."

"But they didn't come with you on this trip?"

"They wanted to, but both of them have summer jobs and couldn't get time off. They were really disappointed not to be able to come."

Payne hooked Ellen's arm through his, and companionable silence blanketed them. An occasional car passed by, but no one else had ventured out to walk after the storm. The soothing strains of classical music flowed through the open windows of a two-story house near the second corner of the block.

Ellen tapped his arm. "I think Olivia is warming up to you a little bit."

"Oh, then that was just a friendly game of twenty questions back there, huh? That's why she didn't shine an interrogation light in my eyes." He slapped his forehead. "Now I get it."

"She can be determined, for sure."

"Tenacious. Relentless. Obstinate. Like a dog with a bone." Payne rattled off descriptions like a cashier counting off dollar bills.

"Okay. Okay," Ellen laughed at his characterizations, but she knew he had a point. "She is a determined young woman, and she's been very frustrated with all of my 'I don't knows' when she asks about you."

They turned the third corner.

"How about you? Were you frustrated not knowing anything about me? Like what I do for a living or where I live?"

Ellen licked her lips. "Well, don't take this the wrong way, but I really hadn't even realized it until she pointed it out. I just enjoyed talking with you about whatever topics came up." She folded her arms in front of her. "When I realized that after talking for hours over three days, we didn't really know the normal information about each other, I felt—I don't know—"

"What?" His soft voice encouraged her.

"I guess I felt a little sad. I mean, I think I said something to her like, 'it must not be too important if we didn't exchange phone numbers.' I was trying to placate Olivia, make her understand that this—whatever it is between us is just a—I don't know. A summer dalliance—"

"A dalliance?" Payne frowned.

"Yes, maybe a flirtation. I don't know—a distraction."

"You do love your words, don't you?" He ran his hand through his hair. "Is that what you think this thing is?"

They'd completed the walk around the block and faced each other back in front of the house.

She shrugged and didn't meet his eyes because his voice had changed, challenging her words. "I don't know what it is."

"Do you want it to be just a flirtation?" Payne persisted.

"I don't know." Even as she said those words, she knew she wanted whatever this was with Payne to be more than a flirtation. Yelling and laughter coming through the front window reminded her of the young people waiting for them. "We should go in. We've been gone for a while." But before she could turn toward the door, he pulled her to him and covered her mouth with his.

Caught off guard, she stiffened for a split second but relaxed into him as a tiny sigh escaped from her throat. She'd wanted to be in his arms since before dinner when she opened the door to let him in. She slid her hand up to the sandpaper of his five o'clock shadow, holding on to his shoulder with her other hand.

Dropping the umbrella, he slid his hand up her back to hold her head and shifted his stance to be closer to her. For Ellen, nothing existed except Payne. She forgot that her daughter waited inside the house. She forgot about the uncertainty of this summer romance. She forgot about the misty rain. She knew only that Payne was real and was holding her, so she kissed him with all the pent up longing inside of her.

He dragged his mouth along her cheek planting feathery kisses. His lips reached her ear and hovered, teasing her with the promise of a kiss. He rubbed his thumb against the side of her neck. "Now do you know if you want this to be just a flirtation?" His whisper sent shivers dancing in her heart.

Chapter 14

"Oh, Payne." She kissed his palm and rested her forehead against his chest, trying to steady her breathing. His racing heartbeat kept pace with hers.

More muffled laughter came from the house. He lifted her chin. Unclenching his jaw, he brushed her lips with a quick kiss. "Come on. Let's go inside."

He picked up the umbrella and guided her toward the front door, his mouth pressed into a straight line.

Olivia greeted them from the circle surrounding the game. "Hey, Mom, you're back. Is it still raining?"

"Just misting right now." She fluffed her hair, trying to shake off the light sprinkles.

"Mrs. Shepherd, we've only just started the game. We'll add you and Payne in, okay?" Tristan scooted over on the couch to make room.

"Thank you, Tristan, but I think we'll go sit on the glider on the back porch for a while. How does that sound, Payne?" She glanced at him, hoping for a smile of reassurance.

He nodded, leaning the umbrella near the front door. They reached the door to the back porch as Susanna began to argue with Samuel for not choosing her definition of *pixilated* as the best one.

The glider, hugging the brick wall underneath the deep porch, was well protected from the inclement weather. "The cushions shouldn't be damp so far under the porch. I think we'll be fine." She sank onto the floral canvas and curled one leg under her so that she could face Payne. He took a seat a few inches away from her, leaning his head against the pillowed back.

Although dusk approached, complete dark wouldn't settle until almost ten o'clock. The storm clouds made it seem later than eight.

They sat in silence for several minutes. Ellen understood he waited for her to answer his flirtation question. She knew she had to address the topic. "I don't know how to answer your last question, Payne."

"I didn't mean it to be difficult." He threaded his fingers at his waist and stared out into the darkness of the backyard.

"It isn't difficult. It's just that I could answer it with two different answers."

He shifted in the glider to look at her. "All right. Give me both answers."

She licked her lips and pushed her hair back. "Okay. On one hand, whatever this is between us does sort of feel like a simple flirtation. As much as we've talked, we haven't really shared about where we live or exchanged phone numbers or email addresses." She smoothed her skirt.

"I mean, I know you played in your high school band, but until tonight I didn't know what you do for a living." She snapped and unsnapped the bottom snap on her jacket. "I know you're working on some kind of a project in Africa, but I don't know how long you'll be there."

He rescued the snap and closed his hands over hers.

She heard the phone ring inside the house. "I'm in North Carolina, and you're in Africa or Maryland. Those locations don't exactly make seeing each other again a walk in the park, do they?"

She looked up at him. "I know you have a godson, but I don't know if you have any children."

In an instant, a tiny flash of something flickered across his face. Was it pain? His hands tightened the grip on hers. Before she stopped to think, she blurted out, "And I don't know how important that blond woman is to you." She winced. Why in the world did she bring up that woman?

He blinked and frowned. "What blond woman?"

118

"The woman on the street with—I guess he's your godson, but he called you Uncle Payne. And she was standing beside you on the church steps after the wedding. On our way back into town, Olivia and I drove by the church yesterday just as the wedding party walked out, and I saw you."

"You saw me on Saturday?" He jerked his head and narrowed his eyes. "You saw me, but—"

"Yes, I saw you standing tall in a fancy tuxedo at a wedding, talking to the blond woman."

He threw his head back with a guffaw. "That woman is Michael's new mother-in-law." He stretched his arm along the top of the cushions and leaned toward her, making it easy for her to see the mischief lighting his eyes. "If I ever see her again, I'll have to thank her for making you jealous."

Ellen straightened her spine and raised an eyebrow. "I didn't say she made me jealous."

"You didn't have to."

"You—"

The sliding glass door opened, and Olivia emerged holding the phone. "It's long distance." She wore a mischievous grin on her face. "Laurel needs to talk with you."

This should be interesting. She wondered what Olivia had said about her mom's new friend.

She mouthed, "Sorry," to Payne and accepted the phone. "Hello, Lu Lu. How are you?"

For the next several minutes Ellen remained mute while Laurel shot question after question generously sprinkled with a few opinions about "this man you've met." At last, Laurel took a breath and gave her mother a chance to reply to her questions. "Yes, I've had lunch and breakfast with someone I met in Galway." A gasp followed by another question or two. Ellen closed her eyes.

"Yes, he came to dinner tonight, but did your sister happen to tell you that she was the one who invited him?" More words crackled over the connection.

"Well, it sounds like you have the scoop already. You don't need any more information from me. Let me speak with your brother now, please." She glanced over at Payne and with an apologetic smile. He took her free hand in both of his.

She heard her son's strong voice on the other end. "Hello, Sweetie. How are you?" After Laurel's frantic questions and remarks, Scott's quiet words comforted her spirit. "Yes," she hesitated. "He's here right now."

"Scott, I really don't think you—" She took a deep breath. "Okay. Fine." She handed the phone to Payne. "He wants to talk with you."

Payne took the phone with one hand but held onto hers with the other. "Hello? This is Payne Anderson." He winked at Ellen. "Yes, I've been enjoying getting to know your mother." Payne grinned. "Yes, I can see that she's a special person."

"Hey, that's enough. Let me have it." Ellen grabbed for the phone, but he turned away from her, capturing both her hands with one of his.

"Thank you, Scott. I enjoyed talking with you, too." He handed the phone back to Ellen and rested his arm behind her on top of the glider.

"Scott, really. Listen…how is everything at home?" Ellen frowned. "She wants me to what? A foreign exchange student won't want to stay with me. She'd be bored stiff without someone her age around, and you and Laurel will be away more than you'll be home. Just tell Diane we'll discuss it when I get back.

"And you're coming to pick me up on Saturday, right? I left all the flight information on the refrigerator. Just call before you leave to make sure the flight's on time. See you soon. Love you. Let me say, 'bye' to Lu Lu, okay?"

Her daughter had used the time off the phone to think of more questions. "Oh, Laurel, don't start up again. I'm fine. I'll see you on Saturday. I love you. Bye bye, Sweetie." She pressed the off button, let her head drop against the cushion, and sighed. "Sorry about that."

"No need to apologize. He was just checking out the competition, you know, being the man of the family. He seems like a good kid." He smoothed the hair back from her temple. "Now, what were we talking about before your offspring interrupted us?

Oh, I remember." He grinned. "Jealousy."

She shook her head. "Not jealousy. Curiosity."

"Semantics."

She opened her mouth to continue the argument, but he pressed his finger against her lips.

"I believe you were in the middle of answering my question about whether this thing between us is as flirtation or not." He clasped her hand in a loose hold.

Scrunching her brow, she looked at him and blinked. That conversation seemed so long ago.

"You were explaining why this thing between us feels like a flirtation, and you said you had two different answers. So now tell me the different answer, why this doesn't seem like a flirtation."

Rather than answering him, she contemplated the way he held her hand with one of his, his other fingers always moving, tracing her fingers, drawing circles in her palm, lightly caressing her wrists. She wished they could just sit here together and not talk about topics that made her heart race. But he waited for her answer.

Meeting his gaze, she didn't see the teasing, assertive man she knew he could be. Instead, he watched her with soft, expectant eyes. She reached over to brush away a few sparkling droplets still lingering in his hair. His mouth turned up into a tiny smile encouraging her to speak.

She took a deep breath and began. "Okay. I enjoy being with you. Last Thursday, after talking with you for three days in a row, I missed you all day long." She laughed. "I know it sounds silly. I mean I barely knew you. I still barely know you, but I missed you anyway. I even went in to Galway on Friday hoping you'd be there again, but you weren't."

His eyes widened, and his mouthed dropped open. "After you hid from me on Wednesday, you wanted to see me on Friday?"

"I told you it was silly." She folded her arms in front of her and focused her attention on the backyard.

"We had preliminary wedding stuff all day Friday. Breakfast, then pictures and then the rehearsal dinner. I had to be with the wedding party from morning till night. And I don't think you're silly." He rubbed his chin. "I went in to Galway to look for you on Thursday although you told me you were going shopping for yarn with Olivia. I even went to that little pottery shop, and—" He slammed his mouth shut and shook his head. "Anything else?"

She swallowed. "I enjoy talking with you. I enjoy being teased by you—a little, and I love making you laugh. You've..." She looked away from him again.

"I've what?" He nudged her chin with his knuckle, turning her face toward him.

"After Steve died, I suppose I sort of shut down in a way. I grieved. I helped the children grieve. I ran the shop and served on every committee that needed a breathing body. I just stayed busy, busy, busy." She rubbed her forehead and shrugged. "So my life has felt full, but I haven't realized how much I missed the interaction between a man and a woman." She studied the band with three sapphires on her right ring finger. "I feel like I'm coming out of a fog." That's exactly what he's done for her. He'd brought color back into her life. His smile raced her heart. His fingers on her wrist tingled her skin. His kisses—she had to stop thinking about them. "You've sort of woken me up and reminded me what the attention of a man can be like."

"I'd like to remind you of other things between a man and a woman."

Chapter 15

She shivered as he lowered his mouth toward hers, but Tristan slid open the glass door and shattered the intoxicating spell surrounding them. "Mrs. Shepherd, Samuel and I are leaving now. Early class in the morning. Thanks for dinner. Bye, Payne."

Susanna popped her head out of the door, too. "I'm shoving off as well. I need to read a few chapters before my lit class tomorrow. Thanks a million, Payne, for bringing the ice cream and the flowers. They're lovely."

"I'll see them out, Mom, then I'm going to read some, too." Olivia closed the door behind her.

"That sounds like my cue to leave, but I think we're just getting to the interesting part of our conversation." He leaned toward her again, but she put both hands against his chest to stop him.

"Yes, I agree with you because it's your turn to talk now."

"What?" Surprise knitted his eyebrows.

"I've talked a lot. Now it's your turn to talk."

"About what?

"About why you said you don't laugh a lot. About what happened in church today. About whatever you want to talk about. I don't want you to leave yet, but I just can't keep kissing you."

"Why? I like kissing you. I want to keep kissing you, too." He gazed at her with an intensity that sizzled her insides.

"Well, you can't." She shook her head. "I can't let you."

"Why?" He stroked her arm and drew circles in her palm.

"Because it's too hard to stop." She ran her free hand through her hair.

"Who says we have to stop?" His mouth moved into a lazy grin.

"I do." She pulled her arm out of his grasp. "Payne, stop. You're making me crazy."

"Good." He gently followed the outline of her cheek with his thumb. His slate eyes looked almost black. "Because you're doing the same thing to me." He hooked a lock of her hair around her ear, fingering the satiny strands.

Ellen reveled in his intoxicating touch for only a few seconds before she pushed his hand out of her hair, holding it in both of hers. "Payne, please. You're not making this easy for me."

"It could be really easy with us, Ellen." Quiet and firm, his voice carried a trace of a question.

"No, Payne. No, it couldn't. I'm not—I can't." She drew in a long breath, and held it, contemplating her words. "As much as I want to play this out, to kiss you and be with you and have you hold me, I can't. I know I'm a widow with grown children, but I can't. I'm not a one night stand. I never have been, and I won't start now."

Payne sat still for a moment watching her. "Believe it or not, I knew that about you. Pretty much from the first time I saw you." He blew out a long, slow breath, wiping his palms on his thighs. "I apologize for making you uncomfortable, Ellen."

"I'm not uncomfortable with you, Payne." She leaned her head back against the glider. Again silence fell between them emphasizing the night sounds. Insects were calling. A soft breeze rippled through the rose bushes laden with heavy blossoms. She remembered the pinks, reds, and yellows adorning the stems now half hidden in the shadows. She found the Big Dipper and searched for the little one until Payne moved.

Her heart clinched in her chest. Was he leaving? Was this the end?

But Payne simply changed positions on the glider to face her again. Relief rushed through her like rain coursing in a downspout.

"I'm not ready to leave yet either." He smiled at her. "So let's talk."

He glanced down at her hands folded in her lap. "When did you stop wearing your wedding band?"

That question was out of left field, but if it kept him here, she'd answer it and any others, too. "About a year after Steve died. A friend of mine who's also a widow told me it'd be easier if I took it off."

"Easier to date again?"

"No. Of course not. I didn't want to date. Easier to let Steve go. To get through the grief."

He clinched his jaw, and then rubbed his hand over his eyes. "Yeah. I know about trying to get through grief."

Ellen waited for him to continue.

"Oh, Ellen. Do you really want to know about my sordid past?" A haunted look marred his face.

"Only if you want to tell me. Payne, I'll listen to whatever you want to talk about."

Bolting to his feet to move away from the glider, he turned his back to her, his hands shoved into his pockets. "I haven't talked about it for years. I've done everything I could not to think about it." He stared out at the darkened backyard for several minutes before returning to sit near the arm of the glider. Resting his elbows on his knees, he covered his face with his hands.

Ellen slid over to him, slid her arm through his and squeezed his forearm. She rested her cheek against his stiff shoulder. "Payne, you don't have to tell me anything."

"That's just it. I know I don't have to, but I want to tell you. I'm torn up about it, though." An anguished laugh escaped from rigid lips. "I want to tell you to get it out, but at the same time, I don't want you to know." He sighed and closed his eyes. "It's not a happy story."

Ellen remained quiet, leaning against him, holding his arm. She felt his body tense, and then he spoke.

"I was married a long time ago. She was a secretary in the environmental studies department. I was beginning my last year of my Ph.D. work. Man, it was a stressful time. And then we made it worse with an unplanned pregnancy." He grabbed his knees.

"Anyway, she had a ball planning the wedding. My parents were less than enthusiastic but did their best to welcome Cindy. I wasn't a lot of help because I was busy writing my dissertation. She pulled the wedding together in less than a month. We didn't have time or the money for a honeymoon." He jerked his head toward his shoulder. "She just moved into my apartment."

"The pregnancy was not an easy one. At five months along, she had to go on partial bed rest. She finally quit her job making money even tighter. She hated being stuck in that apartment. She was jealous of the time I spent away from her. Jealous of the secretary who took her place. Jealous of my dissertation directors."

He rubbed his hand across his eyes. "I didn't exactly help her overcome her jealousy. My dissertation consumed me, and I was running low on patience."

Ellen stroked his back with a gentle touch. *Lord, help him get through this story. Help me comfort him.*

"He was born three weeks early, but the months leading up to it seemed like an eternity." He massaged his temples.

"The baby was tiny but healthy. He was fine, beautiful. I loved him immediately. All that frustration with Cindy's harping evaporated. All of those months of nothing but stress just blew away with one look at him. Does that sound hard to believe?" He raised his head to look at her.

"Absolutely not. I know exactly what you mean." She covered his hand with hers.

He sighed again and leaned back. He gripped her hand tightly and closed his eyes.

"I think Cindy felt the same way, too. I think we both tried hard at the beginning, and things went well for a while. But then Jamie got colic. For a solid month, he cried himself to sleep, woke up, ate, cried himself to sleep. It was horrible. I couldn't get anything done at the apartment, so I spent most of my time either in the science building or in the library. Whenever I was at the apartment, we fought. Both of us were exhausted all the time.

"I helped when I was at home, but my focus was on the dissertation. I figured my responsibility was my paper, hers was the baby. Wouldn't win any votes for fatherhood of the year, I'm sure, but I kept thinking, 'let me finish the last step of the program and then I can really help out.'

"Then all of a sudden one day, he stopped. He was a happy baby again. It was like someone flipped his colic switch off, and he was fine. Anyway, things began to look up a little. I think we both tried because we loved him, but we were discovering that we didn't have a lot in common.

"Things seemed better because Jamie wasn't crying. I finished my dissertation, graduated, and started looking for research jobs. A small college outside of Cleveland offered me a position. We moved to a little rental house right off campus the beginning of January. She hated it. It was probably one of the snowiest years of that decade, and she was cooped up in a tiny house all day long. Didn't know anybody and couldn't go anywhere. I worked all the time." Lost in his haunting memories, he opened his eyes, staring straight ahead. His breathing changed to short, shallow puffs.

Ellen recognized the misery emanating from his rigid body. *Oh, Father, give him the strength to say the words. And help me to hear them.*

She laid her hand on his knee, and he flinched, confirming her suspicion that he'd forgotten her. Glancing quickly at her, he pushed out a long, hard breath and swallowed.

"I came home one night from a full day at college, and she had her bags stacked at the front door, packed and ready to go. She said she was going back to Virginia. I'd been gone all day. Why didn't she leave while I was at work? She had all day to leave, but she loved drama. She seemed to enjoy counting off every single reason why she was miserable. Why I wasn't the husband she wanted or needed. We yelled at each other for, I don't know, maybe a half hour." He rubbed the heal of his hand down the middle of his forehead to the tip of his nose and back again.

"She was determined to leave and leave with the baby even though she didn't exactly enjoy being a mother. She hated changing diapers, getting up in the middle of the night, wearing shirts with spit-up on them. If she was so miserable, why didn't she just go by herself?" He shook his head. "Why did she have to take Jamie, too? He could've stayed with me. I could've worked out something with my schedule at school. If only…"

He leaned forward again with his elbows on his knees and covered his eyes with his palms. Ellen cradled him, laying her head against his shoulder.

"Our fight got louder and louder, and Jamie started to cry. His cries somehow calmed us down, and I convinced her to wait to leave till the next day. I thought I did anyway. Snow had started falling again as I drove home from work that night.

"I thought we'd called a truce, but she was just biding her time. I fell asleep on the couch between midnight and one, so she left sometime after that. A police officer woke me up about six the next morning and told me about her accident. She had spun off the road and slammed into a tree. Died instantly." He licked his lips. "The impact," a shudder rippled through him. "Jamie was thrown from the car seat. He died two days later."

Chapter 16

Ellen laid her temple against his sagging shoulder. "Payne, I'm so sorry." *Please, God, help him let go of this terrible grief. Help him lean on you, Father. Show me how to help him. Please give me the words to say.*

He pushed back hard against the glider, spent from reliving the tragedy. "So there you have it. The whole awful, ugly truth." He covered his eyes with his forearm as if to block out the images he'd described to her.

"It's heartbreaking, Payne."

"It's worse if you lived it."

"I don't know how you lived through it without God's help." Her hand closed over the fist he held against the cushion.

"I did ask for His help at first," he ground out the words. "I begged Him to heal Jamie, to save him. I promised to be the best father, to live my life for Him, to do whatever He wanted me to do if he'd only save Jamie. But He didn't. Jamie died anyway, a sweet, innocent baby."

He shuddered. "So I didn't see any reason to keep talking to God. He ignored me during the worst time of my life. I figured He wasn't interested in me, so I wasn't interested in Him." Trembling hands slid down his thighs to grip his knees.

"Payne, I don't know what to say to you that doesn't sound like a platitude. I just know that for me, I was thankful to have God. He didn't magically take away the pain, but He helped me get through it. That's one of His promises, not that we won't have troubles, but that He'll give us peace through them."

"That's great for you, but our situations were kinda different, don't you think?" His words dripped with sarcasm. "Cindy and I were screaming at each other hours before she died. You loved your husband."

"Yes, that's true. I did love Steve, and we had a great marriage, but I was really angry at him before and after he died."

"You were mad?" A raised eyebrow challenged her over his shoulder.

"Yes. Steve hated going to the doctor. He'd experienced some problems but never mentioned them to me until he was diagnosed. By the time he finally got an appointment to see his doctor, he was already in stage four." She closed her eyes against the memories. "I was so angry at him. His stubbornness and fear stole time we could have had together.

"But I couldn't do anything about that anger. I couldn't yell at him or be mean to him or not help him because he was so sick. Nursing anger at a sick person is not exactly Christian-of-the-year behavior, is it?" She worried a hangnail on her middle finger until Payne closed his hand over hers.

"So I did the best I could to ignore how I felt and did whatever he needed. Then—after he died..." She dragged her teeth against her bottom lip. "My temper came back full force because he left me with three teenagers, the farm to run, the yarn shop, and all the decisions I had to make without his input."

A sound resembling an anemic laugh broke out of her mouth. "You know, I was even angry at other people, people who still cheered at baseball games and enjoyed ice cream cones and laughed at stupid TV shows. They kept living their normal lives, and my world had crashed and changed forever. Yeah, I stayed angry for a long time." She dragged her fingers through her hair. "I couldn't even pray. I could barely get out 'Dear God' over a meal much less pray for help and strength." She twisted the silver bracelet on her wrist.

"But dear, sweet friends prayed for me. They were faithful, and God was faithful to me even when I wasn't." Tilting her head, she looked at him. "So yes, our situations were different, Payne, but I do know about grief wrapped up in anger." She bit her lip again. *Please give me words for him. Don't let me ruin this special time You're giving me.* "Don't you want God to help you let go of this anger and bitterness?"

She waited for him to answer, but he seemed more interested in the rustling rose bushes than revealing more of his thoughts. She respected his silent wish and changed the subject. "You never did tell me about church today. Was the sermon really about drawing near to God? Because, Payne… that's what I've been praying for you."

He gave a short chuckle and nodded. "I figured."

"God wants you to come to Him. He loves you, Payne. Let His love back into your life." Her words ended in a whisper.

"I want to. I think I want to. I don't know if I can. I'm so tired of carrying all this junk with me." He leaned back against the glider to look at her. His exhaustion reminded her of the first time they met.

"Then give all of it to God. Jesus says to come to Him if you're weary or burdened and He'll give you rest."

"It sounds so easy, but—"

"It is easy. You just have to decide to do it." She hesitated for a few beats and then shook her head. "Payne, I'm not a theologian by any stretch of the imagination. I wish I could recite a specific Bible verse that would convince you what I'm saying is true." She stopped to gather courage to continue.

"I don't know why Jamie died while other children survive car crashes. I only know God is sovereign, and I accept that I'm not going to understand everything He does. I also know He wants a personal relationship with all of us, including you." She laid her hand on his arm. "He wants you, Payne, because He loves you."

Payne's eyes fastened onto hers as he listened intently to every word she spoke. When she'd finished, she saw tears glistening in his eyes and knew he'd believed her.

He nodded. He stretched his legs out, laying them on top of the ottoman in front of the glider. Encircling her with his arm, he pulled her to him.

Grateful that he'd listened without taunting, Ellen snuggled close to him, exhausted, too. Resting her head against his hard chest seemed like the most comfortable place in the world.

Except for the night sounds, silence settled on top of them. Her eyelids weighed a hundred pounds, but she fought the urge to let them slide together as long as she could, wanting to be awake if he decided to talk again. Before she succumbed completely to sleep, a thought occurred to her. "Payne, it's really late. Is someone waiting up for you? Should you call?" Her voice, soft and drowsy, betrayed her nearness to slumbering.

Payne chuckled and brushed wisps of hair away from her temple. "No one has waited up for me in a long time."

Before Ellen could think, she whispered, "I'd wait up for you," and nestled more closely to him. She spread her fingers over his strong heart beat, and he covered her hand with his.

Chapter 17

Ellen's question surprised Payne. She'd been so still and quiet he'd assumed she'd fallen asleep. Yeah, the question caught him off guard, but her simple statement that she'd wait up for him had rocked him to the core. Would she really? How could she have anything to do with him now, knowing the vile details of his past and the grief he dragged with him like a rusty anchor? He tightened his arm around her.

How he wanted to give up that grief and anger. For years those feelings had threatened to consume him, but he'd managed to control them. At least he thought he had. He'd buried them way down deep inside him in a place where they couldn't haunt him. No, those negative emotions didn't preoccupy him anymore, but they did rule him in the way he interacted with people.

Deciding he wasn't good at relationships, he avoided them. He allowed his work to keep him from family during holidays, and his parents resigned themselves to seeing him once or twice a year for only a day or two. He had colleagues but no real friends. Only Charlie and Kate had doggedly refused to be pushed away. He acquiesced to their friendship because he secretly enjoyed their visits, but he never understood why they'd stuck by him.

And now he couldn't understand why he felt so drawn to this woman snuggled beside him on the glider. Why, after so many years of tending an impenetrable fence around his emotions, of pushing people away, had he pulled a one-eighty? What was it about her that reached out to him like nobody else? Her smile, maybe. Her kisses, definitely. What about her prayers?

Was it a God thing like she had mentioned during that first

conversation? She said she'd prayed before they met, and she had been praying for him this week.

Payne knew what he had to do. He had known it since the church service this morning but had done his best to ignore the feelings. He could not disregard the rapid fire beating of his heart now.

He closed his eyes to pray for the first time in years.

God, am I here with this woman because you want to get my attention? Are you using her to help me find my way back to you? He chewed his top lip, and one tear marked a trail down the side of his cheek. He squeezed his eyes tight and gritted his teeth. *Okay. All right. I give up. I don't want to hurt. I don't want to be angry. I still miss Jamie. I still don't understand why you took him, but I'm giving the anger and grief to you now. I don't want to carry that baggage one more day. I'm worn out with it. I want to be free of it. I want Your peace. I do. Please forgive me for all of those years I turned my back on you. I'm so sorry. Please help me live in Your peace.* He dropped his heavy head onto the back of the glider cushion and waited.

As he waited for peace to engulf him like a perfect wave on a Hawaiian beach, another song on the Leeland CD floated into his mind. How did those lyrics go? Something about being cradled by a Savior. What else? He could hear the melody, but what were the words? Something like being at a table, not belonging. That's exactly how he felt. With his past, he knew he didn't belong. *But I want to. God, I want to.*

He knew he didn't belong in the peace that he begged for and he'd done nothing to deserve, but he wanted it. Where was the wave? Why didn't he feel God's peace already? *God, did I say something wrong? Did I pray the wrong way? I'm sorry. Please, Father, I'm ready.*

Ellen slid her hand across his chest, and he noticed his heartbeat that had been clamoring against his ribs for the last ten minutes had slowed to a resting pace. His fingers had released the tight fists. The muscles in his forehead relaxed, and he'd stopped grinding his teeth.

God, is this peace? Really?

He'd expected a crash of feeling, sort of like fireworks in his soul, he guessed, but this new sensation felt more like…what? Like feathery touches of light on every part of his body and mind. Peace. This is what it feels like.

Thank You, God. Thank You. He wiped his eyes with his free hand and kissed Ellen on top of her head. He surrendered to the peace mingling with fatigue and closed his eyes, grateful for a God who hears and answers prayers.

ༀༀༀༀ

"Mom! He stayed here all night?"

Both Payne and Ellen scrambled upright on the glider as Olivia's shriek disrupted their peaceful sleep. Somehow, Payne's chin came down hard on Ellen's head as she fought to sit up straight and face the storm that had shattered their silent morning.

"Ow!" Disoriented, Ellen massaged the top of her head.

"You have a seriously hard skull." Payne rubbed his chin, and she heard the sandpaper like sound of his fingers against the dark stubble.

"What about your chin? Oh, no. My contacts are stuck to my eyeballs." Cupping her palms against her eyes, she repeatedly blinked to moisten her contacts, but the absurdity of the situation got the best of her. She lost the battle to control the giggles that bubbled in her throat.

"Mom, did you hear me?" Olivia circled the ottoman. "You're not answering me."

"Oh, Livie, it's obvious, don't you think? Yes, Payne stayed here last night. We fell asleep." Tears filled her eyes as the giggles turned into outright laughter.

"Mom, stop. This is serious. He spent the night here, and you're laughing about it?" Olivia stood in front of them with her hands on her hips, dressed for a run in shorts and an old sweat shirt.

"No, no. I'm not laughing about that. Livie, it's okay. He didn't even kiss me."

135

"Not because I didn't want to." Payne inserted his two cents.

"Payne." Ellen couldn't stop laughing, but at least the tears were helping to loosen her contacts. Thank goodness she still sat on the glider. The aerobic workout sapped her breath and reduced her legs to useless appendages.

"Mom! Stop. Get a hold of yourself. You haven't had a laughing jag like this since before—" Her eyes flying wide open, Olivia slapped her lips together.

Payne's warm, steadying hand pressed against her back underneath the jacket and Olivia's reminding her of Steve served to help her get control again. She breathed deeply and said, "I'm sorry, Olivia."

"You know you would be having a fit if Tristan and I had spent the night on that glider. I can hear you right now. 'What are the neighbors going to think? You're supposed to be an example, not a stumbling block.'" Olivia shook her head and calmed her voice. "Mom, I can't believe you."

"Olivia, I'm sorry. You're right. I would be upset with you. But I'm your mother, and you're not mine." She straightened her back and met Olivia's stare. "We talked for a long time and just fell asleep. We didn't plan to shock you like this so early in the morning."

Olivia let out a frustrated snort. "It's almost seven o'clock, and I'm going for a run." She turned to step away as she said under her breath again, "I can't believe this, Mother."

"Wait, Olivia." Payne stood.

Olivia stopped and faced Payne, crossing her arms. A stubborn expression hardened the delicate features of her face.

"I apologize for putting your mother's reputation in jeopardy. She's a special woman, and I never want to do anything to harm her. I sincerely apologize to both of you."

Olivia flattened her lips, studying the floor.

Ellen's heart filled as she watched Payne humble himself to her rude daughter.

He shoved his hands in his pockets. "I'm leaving for Africa tomorrow, and I'm hoping to spend more time with her today, if that's all right with you. I'd like to take both of you to lunch. That is, if you'd want to come."

At the mention of Payne's trip back to Africa, a heavy sadness ballooned inside her heart, but she refused to give attention to the sadness yet. She willed the growing gloom to deflate while she watched Olivia struggling with her feelings.

Shuffling her feet, Olivia repositioned the black sports watch on her wrist. "I don't know. Mom, you can go ahead. We didn't make plans for lunch."

"I hope you'll come, too, Olivia." Payne offered a tentative smile.

She jerked her ponytail to tighten it. "I'll think about it." Before stepping into the backyard for her run, she threw a quick, "thank you," over her shoulder.

Chapter 18

Standing, Ellen tried to smooth her skirt, but the wrinkles liked the soft fabric and dug in their heels. "I'm sorry about that laughing jag. I've been known to do that years ago. It's completely stupid and inappropriate, I know. But," she shrugged. "I just couldn't help it."

He chuckled, pulling her toward him. "I was a little scared you were going off the deep end—realizing you'd spent the night with a strange man and all."

She swatted him on his shoulder, and he tightened his hold on her. Nestling his chin beside her ear, he whispered, "Thank you for last night. You don't know how much it helped me."

She nodded.

"Something else helped, too." He ducked his head and dragged the toe of his shoe over the Oriental rug, his breathing short puffs.

God, what happened last night? What is tying him in knots? Please help him get the words out. "Payne?"

He turned his gaze back to her, and she saw his struggle to speak. She cupped the rough surface of his cheek.

He cleared his throat. "I, ah, I had a little talk with God, if you can believe that." He fiddled with the point of her collar. "I told Him about all the anger, all the hurt and grief. I asked Him for His peace, too. I, um, I think I'm going to be okay."

Her mouth dropped open for a split second before shock gave way to pure joy.

"Payne, I'm so glad." She beamed at him and trailed her fin-

139

gers to his chin.

"You know, I think you were right when you said that maybe God had brought me to your table in that café. He wanted you to help me." He gave her a quick squeeze and stepped back. "Hey, do you want to have—"

"Yes." She clapped her hand over her mouth and giggled. "Did that sound too eager?"

"It sounds just right." He pulled her to him again.

ℰᎧℰᎧ⳩⳩

Payne burst into the house feeling better than he had in fifteen year. Free, light—happy. Yes, wonder of wonders, he felt happy.

Wearing pajama pants and a t-shirt, Charlie leaned against the kitchen counter waiting for the stream of coffee to fill the carafe. He turned toward the sound of the backdoor slamming and cocked an eyebrow. "Well, well, well. We were just about to issue an all points bulletin for you." A wicked grin engulfed his face.

Payne ignored the remark and grabbed his friend in a massive bear hug. "Thank you," he whispered.

"Hey, if you like that one, I'm just getting started. Believe me." Charlie patted his back.

"Thank you for not giving up on me. Thank you for praying for me."

Charlie relaxed against his buddy and for once had no teasing comeback. Entering the kitchen, Kate froze when she saw the two men. "What's wrong, Payne?"

Payne released Charlie and crushed Kate against him.

"What is it, Payne?" She pushed back from him. "Is something wrong with you or with Ellen? Weren't you with her?" Concern jumbled Kate's brows.

"Nothing's wrong. Everything's so much better. Or at least I think it's going to be." He glanced over at Charlie. "I stayed with Ellen last night. We talked till sometime this morning and fell asleep on the back porch glider." With twenty-five years of history between them, Payne knew Charlie struggled with silencing the joke that trembled on his lips. He appreciated that his friend recognized truth and practiced restraint for once.

Payne gripped Kate's shoulders as he held her gaze. "Thank you for praying for me all these years, Kate. I'm sorry you had to pray for so long without any fruit for your labor." Amazing how Bible truths came back to him when he gave himself up to it.

Tears sprang to Kate's eyes. "Payne, what happened last night?"

Payne kissed her cheek and leaned against the counter. He accepted the fragrant mug of coffee Charlie offered him and shrugged. "We just talked. I told her about Cindy and Jamie. The whole story. All of it. And she just listened." He raked his hand through his hair, leaving it tousled and standing on end.

"When I finished the sorry story, we talked about grief—hers and mine. She lost her husband to pancreatic cancer a few years ago. She reminded me of how God can work through all the hard stuff in life and how other people pray for you through that hard stuff. When you can't or won't pray yourself."

"She sounds really special, Payne." A few tears shined on Kate's lashes.

"You'll have a chance to see for yourself if you come to lunch with me today. I'm meeting her in Galway along with her daughter. Maybe. Want to come?"

"Does it ever rain in Ireland? We'll be there with bells on." Charlie grinned and slapped his friend on his shoulder.

※※◌◌※

After a quick shower, Ellen perched on the arm of the couch for Olivia to finish her run. She didn't have to wait long. Olivia stomped into the house and launched her attack without preliminary questions or niceties. "Mom, I'm so angry with you. Shocked and disappointed, too. I would have never asked that man to dinner if I dreamed he would have ended up staying here all night."

"Olivia, we've been through this. I told you we talked and talked and fell asleep on the glider. I agree that from the outside it may look bad, but nothing inappropriate happened between us. I'm sorry that I shocked you so badly this morning, but you did a pretty good job of scaring us half to death, too, you know." Ellen made a face at her attempt at humor, but Olivia's foul mood couldn't be deterred.

"Well, if you 'talked and talked,' I suppose you got his vital statistics this time?"

Ellen stared at her. *Does she mean how old he is? How tall he is?*

"Mother, do you have his cell phone number, his email address, his office number, his home address?"

Ellen realized they still hadn't swapped contact information and, therefore, couldn't answer Olivia's questions. She shook her head. Ellen rose and walked into the kitchen for some orange juice, and Olivia followed her.

"Mom, you don't know this man from Adam. You have no way to check out if what he's telling you is true. I can't believe you were with him for hours and still didn't get his phone number." Anger turned to concern in Olivia's voice.

"We had more important things to talk about." She filled two glasses with juice.

"More important things like what?" Although curiosity softened her daughter's voice again, Ellen heard a touch of uncertainty, too.

She offered a glass to Olivia. "He told me about how his wife and infant son died in a car accident. I talked about your dad. We talked about trying to live through grief. I told him about how God helped me through the horrible times after your dad died."

Her chin wobbling, Olivia squeezed the juice glass between both hands, but she didn't break eye contact with her mother.

She swallowed and pressed her lips together. "I'm sorry. I didn't know—I."

"It's okay, Sweetie. I know you didn't know." She thought a moment. "I don't understand what all this is about." She hesitated as she remembered what he'd said a few minutes before he left. "In fact, he said something about believing God had brought us together to help him with his grief. Maybe—maybe that's all this week has been about—helping someone turn to God again."

Is that all, God?

No, no, not 'is that all.' Helping Payne come back to God was a tremendous achievement done only with God's hand, of course. If that was the reason they'd met, she'd be thankful to be part of God's plan.

All those pretty sentiments sounded very Christ-like and exactly what she should say out loud and even think to herself, but Ellen realized she wanted more for herself from this week with Payne. Every time she saw him, all her senses stood on alert, waiting for him to smile or laugh or take her into his arms. She wanted this crazy dream to continue beyond Galway.

But how could it in reality? They lived in different states. Tomorrow he had to return to Africa. Then he'd be halfway around the world, not just a few states away. How long would he have to work in Africa?

Neither of them had spoken about what happens next. Maybe he didn't want to break the spell of this romantic interlude. Or maybe he didn't see the need to continue their acquaintance after tomorrow.

If he were a globe trotter, maybe he knew women everywhere he stopped. A woman in every port? Did she really believe that characterization of Payne? She didn't want to, but little doubts waved red flags, threatening to wash her in gloom.

Ellen shoved those negative doubts out of her mind. She had today to look forward to, and she resolved to enjoy every minute she had with Payne.

Olivia narrowed her eyes. "Mom, what is it? Why do you look so sad now?"

Ellen shook her head and forced the corners of her mouth toward her cheekbones. If she looked happy, maybe she'd feel happy, too. "I refuse to be sad today. I'm going to enjoy the last day with Payne. Please come to lunch with us, Livie. I convinced him to ride in on the City Direct instead of picking me up, so he won't have to hunt for a parking place. I'll meet you after your morning class, and we'll walk over together. Sounds good, right?"

Olivia rolled her eyes. "Fine." She drew the one syllable word out for several beats. "It *was* nice of him to invite me." She sagged her shoulders. "I guess I'll go."

Chapter 19

Ellen spotted Payne waiting in front of Darcy's Café as soon as she and Olivia turned onto High Street. At the sight of him, her senses flashed on alert, reminding her of those allergy commercials with one foggy scene followed by a clearer, enhanced scene after taking the medicine. That's what this man had done for her in the past few days. He'd brightened her life.

"Hello, ladies." Smiling, he glanced at Olivia. "I'm glad you're joining us." He hadn't moved to touch Ellen, but his warm gaze lingered on her face. "I hope you don't mind, but Charlie and Kate are coming to lunch, too. He's my college roommate, Olivia. Their son, my godson, is the reason I'm here in Galway."

At the mention of Payne's friends, Ellen's heart flip-flopped, and she tugged at the side seam of her new turquoise sundress. Did they know about his spending the night at her house? If they did, what did they think about her? Good grief, she'd envisioned a different kind of lunch today. She wanted to enjoy her last hours with Payne, not make small talk with strangers who probably thought she was some lonely woman who threw herself at eligible bachelors.

Pointing to the back, he held the door, and Olivia followed the direction of his fingertips. "They're waiting for us at that round table." As Ellen crossed the threshold, he rested his hand at the base of her neck and leaned close to whisper, "You look beautiful, by the way. Sharp dress." He squeezed her shoulder. "I'm glad you're here."

"Me, too."

His simple confirmation allayed her anxieties. So did Kate

herself. Kate's wide-set brown eyes crinkled with her smile, and she grasped Ellen's wrist. "We're so happy to meet you."

Payne pulled out the chair beside Kate for Ellen, offered the next one to Olivia, and then claimed the seat between Olivia and Charlie for himself. Momentarily disappointed that Payne didn't sit beside her, she pushed negative thoughts out of her mind as she'd done earlier that morning, determined to savor all aspects of their lunch.

Enjoying lunch proved to be an easy task. A natural-born story-teller, Charlie entertained them with tales about his and Payne's college escapades. Ellen watched Kate laugh at every story as if she were hearing it for the first time. When their eyes met, Ellen couldn't help an arched eyebrow. Kate shrugged. "I know I should be tired of these stories by now, but I think they're still funny. The best part, though, is how much they enjoy telling the stories." Kate turned toward her husband, "Hey, you haven't told the snowstorm and broom story yet." Both men glanced at each other, grinning.

"Well, that's really Payne's story." Charlie swallowed some of his water with lemon.

"No, it's about your car, if you can call it a car." Payne bumped Charlie on his shoulder.

"Hey, that Bug got us everywhere we needed to go, thank you." Charlie protested the insult and straightened in his chair as if to defend the honor of his Volkswagen.

"True. It just didn't always get us back." Payne winked at Olivia, and jealousy fluttered for a quick second in Ellen's chest.

Their food arrived, putting the snowstorm story on hold. When the waitress left the table, Charlie grabbed Payne's and Kate's hands. "Let's pray, people." Ellen recovered quickly from her brief surprise that a friend of Payne's would be so quick to pray out loud. Comfortable praying in public, Charlie offered a heartfelt, original prayer, no trite phrases or memorized rhymes.

Thank you, God, for giving Payne Christian friends. Thank you for being sovereign. A warm peace settled in her heart. God would take care of Payne's renewed Christian faith after they said their goodbyes.

A bittersweet thought, though as she acknowledged her role in Payne's life might be coming to an end. He'd return to Africa in the morning, and they had no plans after this lunch.

Open to prayer, Payne had allowed God back into his life. He had Christian friends who loved him and, no doubt, prayed for him. He'd be fine without her. But would she be fine without him?

Kate brought Ellen back from her reverie with another request for the snowstorm and broom story. Olivia, breaking a piece of brown bread, surprised Ellen by adding, "Yes, Payne, let's hear it."

"Well, it's really not that much of a story. We were coming back from a fraternity function—"

"A fraternity function?" Kate tut tutted as she stirred her potato and leek soup.

"A. Fraternity. Function." Payne emphasized each word. "A snowstorm had begun during the, ah, event, and Charlie's windshield wipers didn't work, and we had to figure out how to get back across town in the blinding snow."

"Let me tell it. I can do it better than you can." Charlie laid down his fork so that he could use both hands to enhance the story. Payne leaned back in his chair and winked at Ellen. She realized he'd maneuvered the conversation so that Charlie would tell the story for him.

"All right. Listen up. We came out of the 'fraternity function' about two in the morning. We hadn't noticed it, but the snow had been falling for probably an hour or more. Three or four inches of snow swamped my car."

"Three or four inches! It gets deeper every year you tell it." Giggling, Kate shook her head at her husband.

"Darling, who is telling this fine tale?" Charlie slid forward in his chair. "Okay, so we didn't have a yard stick, but my car was covered anyway. We cleared the windshield off with my little scraper and rolled out into the street, headed for the dorm. That's when I realized my wipers were shot. I tried to see by sticking my head out the window, but the wind and snow were so fierce that I thought I was going to lose my contacts. I couldn't see for the snowflakes and the tears streaming from my eyes."

"Anyway, my buddy, Payne, had a brilliant idea. He said we needed a broom or something to keep the windshield clean. At that very moment, Jack, another fraternity brother spotted an old broom propped up against a gas station. We took a detour into the parking lot and grabbed that broom."

"You stole the broom?" Concern laced Olivia's words.

"We borrowed it," Payne inserted. "Seriously." When Olivia's face remained in skeptical mode, Payne continued, "Jack refused to help sweep the windshield because he was certain he'd get pneumonia, so we made a deal that I'd sweep if he'd take the broom back the next afternoon. I doubt anybody missed it, though, because half the bristles were gone. The remaining few that managed to cling to the broomstick curved at the bottom like a capital J. It resembled a broom but wasn't exactly the best representation of one."

"How would he get pneumonia sweeping the windshield?" Ellen wanted the whole story.

Charlie swallowed the last bite of his sandwich. "That's the hilarious part." He pushed back his chair and stood at the table with his feet apart, holding an invisible broom. A few heads around the room turned toward them. "Payne stood up through the sun roof, sort of like a gondola guy, and swept back and forth and back and forth so that I could see to drive." Charlie's eyes shimmered as he remembered, laughing at the scene in his mind. He sank into his chair.

"I didn't have a hat or a scarf or gloves. I thought I was going to freeze to death. I can't believe I didn't catch my death that night." Payne's broad grin belied his health worries.

"Hey, same here. The snow kept falling in on top of me, too, you know." Charlie thumped Payne on his shoulder. "Anyway, the campus police stopped us just as we were turning onto Hill Street in front of our dorm. He listened to our sob story about broken wipers and then helped us find a parking place. So there you have it. The snowstorm broom story."

Ellen and Olivia started clapping, but Kate warned them, "Don't egg them on. They have tons more stories just like the ones you've already heard. They'll stay talking all day if you let them. And, Charlie, dear, we can't stay all day. I wanted to go back to that sweater store we found out on that road going to Bushy Park, remember?"

Charlie nodded his head. "I remember. We have to buy Christmas presents in July, right? Then we have to figure out how to pack all the stuff we bought. That ought to take most of the evening." He blew a kiss to his wife.

Kate leaned over to Ellen and whispered for her ears only. "I'm so glad we had this chance to meet you. We love Payne, and we love seeing the change that's come over him since he's met you."

Ellen opened her mouth to speak, but nothing came out. Kate grabbed her hand and squeezed it. "I hope we'll get to meet again sometime."

Ellen agreed with her, but she doubted the reality of a future meeting.

Olivia dropped her napkin onto her plate and stood. "Mom, I'm meeting with my study group this afternoon, so I need to get going, too. Everyone's coming over to the house, okay?"

"Sure." As she stood, Kate pulled her into a quick hug. Before she stepped out of that embrace, Charlie grabbed her, kissing her cheek. "It was a real pleasure to meet you, Ellen." He glanced over at Payne, "Hey, pal. We've got to leave for Shannon early in the morning, remember?" Payne nodded, and the three of them left with the check in Charlie's hand.

Ellen laughed at the retreating figures. "Quick exit, huh? Seems like they'd practiced."

"I'm sure Charlie and Kate had a planned departure method, and Olivia just took her cue from them. I think they're giving us alone time together." He smiled down at her. "Charlie's paying for lunch because he lost to me at arm wrestling, but we could still get dessert, if you want?" He brushed her hair behind her ear and toyed with her silver hoop.

Caught off guard by his touch, Ellen forced her attention back to the conversation. "You arm wrestled for the bill?"

He nodded. "We always do. Next time, I'll lose and I'll pay.

That's how it works."

Ellen laughed thinking about the two grown men arm wrestling to dodge paying for a meal. And because she had the whole afternoon with Payne. "We can have dessert or take a walk around the Square."

"Here's a great idea. Let's have dessert first and then take a walk. Sound good?"

"Sounds good."

They lingered over chocolate mousse, and she described her farm and her concerns to him. He challenged and encouraged her with questions and ideas.

After the mousse, they headed out toward Eyre Square. Sometimes he took her hand or put his arm around her shoulders as they strolled from shop to shop, but he never tried to kiss her. Sometimes they talked. Other times they simply enjoyed each other's silence.

As the afternoon slipped away, Ellen realized they were both avoiding the obvious. Deciding to tackle the pink elephant, she turned toward Payne. "Our day is fading. I suppose I need to get back to Olivia, and you need to pack."

He nodded and rubbed her forearm. "I know. Packing won't take long, so I'm not worried about that. Are you ready to say 'goodbye'?"

So, it was going to be 'goodbye,' not 'til we meet again' or something less final. "No. I'm not ready, but the time is getting closer and closer, you know. And the City Direct doesn't run all night."

He ran his hand behind his neck. "Yeah. I know." He cocked his head. "What about this? What if we take the City Direct back to Charlie and Kate's house? Then I'll drive us back to yours. We can see what Olivia wants to do for dinner. Okay?"

"Okay." Ellen expected she'd agree to any plan he had.

Chapter 20

Switching the City Direct for the car took less time than anticipated. Payne left a note for Charlie and Kate, still out shopping for souvenirs. Arriving at Tohlfair, they found the study group gone and Olivia in the kitchen adjusting the heat under a pot. "I kind of thought you might be joining us." Olivia directed a shy smile at Payne. "I hope you like pesto. It's bottled, though. Not as good as Mom's homemade, but it'll do."

"Pesto with angel hair. I love it. Thank you, Olivia, and don't worry. Your mother and I won't surprise you by being on the glider tomorrow morning. I've set myself a time limit tonight."

Olivia broke the dried pasta in half and tossed the pieces into the rolling water. "Good. I don't think I could take another scare like that."

During dinner, they listened to a Van Morrison CD and talked about Olivia's studies. As they cleared the dishes, Olivia surprised them both with, "Are you going to give my mother your phone number or email address or anything like that before you leave? I keep asking her, and she keeps telling me that neither of you have talked about stuff like that."

"Olivia!" Ellen, color flooding her cheeks, reprimanded her daughter.

Olivia dipped her head. "I'm sorry if you think it's none of my business, but I'm just curious for my mom's sake."

"As a matter of fact," Payne reached into his back pocket for his wallet. "I keep forgetting to give your mom one of my cards. It has all of my contact information." He handed the card to Ellen. "Now, I need yours."

Satisfied, Olivia produced a pen and a slip of paper for Ellen. "I guess I'm not needed here any longer, so I'll retire to my room." She faced Payne. "I enjoyed meeting your friends today, Payne. Thanks for inviting me. It's certainly been—" She hesitated, "Interesting, I suppose, to get to know you. I hope you have a good trip tomorrow."

"Thank you, Olivia. I think you're interesting, too." Smiling, Payne winked at her.

She gave her mother a quick hug and retreated up the stairs. Ellen moved into the den and sat on the sofa. Payne followed her but sat with a little distance between them.

An awkward silence descended on the room. She glanced at him.

"What is it?" Payne had turned toward her, watching her face.

She pushed her hair back with her palm, searching for how to explain her feelings. "I haven't felt self-conscious with you since the first day we met. Well, maybe right after that stupid first kiss."

"That first kiss wasn't stupid."

Her insides melted.

She didn't want to think about that kiss, especially the humiliation after it. She shrugged. "Now I'm starting to feel a little weird, though. Like, what comes next?"

"What do you want to come next?" He rested his arm along the top of the sofa.

"What do *you* want to come next?" She didn't want to have to spell it out for him.

"I asked you first."

"For Pete's sake." Ellen decided to plunge right in. She knew she had a slim chance of ever seeing him after tonight, so she had no reason to hide her thoughts and emotions. "Okay. I wish we could see each other when you get back to the States, but I really don't see that happening. So I'm thinking it might be a little awkward and sad, too, saying goodbye."

"Why will it be awkward?" His eyebrows bunched together over his dark eyes.

She hesitated. Maybe it wouldn't be awkward for him. Maybe he was ready to leave and say bye right now. Shaking her head, she decided to step out in unfamiliar territory, to plunge ahead with her original thoughts, before doubts in her mind grew louder.

"I'm thinking about the promising to keep in touch. We both lead busy lives in two different states. And we might want to keep in touch, but that can be difficult. I don't enjoy talking on the phone very much. And while I do email, I don't like it too much either. I like face-to-face communication or old fashioned real letters with stamps and return address labels. They're more personal than email."

He searched her face for a minute. "Well, let's not promise to email or call, so that if it doesn't happen, we won't feel guilty. I can't guarantee consistent emails anyway because when I'm out in the field in Africa, the internet is hit or miss. It could be a while before I can email regularly. How does that sound—not promising to email, I mean?"

Her pulse staccatoed under his intense scrutiny. Was he holding his breath?

She dropped her gaze to her fingernails to steady herself, pushing back her cuticles. "I know I said I don't like emailing, but I don't really like the not-promising-to-email plan either."

He let out his breath, laughing. "Well, that's good. Neither do I. We'll email or call or both when we have a chance. How's that?"

"Better, I guess." Marginally better. He'd seemed a little different today. Although still attentive and charming, he hadn't kissed her since this morning. Wait, he'd kissed her on top of her head when he left. He hadn't really kissed her since—since when? Since right after their walk last night. What did that—

"Ellen, come back to me. Where were you? Did you hear what I said?" Payne tugged her earlobe.

"I'm here. I'm here." The smile she offered him was more of a straight line than a curved one. "Sorry. What did you say?"

Payne laughed. "We have another option. We could plan to meet somewhere in the States when I get back. How do you like that?"

Ellen's heart leaped. "That sounds good, but sometimes it doesn't work."

"What do you mean?" He frowned again.

"Well, I've seen this option played out in movies. The main characters plan to meet at a certain time, and one of them comes too late; or he's at the big water fountain on the east side of town, and she's at the little one on the west side; or she's in a wheel chair and can't make it to the top of the Empire State Building, and he thinks she's stood him up."

"You're being a little bit negative, don't you think. We'll just have to be better planners, right?"

Yes, a negativity knot multiplied in her chest, threatening to rule her emotions. Her week with this man was coming to an end. She felt the close of something special with her entire body. A crazy idea blossomed in her mind. "Will you be back in the States by Thanksgiving?" Maybe having something to look forward to would help her get over missing Payne. Because she knew she'd miss him.

"Thanksgiving? If all goes well, I should be back by the end of August. Beginning of September at the latest. Why?" He leaned toward her. "What did you have in mind?"

She lost her thought for a moment thinking he might kiss her. "I…I was thinking maybe you could come to my house for Thanksgiving, that is if you were back and if you didn't already have usual plans. I mean, we wouldn't end up at the wrong fountain or somewhere else at the wrong time." She plucked at the tassel on the corner of the sofa pillow.

"I don't have usual plans for Thanksgiving. Sometimes I go to my parents. Sometimes they visit my sister. Charlie and Kate usually invite me to spend it with them. But I'm never a definite for them either." He rubbed his knee. "Thanksgiving seems like a long time away."

"True, but you're going to be in Africa for part of that time. It looks like I might have a foreign exchange student which means September and October could be really busy, not to mention how crazy a yarn shop can be during those months. Everybody's in a frenzy wanting to start and finish Christmas presents."

He narrowed his eyes. "How big of a shindig are you talking about?"

She crossed her arms in front of her. "Look, you choose a different time if Thanksgiving is a bad idea. I thought—"

"How many people?"

She swallowed. "Sometimes we have between twenty and twenty-five, give or take."

His eyebrows shot up. "Twenty or twenty-five?"

"It's mainly extended family and a few displaced people who might not have another invitation. Olivia will still be here in Galway, but you've spoken to Scott on the phone. You could bring a friend if it would make you feel more comfortable." Grasping for straws, she didn't have any better idea. Time with Payne ran away from her, and she couldn't stop the evening from ending.

"Bring a friend?" His eyes twinkled, and his huge grin creased his cheeks. He had the nerve to laugh at her.

"For Heaven's sake. What's so funny about that?" She slapped her hands on her hips. "Help me out here. I'm trying to come up with a plan, or do you have a better one?"

He leaned toward her, grabbing her hands. What took him so long?

"Thanksgiving's a good plan. It just seems like a long time from now." His thumb swished across her palm. She bit the inside of her cheek to withstand the zings coursing through her body. "But you're right. I'll be busy in September writing up the notes from my project. I'm not scheduled to teach fall semester, though. That'll help."

He studied her fingers, caressing them. His voice dropped to a softer pitch when he spoke again. "It's almost time for me to get back to Charlie's, but I want you to know this week with you has been special to me. Real special. So much has happened." He raised his eyes to meet hers. "Thank you for praying for me. I'm not completely where I need to be, but I'm on my way. That's more than I could say for a long time. You're the reason for that."

She shook her head. "God's the reason, Payne, not me."

"You were the one He used to get my attention, Ellen. I need to process all that's happened. Africa will be good. Have some alone time. Think." He tightened the pressure on her hand. A muscle in his jaw jumped. He straightened against the couch and licked his lips. "I've got to go. If I don't—" He stood and pulled her up, too.

The end had come so fast Ellen felt as if she'd been ambushed. She struggled to keep her breathing steady. *Dear God, Help me do this. Help me say 'goodbye' to Payne.* He draped his hands on her shoulders. His thumbs stroked her collar bone, but he held her away from him.

"So, let's see. We'll email when we can—no promises to email every day or even every week. Remember it'll be a while before I'll be able to email regularly or even at all. And I'm coming to your house for Thanksgiving, right?"

She didn't trust herself to speak through her constricted throat. She nodded.

"Okay, then." He dragged his fingers through his hair, crossed his arms, and cleared his throat. "Okay, then."

He wiped his hand across his mouth and shook his head. He shoved his hands in his pockets, glanced toward the door.

Where was the awkwardness coming from? Was it the end-of-the-date goodnight kiss? Did he not want to kiss her tonight but was thinking that she expected one? Why did he seem so uncomfortable all of a sudden? Fine. She'd help him. She refused to watch him squirm, waiting for him to make the first move.

"Payne, this has been a special week for me, too. I'm really glad you eavesdropped and interrupted me in the café that first day." She forced a teasing smile. "And I'm glad to have met Charlie and Kate. I like them a lot." Ellen thrust her hand toward him.

Some kind of emotion passed over Payne's eyes, but Ellen couldn't determine if he were going to yell at her or laugh. He burst out laughing. "That's exactly what you did the first day we met. I guess it's time for me to go, huh?"

"No! Good grief. You looked like, like you were under duress or something. I wanted to help you out. I wa—" He pulled her to him, and she wrapped her arms around his waist.

He spoke against her hair. "You're right. This is hard. And awkward. And I wish I didn't have to leave, but I do." Leaning back, he clasped her face with both hands and traced her high cheekbones. "Sweetness." He crushed her to him once more, brushed her lips with a light kiss but let her go as he hurried toward the door. Hesitating before opening it, he turned back. "Till Thanksgiving, right?"

She nodded, and he stepped out into the night.

Ellen sank back onto the sofa. As much as she felt like crying, she squeezed her eyes closed before the tears could form. True, she felt bereft, a little confused over Payne's actions tonight and already lonely, but she had four more days to spend in Galway with her oldest daughter. She resisted the urge to wallow in self pity and ruin her vacation. Payne had accepted her invitation to Thanksgiving and that would have to carry her through the next few months *Thank you, God, for this time with Payne. I'm trusting you with what comes next.*

ഇ�ഇ�ര�ര�

Payne sucked in huge gulps of damp air as he jogged to the rented Volvo. Trying to be a gentleman tonight, he'd refrained from kissing Ellen except for that brotherly goodbye peck. Not folding her into his arms and kissing the life out of her was one of the hardest things he'd accomplished in a long time, but stopping once he'd reveled in her response would've have been harder.

He'd recognized the confusion in her eyes, but he couldn't explain everything to her tonight. He couldn't even explain everything to himself yet.

He needed time to think through the last few days in Galway—meeting Ellen and discovering his attraction to her, attending church and praying to God for the first time in years, realizing he wanted to be close to God again.

And realizing Ellen was important to him.

These new revelations unsettled him, sitting on his shoulders like a new coat—not uncomfortable but something to get used to. He already missed Ellen. How could he wait till Thanksgiving to see her again?

Chapter 21

"Ellen, what do you think? Ellen?" A sharp, nasal voice interrupted Ellen's thoughts.

As she often did in the three weeks since she'd come back from her trip, she found herself daydreaming about her encounters with Payne. Sometimes she drifted back to Galway in the middle of helping a customer in her yarn shop or, like now, in the middle of a meeting. She pulled herself back from Galway. "I'm sorry, Tamra. What did you ask me?"

Tamra Creech's voice raised a notch as she enunciated each syllable. "I said, 'what do you think of the latest proposal for the coffee shop?' School starts in just over a week, Ellen. We have to hit the ground running."

Ellen stared at Sally, pretending to listen but the brown circle of lip pencil outlining Tamra's coral lips distracted her. Fascinated, she focused on the ring forming the words instead of on the message. Identical coral strips of blusher indicated hidden cheek bones. Black eyeliner dominated her tiny, set-too-close-together eyes. Tamra's brown hair streaked with blond highlights was teased up above the crown of her head, curving down to cradle her chin. Chandelier earrings swished as she emphasized her words.

As the school's liaison to the school board, Tamra was an organizer, an i-dotter, and a t-crosser. She meant for everything to be done and to be done properly.

Too bad her makeup pallet resembled Emmet Kelly's.

Ellen chastised herself for the bad attitude. *Father, forgive me for that mean-spirited thought and for this perpetual funk I'm*

159

in since I've been home. Please help me to concentrate on this conversation.

The brown circle continued its calisthenics. "We need to have everything in place. A good idea is one thing, Ellen, but a good idea that works is quite another." With French tipped nails, Tamra tapped her animal print covered ink pen against the faux leather note pad, as if to add weight to her point.

Ellen had suggested to Tom Daughtry, the high school principal, the idea of opening a student-run downtown business over two years ago. She needed something to work on to propel her out of her depression. She and Steve had often dreamed of a student-run business in town, and she was determined to make it come true.

After reviewing her business proposal, Tom had cautiously agreed to support the plan and enlisted the necessary teachers to help. He'd also accompanied her when she explained the endeavor to and asked for permission from the school board to try this new course in education.

Finding a business owner to join the team proved easy in Noah Woodard, a great-great grandson of one of the original founders of Bandon. With a soft heart for the high school as well as his hometown, he also had a vacant store-front ready to host the venture with the school.

"Tamra, I agree that we need to hit the ground running next week, but everything is ready. The latest proposal is solid." She nodded to the business department chairperson and the consumer sciences chairperson. "Mr. Schmitt and Mrs. Holly sketched out the preliminary plan last December. They fleshed out the business plan with the help of some of their best students, and the school board approved the proposal last March." Ellen ticked off by heart the steps of the process that Tamra already knew, having been involved with it ever since the school board had approved the project.

"Volunteers from the woodshop classes made minor repairs to the shop front throughout the summer. It's ready to go. The students who are participating in this adventure know the rules, the expectations, as well as the risks."

"I hope you understand your risk, Ellen. You're the one fronting the money for this 'adventure' as you call it with money from Steve's insurance policy. Let's not forget that this 'adventure' is still a class, and the students need to remember that, too."

This woman rubbed Ellen the wrong way. Ellen barely kept her temper in check. It was no one's business but hers and her children's what she chose to invest in. Steve's vision of teaching business entrepreneurship to high school students from the ground up had the support of the school board, teachers, students, and parents. They had planned it together. She wasn't walking down this new path on a whim or without a lot of prayer surrounding it either.

She counted to five and narrowed her eyes. "Yes, I've backed this venture with some money, but don't forget that Noah is giving the school the use of his store rent free for the first three months and then renting it to us for next to nothing indefinitely. He wants this experiment to work, too. It's good for the town to have one less empty store front, and it'll be a great opportunity for the students also."

She forced herself to soften her tone before she continued. "Tamra, we are good to go. Of course, we're expecting a few wrinkles for the first week or so. No one has tried anything like this in Bandon before. But if people will be patient, we have a good chance of succeeding." Most of the teachers and administrators nodded their agreement, adjourning with little more discussion than to put a weekly update check meeting in place for the first four weeks of operation.

Ellen exited the building, heading to the yarn shop to visit with Agnes and check on yarn orders. Agnes McKnight, one of her friends who had run the shop during the Ireland vacation, had loved the job so much that she'd convinced Ellen to keep her as store manager. Lonely and close to slipping into a depression after her husband of fifty-four years, Henry, had died in early February, Agnes grabbed the opportunity to work in the yarn shop with both hands. She'd said more than once, "I love my new job. My heart is a little bit lighter here in the middle of all this yarn."

Having a full-time colleague in the shop had proven invaluable to Ellen. With Agnes in the shop, Ellen had more time to help with the coffee shop and more time to plan the future of her farm. Equally talented in crochet as well as knitting, Agnes helped calm frustrated customers, taught classes, and listened with thoughtful insight to Ellen's new ideas for the shop.

"Hello, Dear." Agnes's head popped up from a pattern book as Ellen entered the front door. "Wow. You look a little frazzled." Agnes' eyebrows pulled together over bright, blue eyes. Her silver hair sported a short, spunky hairdo that belied her age. She didn't look like a little old lady who knitted and crocheted. With the fun, bold colors of her t-shirt and swingy skirt and the chunky bright pink beads around her neck, she looked more like she belonged in a boutique located near a college campus.

"I just finished my meeting with the coffee shop advisors. Tamra Creech shared her fifteen cents' worth." Ellen grimaced.

"Say no more. That woman makes me want to growl sometimes. We served in the garden club together a few years ago. Not to start gossiping, but I just know what you mean, Darlin'." Agnes pursed her raspberry tinted lips, eyes sparkling. "I also know something that might wipe that frazzled look off of your pretty face. Guess what it is."

Ellen smiled. "I love having you in this shop." She kissed the older woman's cheek and set her pocketbook near the cash register. "Okay. Let's see. Did they pull the ticket at the library today, and I won the gas card give away?" The hardworking friends of the public library sponsored fundraisers almost every other month, and Ellen supported every one.

"No. Better than that." Agnes turned to move away from Ellen. "I can't wait for you to guess. Ta daaaa!" She pointed to a back corner of the shop. "A great big box all the way from Ireland arrived today." She clapped her hands tinkling the tangle of bracelets on her wrists and giggled.

Ellen squealed with delight.

Agnes pushed the box out of the corner with her lime-colored sandal. "I think you know what's in it. I made myself not open it even though mail technically falls under my job description. I saved it for you."

Ellen rushed to the box and traced her fingers over Grainne's return address. "Great! I can't wait to see those yarns. You're going to love them. And they're here just in time for the next prayer shawl meeting. Hand me the paper scissors, please, and I'll strip the sealing tape."

The yarns had dimmed in her mind's eye, but the vibrant colors nestled in the box thrilled Ellen again. Agnes stroked the silk and wool skeins, reveling in the unusual softness. "These are marvelous. Your description of them didn't do them justice, Boss."

"I know. You really have to experience these jewels. When Olivia and I saw Grainne's yarns, I knew they were special. Eastern North Carolina and wool don't exactly mix for most of the year, but I couldn't pass up these yarns. We have to display them with some fabulous patterns. I need you to help me choose a few to highlight, okay? Can we do that as soon as possible?"

Ellen's hands emptied the box of its exceptional treasure, but her mind had slipped back to the day that she and Olivia had met Grainne and discovered her talents with wool. Then, of course, already in Galway, her memory skipped easily from that day with Olivia to all the ones with Payne.

Chapter 22

Ellen succumbed completely to reflecting on her time with Payne during her drive home. She smiled remembering him that first morning. He really did look like some kind of derelict with his dusty, worn clothes. It's a wonder the owner of the cafe allowed him in. It's a wonder her avoid-confrontation mentality didn't send her running for the door with his first cracks about prayer.

A picture of him when he bumped into her in the pottery shop floated into her mind. If she concentrated hard enough, she could smell his clean, spicy scent and feel his strong arms steadying her.

During the ten minutes' drive home, many pictures of her time with Payne flickered in her thoughts, but she stubbornly avoided the memory of their first kiss. That image still vexed her.

As she rounded the curve a half-mile from her house, the neighbor's psycho German shepherd pounced out of the ditch, yelping and chasing the mini-van to the end of his yard. Never mind that the crazy dog was as consistent as daybreak in his Cujo antics, Ellen, snatched from Galway with a jolt, still gasped and strangled the steering wheel.

Turning into her driveway, she put the van in park and retrieved the mail from her box. Knowing she wouldn't find a letter from Payne didn't stop her from hoping for one as she flipped through the envelopes and mail order catalogs.

She inched down her long paved path to her house, allowing her mind slide back to Ireland. On their last afternoon together, she and Payne had strolled down the promenade in Salthill, the sea-side area of Galway. They'd snuggled together against the brisk, salty breeze blowing in off of Blackrock Beach.

Taffy, her soft-coated Wheaten terrier jumped on the bottom of the door-frame, greeting her with excited licks when she opened her door. "I'm happy to see you, too, but wait a minute, Taffy." Ellen laughed and pushed against the dog's muzzle. "Let me grab my stuff."As she rounded the back of the van, a puff of wind fluttered into the garage, bringing another assault on her senses. The wind blew from her neighbor's farm, bringing the sharp, earthly scent of cows with it.

Definitely not in Galway anymore. Essence of bovine instead of crisp, salt air.

After visiting a few minutes with Taffy and feeding him, she dragged herself into the kitchen, buoyed by the attention of her loving dog. She dropped her mail onto the counter and opened her freezer. She seized the carton of dark chocolate, chocolate chip light ice cream. Since the carton held only one or maybe one and a half servings, she grabbed a spoon and dug into the chocolate therapy, skipping the bowl. One less dish to wash.

Leaning against the sink, she enjoyed the frozen treat melting on her tongue. She exhaled a weary breath as her neck muscles loosened and her shoulders sagged, She noticed her computer, the sleek, black screen dominated the kitchen desk. It beckoned to her, and she remembered the last night with Payne, discussing emails and making plans to see each other again.

She licked her spoon.

"Stop taunting me. It's not time to email him again."

She'd already emailed him twice in the three weeks that she'd been back in Bandon, struggling both times over stories to share, length of the messages, and tone. That first email she wrote turned into a whole afternoon of writing, deleting, wiping sweaty hands, and frantic prayers. At first, when she'd begun typing, she'd filled the screen with anecdotes from her last days in Galway and the flight home.

After reminding herself that emails weren't supposed to be so long, she pushed the cancel button, deleting the whole note. Emails weren't exactly the best platform for her writing style. She grappled with condensing the best stories into a few sentences. Ending with the hope that his project was going well, she'd pushed the 'send' button, immediately wishing for a do-over.

Although he'd told her not to expect a response from him for a while because of unpredictable internet service in the Ugandan countryside, disappointment still shrouded her the next morning when her account showed no reply from Payne.

She'd restrained herself from writing another email for ten days. In the second email, she described the coffee shop project in a quick paragraph because she'd spent the morning with the two lead teachers assessing last minute details. Even with a short description, she couldn't hide her excitement that the coffee shop dream inched closer than ever to becoming a reality.

Continuing to write without responses wore on her courage, and even though she knew he worked somewhere in the wilds of Africa and couldn't email, doubts jabbed at her self-confidence. She should wait a few more days before sending another message.

Maybe by then she could think about a topic that would be short, informative, entertaining, and make him miss her as much as she missed him. *Whoa. That's a tall order.* Stick with short, for sure, and informative. An email like that wouldn't portray her as some lonely widow pursuing an eligible man, would it?

But wasn't she lonely? She knew the quick answer to that question. Although she filled her time with community ventures and yarn projects and anything else to take her mind off memories of Payne, loneliness stalked her. It waited for her at the threshold of her shop as she helped her customers. It lingered in another classroom while she finished her church meetings, accompanying her on the ride home.

She did miss him, and she couldn't help it. She missed talking to him. She missed his eyes crinkling when he laughed. She missed his hand holding hers, and she missed his kisses.

Dear God, help me stop dwelling on Payne. I have other things to do. Help me to focus on my responsibilities here and not on him.

After tossing the empty carton into her garbage and the spoon into the dishwasher, she snatched the portable phone out of its cradle to call Diane Yates. She didn't want to wait to find out about the foreign exchange students. Not in the mood for pleasantries or chit-chat, she opened the conversation with her objective when Diane answered. "So do I have one or not?"

"Oh, hey, Ellen. I'm fine. How are you?" Diane laughed. "Honey, you know I won't have the final number until next week at the earliest. It might even be the first couple of days in the second week of school. You're still on my backup list unless you want me to move you up to the main list." Diane's voice rose a hopeful notch.

"I'm fine with being on the back-up list. And you put me on the bottom of your backup list, right?" She rubbed her forehead wondering if she had any more ice cream in the overflow freezer in the garage.

"Ellen, it sounds like you don't really want an exchange student. You're making me feel bad." Diane's voice whined.

"Your pouting won't make me change my mind. You know I love you, and I enjoy helping with the students, but I'll be the only one at home this year. The poor student would probably be as bored as all get out with nobody around but me." Ellen flipped through the mail, throwing the junk pieces straight into the garbage.

"No one could be bored at your house. You're busy all the time. Hey, I just remembered. That travel piece you did for the paper was really good. It makes me want to hop on a plane, too."

"Thank you." Ellen had turned in the article to Frank the week after she arrived home, but who knew that a weekly paper could be so full of weddings and funerals and speeding drivers that it took him two more weeks before he could run it?

"But, Ellen Shepherd, I think you left out the most interesting part of your trip." Diane purred like she had a secret that she couldn't wait to share.

"What do you mean, Diane?" Ellen's fingers froze as the last envelope slipped into the trash. Her heart fluttered, dreading Diane's next comment.

"I heard you met some man over there. Why didn't you mention him in your article?"

Ellen heard the grin in the other woman's voice. Her back as straight as a board, she gripped the phone with both hands. She forced a calmness to blanket her words. "Who told you that? And it was a travel piece, not an article describing all the interesting people Olivia and I met over there."

The thought of Diane Yates spreading the tale around town that she'd had a romantic interlude churned the ice cream weighing down her stomach. What would people say if they knew she'd flirted with a stranger in Galway? As much as she loved Diane, Ellen knew she had a penchant for sharing news, and she didn't want to be the conversation du jour.

"When Scott called me back, he mentioned talking with some man who was having dinner with you. So spill it. Who was your dinner companion?"

Ellen knew her son. He probably mentioned Payne after Diane grilled him about what his mother was doing in Ireland.

"Oh, I remember that night." Ellen cooled her voice, adding a nonchalant note. "We had several people over for dinner after an afternoon on the square in downtown Galway." How cosmopolitan did that sound? "Laurel and Scott called while everyone was still there, and, yes, I do believe Scott talked to one of our guests." How could she finish this phone call without Diane thinking she had something to hide? "We had people there from Scotland, Ireland, and from Nigeria, too. We had a great time listening to music and playing games and talking." Enough information. Diane doesn't need to know anything else. "So call me as soon as you know about the students. Okay, Diane?"

"Trying to change the subject, huh? Well, be that way. I have to go, too, but Scott painted a great big different picture about that night than you just did. Maybe I'll have to ask him to clarify his description the next time I see him." Diane softened her tone.

"But listen, honey. You've been alone long enough. If you met someone in Ireland, I say, 'good for you.' If you didn't, there are plenty of men here chomping at the bit to spend time with you. Jim Meadows is one. He mentioned to me the other day how impressed he was with your coffee shop project. He asked me allllll about you." The grin crept back in Diane's voice.

"Dr. Meadows? The school board chairperson?" As far as she could remember, she had never spoken more than a quick hello to him. "I hardly know the man. How do you know him?"

"He goes to my church. We chatted after the morning service a few weeks ago. He's been divorced for, I don't know, six or seven years. He was seeing Kathy Thor—."

"Diane, I'm sorry, but I really do have to go." Ellen didn't want to hear the details of Dr. Meadows' dating life. "Call me when you know something about the students. Bye." Ellen rammed down the receiver button with a determined index finger. Not quite hanging up on Diane, she did say 'bye' first.

The perils of living in a small town. Everyone knows your business and thinks she has the right to give commentary on it. First, Tamra Creech and now Diane.

Jim Meadows? She'd have to steer clear of him. She didn't want to have to thwart his advances if he decided to do more than compliment her. She wasn't interested in Jim Meadows or anybody else, for that matter.

Ellen's mouth dropped, and her hand flew to the base of her throat.

That's not true. She was still very much interested in Payne, but with every passing day and no communication from him, her misgivings grew stronger. Thoughts about his waning interest made her sad, but she had believed from the beginning that their relationship, if it could be called that, was designed by God.

Maybe God had designed it with a two-fold purpose. One, so that Payne could let Him back into his life, and two, so that God could open up a new chapter in her life called **DATING**.

She didn't want to date. She wanted Payne.

But Payne was half a world away and quickly becoming a memory that seemed more fairy tale than real. Did he ever think about her?

What about Jim Meadows? Almost every mental image of him included his hand wrapped around a biscuit from a fast food restaurant. He wasn't obese, but he certainly seemed to enjoy tending his middle aged spread. Payne, in contrast, still looked as trim and fit as Tristan and Samuel.

She caught her breath, ashamed of her superficial musings. She'd never thought of herself as shallow before.

Was it shallow to observe obvious facts?

Dear God, I have to stop spending so much time thinking about Payne. Was the time we spent in Galway the extent of our relationship? I have work to do here, and he's got his own to do, too. Please help him with his project, protect him, and continue to give him wisdom to understand and value his renewed relationship with You.

Chapter 23

She arrived late to the prayer shawl meeting the next week because she'd been helping Scott and Laurel pack for college. Both would be leaving within the next few days.

The prayer shawl group consisted of members of various churches who met once a month at her shop to share tips, ideas, new patterns, fellowship, and desserts. The ladies returned to their respective churches to share what they had learned with other yarn enthusiasts.

Once a month the shawls were dedicated during morning services and given to community members, friends, or relatives who suffered from chronic illnesses, or grief, or other life challenges. No one believed the shawls had healing powers, but the shawls provide tangible evidence of God's love to the hurting recipient.

Ellen loved the ministry and regularly donated yarn to the shawl group as well as to several church ministries.

When she entered *Knit One, Crochet, Too*, all of the ten regular members were seated, working on their various projects.

"Well, hey. Everybody's here tonight." She grinned at the women, thankful for this group who had supported her through the difficult phases of her grief. "I think you deserve a special treat since one hundred percent attendance doesn't happen very often, and I know just the thing. Has Agnes shown you the new yarns from Ireland?" Ellen glanced at her friend as she spoke, but Agnes, mesmerized by the hook and yarn in her hands, didn't respond.

"Agnes?"

Agnes lifted her gaze, a puzzling smile hovering on her lips. She shrugged her shoulders, but something else flickered behind the red, polka dot reading glasses perched on Agnes's nose.

"Agnes mentioned the yarns, yes, but we've got another idea for a treat." A former high school English teacher, Myrtle Brown, was the oldest crocheter in the group. She'd taught grammar, writing, literature, speech, and drama since 1945 when she returned from working in an airplane factory during World War II. After retiring, she enjoyed two years of traveling the world until the new principal, a former student of hers like most people in the town, begged her to come back to the classroom.

She taught for several more years until she refused to return citing the rampant disrespect from some of her students and her fatigue at seeing boys' underwear peeping out from saggy pants.

She never married but, according to town legend, had left her heart in California in World War II. Besides crocheting and making scuppernong jelly, one of her passions was writing a by-monthly letter to the editor of the *Dispatch* on current newsworthy topics.

The gleam in Miss Myrtle's eye baffled Ellen. "I have a dessert, too. I brought some brownies with chocolate chips and pecans. I know you love them, Miss Myrtle."

"Indeed, I do, but that is not the treat to which I'm referring." She giggled like a misbehaving student in one of her classes. "We are here tonight to hear every last detail about your Irish boyfriend."

Ellen's mouth dropped open as all the women chimed in, "Yes, Ellen."

"Tell us how you met."

"What's his name?"

"Is he going to come visit you?"

She glanced at Agnes, silent, but smiling. How did she manage to look hopeful and sheepish at the same time? "What are you talking about?"

"Come now, dear." Miss Myrtle leaned forward and thwacked Ellen on the knee with her crochet hook. "Every one of us has heard the rumors, but we want to hear the truth from you." She smiled and wiggled back into her upholstered chair, ready to listen to a fascinating story.

"Miss Myrtle, really. I don't have an Irish boyfriend." Both points were true. Payne wasn't Irish, and he wasn't her boyfriend either.

Ever the formidable English teacher, Miss Myrtle fixed her unwavering eyes on Ellen and arched a brow. "Are you saying that you did not meet a man during your sojourn in Ireland?" Miss Myrtle rested her project in her lap and waited for the answer.

Ellen could not evade that pointed question, but somehow she had to stamp out this potential fire of wagging tongues. "No, ma'am, I'm not saying that exactly. I did meet a man, but—"

Miss Myrtle cackled with glee. "Well then, girls, we do have a story tonight." She slapped the arm of her chair. "Get on with it, Ellen. I'm ninety years old and counting. Don't keep me waiting."

Ellen chewed on the inside of her cheek. She realized she'd have to share something about Payne with this group of women breathlessly waiting for a juicy story. Miss Myrtle wasn't a little old lady to be put off with a nonchalant, "Oh, there's really nothing to tell."

Despite feeling blindsided, Ellen managed to give the ladies just enough information about Payne to be interesting while skipping over how much he'd invaded her heart. She kept them laughing by relating some of Payne's Africa stories and the broom and snow story from college, but she didn't give them details of the romantic side of her encounters with him.

Only Miss Myrtle was bold enough to call her on her omissions. "These anecdotes are humorous, dear. We've enjoyed every one, but we want to hear more details about the two of you together. Start with what he looks like." Miss Myrtle, as usual, in control of the classroom.

"Oh, Ellen, yes! Is he handsome?"

"Is he tall?"

"Does he have blond hair or black?" Every woman inched to the edge of her seat and leaned forward in anticipation of all the thrilling details.

"He's tall. I guess he's about 6'2" or so. I didn't measure him." Ellen forced the sarcasm out of her voice. Instead, in her mind's eye she saw what he looked like that day in the pottery shop. "Yes, I think he's handsome with dark hair and gray eyes. He's got a tan because he works outside." She trailed off as she remembered how he had surprised her, completely rattling her when she ran into him. She remembered how he had asked her to have lunch with him and how they'd talked for hours. Her heart squeezed with the ache of missing him.

"Ellen? Ellen, dear. Come back to us." Miss Myrtle's sharp voice and a chorus of giggles snatched Ellen back from her memories of Payne. "Where were you, dear?" She smiled like a child who just sneaked a cookie from the cookie jar. "We might not know the exact location of your daydream, but I think we can correctly guess the person who captured your thoughts, right girls?" She elbowed Agnes, and more giggles rippled through the shop. Ellen couldn't believe these women she'd known for years were acting like silly teenagers discussing a first crush.

The bell at the front door jingled interrupting the pajama party. Ellen turned, surprised to see Diane Yates' enormous smile.

"Of course, you're here. I couldn't reach you at home or on your cell phone." She draped an arm around Ellen's shoulder.

"I must have left it in my car. What's up, Diane?" Ellen asked though she had a pretty good idea of what might bring Diane, a self-professed craft klutz, inside *Knit One, Crochet, Too*.

"Good news, Ellen. I have a darling girl for you. She's from South Korea, and her name's Euri. Isn't that great news? I know you're going to love her." Diane hugged Ellen's shoulder, adding a little shake for good measure.

Jaw dropping again, Ellen wriggled out of Diane's grasp. "I thought you said I was at the bottom of your stand-by list. I really didn't think they'd place a student with someone who doesn't have children in the house." Her ambivalence toward this situation grew by the minute. As much as she enjoyed international experiences, she didn't see how this one could turn out positively for the poor Korean girl who probably looked forward to meeting a big American family. Instead, she had drawn the card of a widow who lives by herself for most of the year.

"Ellen, honey, you were the only one on my stand-by list, but that doesn't matter." Diane waved her hand in the air. "And the board will take anyone who shows an interest and passes the security clearance. Anyway, Euri was originally supposed to go to North Grafton, but that placement fell through, and we got her in Bandon. And don't worry. I've implemented a new part to the Foreign Exchange program. Each F.E. student gets a school companion to help them become acclimated to the school as well as the community.

"I sort of handpicked the students I wanted involved with this endeavor, and they had to complete three hours of training. And guess who Euri's companion is going to be?" She clasped her hands together as if in prayer. "That sweet little Robin Taylor, your neighbor down the road." Diane paused for a few seconds, watching Ellen digest the news.

"Won't that work wonderfully? Robin is interested in any kind of foreign affairs, but her family just cannot host a student right now what with the grandfather living with them. Robin's so excited. She's going with me to meet the bus when it stops in Tyler. And, of course, I need you to come, too."

"When?" Ellen gulped, feeling as though she were being swept along a swelling river.

"Oh, I'm sorry. I left out that important detail, didn't I?" Diane laughed. "Thursday, honey. They leave Washington, D.C. on a bus bound for North Grafton High School Thursday morning. We'll pick up five foreign exchange students about 12:30, Thursday afternoon at the high school."

"Seriously? So I have one short day to get the house ready for her? I thought you were going to tell me as soon as you knew something." Ellen's brain throbbed in her spinning head.

"Honey, I'm sorry this is short notice, but I got the call from Mona at North Grafton this afternoon. It'll be fine, really it will." She grabbed Ellen for another quick hug. "You'll do great. It's going to be a tremendous year, you'll see."

The bell jingled again as she opened the door to leave. "See you Thursday, Ellen. I'll pick you up here around noon. We can ride together." And she was gone.

જીજીભ્રભ્ર

Later that night Ellen tried to go to sleep, but thoughts about hosting an exchange student all year swirled through her mind. *God, are you sending Euri to me as a blessing? Is this how You're going to help me get over Payne? If I'm running around after a teenager again, I won't have much time or energy to mope over him. Help me to focus on Euri, Father. Help me to be a blessing to her.*

The prayer brought peace to Ellen, curling on her side and clutching an extra pillow, but it didn't chase away the image of Payne smiling in the middle of the green fields of Ireland.

Chapter 24

Friday morning while Euri slept late, Ellen called Agnes at the shop.

"Good morning. How's business?"

"The shop's fine. Very quiet. How's it at your house? How is our foreign student? What's her name? Tell me everything."

Ellen laughed. "My house is quiet this morning, too. Eurr— Euri Tann is her full name—is still sleeping. She's probably exhausted with traveling half way around the world in the last few days."

"Poor thing. How did last night go?"

"Mostly fine. A little awkward sometimes. She's shy and doesn't generate conversation even though she speaks very good English. She yawned the whole time, but she insisted I open the gifts she brought with her."

"Oooh, sounds fun. What'd you get?"

Ellen enjoyed the older woman's childlike enthusiasm. "You seem about six right now, did you know that?"

"I love presents. What can I say?"

"Her mom quilted a beautiful pocketbook for me. I'll bring it to show you. She also brought an exquisite blue and white vase that just about took my breath away when I unwrapped it from the tissue paper. I'm so thankful it didn't break in transit."

Agnes gasped. "How true, how true."

"She pulled bags and bags of candy and snacks out of her luggage for us to sample. I'll bring some of those for the store, too."

"Aw, she sounds like a sweet girl. I can't wait to meet her."

"She is sweet. She smiles almost constantly and knits, too.

You'll get to meet her when we come in this afternoon. What time did you want to get on the road? You're still going to Emerald Isle for the weekend, right?"

Agnes owned a place at the beach about two hours east of Bandon and spent a few days there at least once a month throughout the year. "Yes, I wanted to check out that crafts fair the Friends of the Beach host every year. As long as I can leave by two-thirty or three, that'll be fine."

ഇ ഇ ଓ ଓ

Later that afternoon, a grinning Euri watched as Agnes inspected the quilted purse and marveled at the delicate stitches. Agnes pushed a piece of Korean candy to the side of her mouth. "Your mother is a true artist. This work is gorgeous. And I love this yummy candy."

"Take a handful with you on your road trip. We have bags of it. Right, Euri?" Ellen smiled at the young girl.

"Okay, I will." Agnes grabbed several pieces and dropped them into her bright yellow straw handbag. "I'm on my way then." She peeked at her white jelly watch. "Maybe I can get a jump on the beach traffic. You two have a great weekend. See you next week. Toodles." Agnes pulled the bag onto her shoulder and left trailing a whiff of White Linen perfume in her wake.

Euri scrunched her brow and cocked her head. "Toodles?"

ഇ ഇ ଓ ଓ

They paused over a basket of cotton and silk blend yarn, choosing colors for a sweater Euri wanted to knit when the bell tinkled at the front door.

Ellen greeted the customer. "Hello, Miss Myrtle. It's nice to see you again so soon. Do you already need more yarn?" Although Ellen had loathed the grilling session at the prayer shawl meeting on Tuesday night—led by Miss Myrtle—she still loved her and always looked forward to seeing her.

"No, I have all the yarn I need right now, dear. I'm here be-

180

cause I've been convicted." In her whole lifetime, Ellen couldn't remember ever seeing the former English teacher looking remorseful, but here she was standing in front of her, a penitent expression ruling her face.

Furrowing her brow, Ellen bit her lip. Miss Myrtle's contrite mood unsettled her. She hoped humor might relieve the disconcerting situation. "Did you eat too many chocolate-covered peanuts?"

Miss Myrtle straightened her back. "One can never have too many chocolate- covered peanuts, Ellen. Don't ever forget that fact." She flattened her palms against the sides of her skirt. "No, dear, it's not a silly thing I've come about. Are you free for a few minutes or should I come back at another time?"

"I'm free right now, but first let me introduce you to my foreign exchange student from South Korea. She'll be staying with me this year. Euri, this is Myrtle Brown. She's the best English teacher I know. Miss Myrtle, this is Euri Tann."

Miss Myrtle reached out her tiny hand and clasped Euri's. "I'm so happy to make your acquaintance, dear. What an adventure you'll have here. If I can help you at all, please come see me."

The young girl bowed her head and whispered a shy, "Thank you."

After directing Euri to another display of yarn and mentioning her lap-top on the desk behind the counter, Ellen turned her attention back to Miss Myrtle whose guilty expression had returned. "Miss Myrtle, what in the world is wrong?

"I'm ashamed of my behavior on Tuesday night."

"Oh, Miss Myrtle—"

"Wait, Ellen. Let me finish." Miss Myrtle cut her off with authority. "I want to apologize for trivializing and making sport of what you experienced on your trip. Love is not a trivial thing, and—" She held up her hand as Ellen opened her mouth to speak. "Even if you refuse to acknowledge the strong feelings you have for that young man you met in Galway, maybe you can admit that you had a romantic adventure at least. Romance is nothing to sneeze at."

Ellen jumped in as the other woman took a breath. "You think I have strong feelings for him?"

"Oh, my word, missy. I'm not deaf. I'm not blind. I'm not

dead yet either. I saw how your eyes softened as soon as you started thinking about him. I heard how your voice dropped and sounded all whispery when you started describing him. I'm just wondering why you act as though it's over?" She stopped and stared out the front window.

Ellen watched the older woman, sensing she had more to say.

Miss Myrtle sighed and looked back at Ellen. "I'm sure you've heard the rumors about my time in California during the war."

Ellen's eyes widened. She'd heard the rumors her whole life—the man had died, the man had jilted her, she had jilted him. Was she about to hear the truth now?

"Some of the rumors are true, of course. It's true that I fell in love there, but he didn't break my heart. Well, he didn't mean to." Her usual ramrod spine sagged.

With one arm supporting her waist and the other holding Miss Myrtle's arm, Ellen guided her to the wingback chair she always claimed at the prayer shawl meetings.

Tugging her hem over her knees, she avoided Ellen's eyes. As she placed her pocketbook beside her sandals, she grabbed a skein of sock yarn out of the basket next to the chair's claw foot and twirled it in her lap.

Fastening her gaze on something outside the front window, she drew a long breath and shared her story. "His name was Lloyd, a graduate of the Naval Academy. I've never seen another man who could hold a candle to his good looks." She turned toward Ellen with twinkling blue eyes. "And I'm including any of your movie stars, too—Clark Gable, Rock Hudson, Robert Redford, Johnny Depp."

Ellen blinked and shook her head. Miss Myrtle found Johnny Depp handsome? Who would have ever thought it?

"His eyes were as blue as the hydrangeas by my grandmother's front door. His blond hair seemed to hold the sun in it. He stood about six feet tall and just towered over me. I was all of 5'3" back then. He had the broadest shoulders. Oh, and he was so strong." She chuckled, covering her heart with her hand.

"Goodness, I sound like a silly teenybopper and so shallow talking about what he looked like. But, Ellen, he was as beautiful on the inside as he was on the outside."

Her eyes shined at the memory of her true love. Her quick breaths and flushed cheeks betrayed the proper lady who sat before Ellen. Beneath the creases in her skin and the gray curls, Ellen could imagine the young girl Miss Myrtle had been when she fell in love with a beautiful soldier.

"He was such a kind man and so interesting to talk to. I can hear him right now, 'What do you think about what's happening in Europe, M?' He called me M, and he really listened to what I had to say, too." She paused, studying the floor.

"I had arrived in Long Beach, California, at the end of May in 1944 because I finished my commitment teaching at the high school. Clara Jenkins and I went together. We were determined to help with the war effort and ready for an adventure, too. We got jobs at the Douglas Aircraft Company."

Ellen gaped at the image of the diminutive Miss Myrtle clothed in cover-alls and wrestling with a screw in the fuselage of an airplane.

Miss Myrtle laughed at Ellen's expression. "No, dear. Do not think that I was Rosie the Riveter. I did not build airplanes. I worked in the payroll department. Although I majored in English, I still had a head for math."

"We met the first Friday night I was in town. He and some of his buddies lounged in a Chevrolet in front of an ice cream shop, and as Clara and I strolled toward the door, they shouted hellos to us. It was all very respectable, mind you. No cat calls or anything like that." The window captured her attention again—or maybe the images from her past ambled in front of the glass. "It makes me think of my favorite word, serendipity."

She closed her eyes and lifted her chin. "Anyway, we met that night and just clicked. They were waiting for their orders to ship out. We were together as much as we could be." She pinned her bright blue eyes on Ellen and smiled. "He took me dancing. Oh, how he loved *The Chattanooga Choo Choo*. On the days we couldn't see each other, he wrote me letters. No cell phones or emails back then, you know." She compressed the end of the skein and released, watching the fibers spring back to their original form.

"At the beginning of August, he received his orders. He had to ship out on the tenth. We knew our time was running out." She dropped the skein back into the basket.

She licked her lips. "We spent his last days of leave together, and one afternoon we shared a box of Cracker Jacks. Back then, the little prizes were something to look forward to, not the paper stuff you get now. He let me tear open the packet, and I poured a ring out onto his palm." She pulled a chain from out of the neck of her blouse and dangled a little ring in front of Ellen. "Can you believe a ninety year old woman wears a Cracker Jack ring around her neck?" A rueful smile lit her face.

Leaning forward, Ellen covered the tiny lady's hand with hers.

"He said, 'This is fate, M. I love you. Let's get married.' People got married in those days at the drop of a hat before the boys shipped out. I said the first thing that popped into my mind, 'I love you, Lloyd, but I always thought I'd get married in my little church in Bandon with all my family and friends standing with me.'

"He didn't bat an eye. He didn't try to change my mind. He just said, 'Okay. You wear this ring, and when I get back, I'll put a real one on your finger, and we'll get married in Bandon. Is that a good plan, M?'"

She let the necklace fall against her bodice and rubbed her forehead. "You don't know how many times in my long life I've wished I'd just said, 'Yes, yes, yes.' I would have been married, a widow, yes, but I might have had—"

"He shipped out three days later, and I went to see him off." She opened her pocketbook and took out a black and white photograph framed in polished silver, handing it to Ellen.

Ellen studied the photo, realizing it showed a twenty-something Miss Myrtle in the arms of her true love, a handsome soldier. Their arms clutched each other, but her upper body faced away from him. Both of them were looking over her shoulder, wearing such sad expressions that tears stung Ellen's eyes.

"Clara took that picture right as the ship's horn sounded the last warning. The first time we saw that picture after she developed it Clara apologized for it and wanted to throw it away. Can you imagine? She said she didn't mean to get a picture of us looking so sad, but I kept it because it was just plain truth."

Ellen handed the picture back to Miss Myrtle. "That suit I'm wearing there was the first big thing I bought with my airplane money. I sent most of what I earned back home, but I paid for that suit on a layaway plan. It was navy blue with a fuchsia blouse."

She traced the image of the suit with a nail painted in pink polish. "I'd never seen any fabric that shade before and thought it the prettiest color in the world. Still do. I wore that suit to see him off and never put it on again. I tried, but I just couldn't." She shook her head.

"Lloyd left that day and was killed two weeks later. One of his buddies who was still waiting on orders came and told me. I had planned on staying in California, but I packed up and came home. Mr. Young, the principal, needed a librarian in the high school library, so I kept charge of all the books until I could get back into an English classroom." She sat lost in thought for several minutes, turning the ring with her shaking fingers.

"And you know what?" Miss Myrtle straightened her chair. "I don't want you to feel sorry for me one bit. I've had a good, long life, Ellen. I loved a special man, and he loved me. Other men courted me. I could have been married if I wanted to, but I just didn't feel that important spark with any other man." She pointed her index finger at Ellen. "That spark is important. Don't forget it."

She patted Ellen's hand. "Well, I didn't come to tell you that whole sad story just to hear it all again. I had a good reason to share it. The other night when you were talking about your special friend, I thought I detected a—oh, I don't know—some kind of sadness or angst or something. I'm here to tell you, missy, if you feel that spark I was talking about—and I think you do, you need to do something. Steve was a good man, and you loved him. But he's gone now, dear." Her words were quiet but firm.

"Forgive me for being so blunt. But it's the truth, honey. Don't end up a ninety-year-old woman with regrets. I have just the one—that I didn't say, 'yes,' when I had the chance. I don't want you to have any. Don't worry what people will say or what people will think. Don't wonder if it's the right time. Don't look back and say, 'I wish I'd done something. I wish I'd said something.' Get up and just do it. Isn't that what the shoe commercial says?" Chuckling, Miss Myrtle rose from her chair and smoothed her skirt.

Ellen opened her mouth to speak, but the older woman shushed her.

"No, don't say a word. I came to give my two cents, and I did. Just think about what I said." She reached for her pocketbook and opened her arms toward Ellen.

Ellen leaned forward, hugged the special woman and whispered, "Thank you, Miss Myrtle."

"You're special to me, pretty girl. It sounds like you might be special to someone else, too. Don't give up, sweetie pie." She waved bye at Euri peeking over the computer screen and left the shop.

ℰ)ℰ)ℰ)ℭℛℭℛ

For several days since Miss Myrtle had shared her love story and admonished Ellen to follow her heart, those words ruminated in her mind. She heard the truth in the wise woman's advice, but she wondered if she'd ever need that counsel. Every passing day took her farther away from Galway and Payne.

But every day also brought her closer to the stronger version of herself that the trip to Ireland had birthed. Those tiny steps toward strength and courage continued here at home. She could think of Steve without the breath shooting out of her lungs, without her stomach reeling like someone had punched her. Tears didn't pool in her eyes at the mention of his name anymore.

Whether the change came from time or Payne or all the prayers sent heavenward on her account, her heart—though cracked and missing a piece—had mended. It waited for the new chapter in her life to begin.

But she needed to have a conversation first.

Chapter 25

The next Sunday afternoon while Euri spent time with Robin Taylor, her appointed friend and helper, Ellen drove to Bandon's cemetery.

Miss Myrtle's truth had echoed in her mind for days. She'd worried about what people might say or think if they knew someone had caught her eye—maybe more than her eye. She'd worried that comments would fly about her forgetting Steve. Ellen worried that people might think her foolish for beginning a relationship during a two-week vacation halfway around the world.

She needed to let go of other people's opinions.

She needed to talk with Steve.

She coasted the van to a stop and allowed herself a minute to buoy her emotions. After a quick prayer for strength, she strode to his grave and sat by the headstone. She rested on the soft grass in silence for a long time letting memories of her husband wash over her. Pictures of him fooling around in college, dressed up for his first job interview, diapering their children while he crinkled his nose filled her mind, and teardrops spilled down her cheeks.

Several minutes ticked by with nothing but the occasional passing car to mar the comfortable silence. She propped her chin on bent knees and plucked leggy blades of grass at the corner of the marker. Her words broke the quiet with soft, hushed tones. "Steve, sweetheart, I loved you so much…I still do." She swiped a damp tissue under her eyes. "I do love you Steve, and always will, but I guess it's different now."

She wadded up the limp Kleenex and crammed it into her pocket. "I never wanted to hurt you, and in my heart I know I can't because you're in Heaven, praising God and enjoying His presence every single day."

"But, Steve, I'm still here, and—well, I met someone who makes me laugh again, who makes me look forward to another day." Her eyes pleaded with the headstone to understand and chewed her bottom lip.

"Here's the thing, though. I haven't heard from him in over a month, so I'm thinking whatever was happening between us in Ireland might have been…might have been just for that time, you know? I kinda wish I could ask you for advice." She shook her head at the irony of that wish.

"Anyway, Steve, God is moving me to a new place in my life. I wasn't looking for it. I didn't want it." She exhaled a slow, unsteady stream. "It's taken me awhile, but…I think I'm ready to explore that new place. I just wanted you to know." She patted her wet cheeks with a fresh tissue and blew her nose.

She stood, whispered, "I love you, Steve," and blew a kiss toward his name carved into the headstone. Turning back to the van, she remembered Euri. For the first time since meeting her, Ellen thanked God for bringing Euri into her life. She didn't have an empty house to go home to. She had a smiling, sweet teenager ready for her own adventure in America.

ഔഔൠൠ

Waiting in the family room, Euri turned off the TV when Ellen returned from the cemetery. "Hi, Ms. Ellen. Robin say party at 5:30. Okay?"

"Sure, Euri. Just let me grab a quick shower, and we'll leave in a little bit."

She hurried past the family room to shield her splotchy face from the teen. She massaged the back of her neck as she ascended the stairs. The last thing she wanted to do right now was attend a welcome mixer for the exchange students. After the emotionally draining afternoon, she longed for a hot bath and an early bedtime.

The hot water pounding on her shoulder muscles succeeded in easing a few of the knots tying up her neck and upper back. She stood under the satisfying pressure for several minutes, forcing herself to focus on the liquid heat and nothing else.

After the reviving shower, she snuggled herself into a white fluffy terrycloth robe and padded into her bedroom to dress. A stray image of Payne popped into her mind, and she wondered what he was doing. She wondered if he had returned to the States yet. She wondered if she'd ever see him again.

She shook her head and threw back her shoulders. The time for day dreaming was over. Her turquoise sundress swung just above her knees as she craned to zip it up.

A hot pink bangle bracelet and plum-colored lipstick added a sparkle to her look. Her outside was ready for a party. Her insides? Not so much.

಼ಿ಼ಿ಼ಿ

Holding a plate with a piece of cheese pizza and a fried chicken thigh, Euri stayed close to Ellen until Robin arrived and whisked her away to a group of South Koreans and locals. Diane Yates hopped in close taking Euri's place, linking her arm through Ellen's.

"You look gorgeous tonight, honey. You know, I wouldn't have put you in turquoise, but that particular shade is beautiful on you. Is it new?" Diane spread the folds of the skirt to get a better look.

From anyone else, that statement might have been a backhanded compliment, but it was pure Diane, saying exactly what she thought with no filter.

"This is the first time I've worn it here." A picture of the lunch with Payne and his friends at the Galleon fluttered across her vision before she could stop it.

"Oooh. Doesn't that sound mysterious? I'm thinking you must have worn it with your Irish man. Am I right?" Diane grinned and hugged her friend's arm. "Hey, look. Here comes Dr.

Meadows. He said he hoped to meet you. I'll introduce you two."

Ellen glanced toward the buffet table to see a man with attention-grabbing jet black hair, on the short side even in his cowboy boots, gliding in their direction. Dr. Meadows carried a plate piled high with pizza slices and a few bits of salad. His fingers were free of rings, but a heavy gold chain encircled his right wrist.

"Diane, I see you've got somebody I've been wanting to meet. Introduce us, please." He reached a hand toward Ellen.

She tightened her grip on Diane's arm before letting go, sending a warning glance to her. She willed Diane not to leave her alone.

"I've heard wonderful compliments about that coffee shop thing ya'll are doing over there in Bandon. Tell me all about it." He stabbed a spinach leaf and tomato triangle with his plastic fork.

Despite the flashing signals from Ellen's eyes, Diane excused herself to check on her students.

Ellen wrapped her arms around her waist and resigned herself to spending time with Dr. Meadows. "Thank you. Yes, our soft opening went well, I think. The grand opening won't happen for another two weeks. But everything looks good so far."

For the next thirty minutes, he ate, talked about the state of the schools, the state of the county, the state of tourism at the beaches. Ellen nodded and contributed monosyllables and a few appropriate phrases every now and then. When she noticed Euri standing by a weeping willow with a few other teens, she extricated herself from Dr. Meadows' monologues with a quick 'goodbye' and what she hoped looked like an apologetic smile and escaped to the willow tree.

When she approached the group, Euri's animated voice surprised her as the teen related a funny story. "Yes, and today, phone ring. I jumped. It scared me so bad."

The group surrounding her laughed at Euri's face, eyes wide, mouth open in fright.

Ellen's heart hammered at the words. The phone rang? When? She hadn't heard it. When was the last time she checked her messages? Friday? Thursday?

Ellen grabbed Euri's forearm, trying not to squeeze too tightly. "Euri. Did you say the phone rang? When?"

"Today before you got home. I didn't answer. Your answer box did."

"Do you know who called?" Stupid question. Of course she wouldn't know. "Was it a man or a woman?"

"I don't know. I didn't listen. Not my business." Euri's eyes widened again, and Ellen saw a glimmer of fear and confusion.

"Hey, Sweetie. It's okay. We'll check when we get home. No problem. I was surprised that someone called. That's all. Don't worry about it." Ellen rubbed her back, and the young girl's face relaxed with relief.

She moved away from the young group, her mind flipping through the possibilities for the mysterious caller. The shop was closed on Sunday, so the call probably didn't concern the business. She'd talked with her children on Saturday, so, unless they'd had an emergency…

An emergency? Don't hop down that bunny trail. Check the phone.

Great idea, but she'd left her cell phone in her pocketbook in the car. Turned off. Breathing in the soft scent of a Cape Jasmine bush, she scanned the crowd, then discreetly exited the garden party through the wrought iron gate, heading for her car.

Pressing the button to turn on the phone proved to be tricky because of her trembling fingers, but she managed it. Deep down, she didn't believe she had an emergency on her hands. She knew the trembling came from the possibility that Payne had called.

She took two long breaths to compose herself as the screen came to life. Yes. She had a message.

The phone accepted her password to retrieve voice mail, and Payne's voice filled the car. "Hey, Ellen. It's Payne. I'm back finally. Safe and sound. Ahhm." He cleared his throat. "I'll try your home phone. Bye."

Ellen's heart, pounding a crazy beat, fueled the grin that split her face. She didn't try to contain it. She didn't want to. She giggled and hugged herself. Payne was back. He was safe, and he'd called her. Why, oh why didn't she keep her phone turned on? How many times had the children chastised her for keeping the silent phone tucked in her pocketbook or lying in the ashtray?

Before she lost her nerve, she punched in his numbers to call him back. After three rings, an automated voice told her, "The voice mail box for Payne Anderson is full. Please try your call again later."

Frustration and disappointment worked to steal her happiness, but she refused to give in to those negative emotions.

Payne was back. Good. He called. Very good. Another message waited on the home phone. Very, very good.

She hit the repeat button to listen to his voice again.

When she returned to the backyard, she noticed that some people had already left, and others were saying their goodbyes. Excellent. If she could find Euri, they could leave as well.

Locating Euri and thanking the hosts turned out to be easier than maintaining the posted speed limit for the twenty-minute drive home. Chatting about the party required monumental concentration because all she wanted to do was think about the phone call and Payne.

Taffy greeted her as she climbed out of the van. Stopping to pet him though her fingers itched to tap the answering machine, she barely noticed the absence of her two cats. Probably already on the evening prowl.

Thankfully, Euri said a quick "good night," skipping up the stairs to Olivia's room, and Ellen sprinted to check the machine.

Sure enough, the little green light blinked in the darkness of the office. She scrunched her eyebrows. Why didn't she see this earlier?

The screen revealed five new messages, but she wanted to hear only one of them. The one with Payne's voice.

"Hey, Ellen. Uhmmm. I thought you'd be home from church by now. Maybe you're away for the weekend since you didn't pick up yesterday." She heard him take a few short breaths. "Ahh. I have… Ah. Well, … Sorry I missed you…" A click signaled the end of the message, and she hit the key to save it.

Yesterday? He called on Saturday, too?

She skipped through the other messages until she found the one from Saturday.

"Hello, Ellen. This is Payne. Ahmm. I'm back." He drew another breath and hesitated. "Ahmm. I'll try again. Bye."

Chapter 26

Monday morning, Ellen perched on a kitchen stool, her thumping heart making her breathing quick and shallow. Payne had left three messages. Short and not informative, but three messages nonetheless. She could wait for him to call again, or she could step out of her safe, boring always-do-what-I-think-I should-do box and try to contact him.

His inbox on his cell was full last night, so stepping out of her box would be Plan B—calling his office at Maryland State. She examined his business card, not as crisp now as when he'd given it to her almost two months ago. Regular handling has a tendency to soften cardstock, the only thing she had to remind her of him. Why hadn't she taken his picture during those precious few days in Galway?

She ran her finger along his office number. Reaching him should be simple.

Ellen grabbed the phone, pressing the numbers before she changed her mind. When the automated voice asked for the extension number, she plugged in those numbers, too. After several rings, the call rolled over to the department secretary.

"Maryland State Environmental Science Department, may I help you?"

Ellen gripped the receiver. "Yes, I hope so. I was calling for Dr. Payne Anderson, but he must be out of the office because no one picked up."

"Okay. Let's see. Would you like to leave... oh, wait. It says here that Dr. Anderson is on a leave of absence."

Ellen frowned. "A leave of absence? But I thought he'd already returned from Africa." In fact, he'd said that twice in her messages.

"I'm sorry. I really don't know. I'm just a temp. This is only my third day." The secretary whispered the last sentence.

Ellen realized she'd received as much information as the secretary could give her. "I understand. Thank you anyway." Ellen hung up the phone with ambivalent feelings. Something about the phrase, "leave of absence," bothered her. What did that mean? Still researching? Spending time with family? Recovering from an illness picked up in Africa?

At least she'd tried to contact him, and she'd discovered he wasn't at MSU this semester. She could call again in a few days when the regular secretary returned. She could try his cell again, too. Satisfying only a tiny bit of her curiosity, she'd succeeded in creating a whole new list of questions.

ೞೞೞೞ

The rest of the day and the next passed with no word from Payne, but she had little time to fret about her disappointment. Emergency calls from the coffee shop and responsibilities with her own store kept her mind from drifting to Payne more than two or three times.

Wednesday morning, she lowered a roast into her crock pot and smothered it with carrots and onions. While a batch of chocolate chip cookies baked in the oven, she sliced lemons for a pitcher of homemade lemonade. All of Scott's favorites. Scheduled for an allergy appointment he couldn't switch, she expected him home sometime in mid-afternoon.

She hoped he'd make it home in time for her meeting with Dr. Hunter from North Carolina State University. Thinking about the meeting made her heart skip a beat. Apprehension ruled her body.

Dear God, please help this meeting go well. Help me to remember all the things I've researched and studied. Give Dr. Hunter listening ears and a soft heart to what I'm proposing.

The trilling of her phone interrupted her prayer. Saying a

quick, "amen," she grabbed the receiver. A booming, familiar voice shaking with excitement greeted her. "Hi, Ellen. This is Blake. Are you busy? I want to drop by for just a minute, if you have time."

"Sure. Come on. I'm just waiting for someone from State. He's supposed to be here in a little bit. Come on over." She wiped the lemon juice splatters from the counter.

"I'll be there in a flash. I'm sitting at the stop sign just about to turn onto Woodhill Road."

"Hang up before you start driving again." Once a mother, always a mother. "See you when you get here."

Ellen had known Blake Thompson since her days as his family's babysitter. Her favorite of all the children she watched, he had a wicked sense of humor, beautiful blue eyes, and a big heart for the Lord. He'd grown up to be a high school and college baseball star, leaving a trail of wounded hearts since he was twelve years old.

But once Callie Richards moved to town, he had eyes only for her. They had begun dating right before his senior prom when she was in tenth grade and married a year after Callie graduated from college. During the next five years, they'd suffered two miscarriages but had obediently surrendered their will to God's regarding the size of their family.

Ellen had faithfully prayed with them and for them during their heartbreaks and had come to love Callie almost as much as she did Blake. She watched his black jeep speeding up her long driveway toward where she stood on the concrete pad near the basketball hoop. The scent of pine straw baking in the September sun wafted by on a slight breeze. Taffy wagged his tail, barking to announce the visitor.

Barely stopping his jeep before he was out, he ran toward her. "Ellen, we're pregnant! We're pregnant. And this time, it's going to be okay. She's four months, and we've just seen the doctor. He said she's fine and the baby's fine. We're gonna have a sonogram next month." His words tumbled out on top of each other as he picked her up and swung her around like ribbons on a May pole.

Laughing, she swatted his back. "Blake, that's wonderful news, but put me down. You'll hurt yourself."

He obeyed her wishes but grabbed her shoulders and hugged her again. "I'm so happy, Ellen."

"I'm happy for you, Sweetie. How's Callie? When's she due?" Out of the corner of her eye, she caught sight of another vehicle moving up her driveway and realized it must be Dr. Hunter from NC State.

"She's great. We're both over the moon. The doc says March first. Isn't that a great date? I just told my parents, and we're going out to celebrate tomorrow night. You're coming with us, too. Okay?"

She straightened her skirt and smoothed her blouse. "No, Blake. That's for family. We'll celebrate another time."

The red Ford F-150 parked beside Blake's jeep, and two men climbed out of the cab.

"Yes, Ellen." He mimicked her. "Tomorrow night. 6:30. Be ready." Seizing her in another massive hug, he kissed her on her cheek and jogged back to his jeep nodding to the men who waited in front of their truck. "See you when I pick you up," he called before slamming the door.

Her huge smile reflected her joy for Blake and Callie. She waved at him as he backed the jeep away from the concrete pad and wheeled it around toward the road. Steeling herself for the next part of her afternoon, she turned her smile toward the two men who'd come to evaluate her proposal.

The future of her farm could rest in their decision.

ജയയരൗ

The driver, maybe sixty-two or three years old, wore faded khaki's and a red golf shirt. His straw hat sat back on his head, and a thick, salt and pepper mustache shaded his mouth.

His younger companion wore olive pants and a white short-sleeved shirt that contrasted with his deep tan. His ball cap, pulled low over his face, concealed most of his aviator sunglasses. Standing with arms folded across his chest, his chin jutting forward, he struck her as unfriendly, maybe slightly arrogant. She abandoned her musings about his challenging stance and what about him seemed familiar when the older man greeted her with introductions.

"Hello, Mrs. Shepherd." He held out his hand to her. "I'm Hank Hunter from NC State. It's nice to meet you in person finally." Releasing his clasp, he turned to the other man. "And this is Dr. Payne Anderson. He's an old student of mine who, I'm hoping, is going to join us in the environmental sciences department, if we can lure him away from Maryland, that is."

At Dr. Hunter's words, "Payne Anderson," white noise swooshed in her ears blocking out all her surroundings except for Payne's face. She lifted her foot to follow her first instinct—sprinting into his arms—but flattened it back in place. Something rooted her to her driveway. Something was wrong. Instead of reaching toward her, he kept his arms folded. Instead of smiling at her and asking if she'd been praying for him, his mouth and clinched jaw remained unyielding, as hard as the concrete beneath her sandals.

Except for the mad pummeling of her heart, her body shut down. Her lungs forgot how to take in air. Her brain stopped processing all thoughts except for how Payne could be here in her yard—and why hostility emanated from him.

What happened to the warm, funny man who had hugged her like he didn't want to let go his last night in Galway? Who was this hard, imposing man standing in front of her, his mouth drawn into a stubborn, straight line? The effects of the jolt ricocheted through her body with quaking tremors.

She remembered this response to shock. She'd experienced it once before—at a surprise birthday party Steve had successfully thrown for her. Her emotions had turned one hundred and eighty degrees in the space of thirty seconds.

At first she'd been furious with Steve because of the silly ruse he'd engineered to deliver her to the party. Anger switched to complete astonishment at facing over fifty friends and relatives yelling, "Happy Birthday!" and "Surprise!" at her. The lightning change wreaked havoc in her emotions. Her hands trembled for the better part of an hour while she greeted the guests.

Now her developing joy at the prospect of a new stage in her life had been ripped away by the world-altering vision of Payne standing in her yard—and by the dawning realization that something had happened to change the Payne she knew and still missed.

She wrapped her arms around her waist. Her fingers digging into her sides couldn't still her quaking body. "Payne."

"Hello, Ellen." He shoved his hands into his pockets, an enigmatic expression plastered on his handsome face.

"You two know each other already?" Dr. Hunter raised his eyebrows, his eyes searching back and forth between them.

"We met last summer in Galway." Payne's words sounded more like an accusation than an explanation.

Dr. Hunter folded his arms in front of his substantial chest and nodded. "Galway. I love that city. My wife and I spent our second honeymoon there about ten years ago. Beautiful place. If I had a ticket, I'd fly there right now." He shook his head. "Talk about a small world, huh?" When neither Payne nor Ellen spoke, he bent down to pet Taffy who wagged his tail beside him. "Well, Mrs. Shepherd, we wanted to talk about making your family's property into a research farm."

"Yes." The lone word from her desert-like mouth surprised her. How could she produce an acceptable response to Dr. Hunter while her brain vibrated like a bowl of Jello? How would she be able to discuss her plans with one ounce of coherence if Payne watched and listened?

Dear God, please help me. What is Payne doing here? This doesn't even make sense. He's taking his sabbatical in Raleigh? Why does he look so unapproachable? Why didn't he tell me he was coming? What do I do? What do I say? I need Your help, Father. I need it right now, please...

She cleared her throat and licked her lips. "Please come inside, and we can talk. I made lemonade." She hoped her voice didn't reveal the chaos inside her body.

Dr. Hunter straightened and adjusted his belt. "Sounds like a plan." He extended his arm, gesturing for her to lead them inside.

Ellen wondered if the older man was as oblivious as he seemed to the tension radiating between Payne and herself. She imagined Payne's dark, gray eyes boring into her back as she led the men toward the front of the house. The thought of sitting down and discussing her farm in front of Payne's confusing animosity toward her churned Ellen's insides.

They ascended the brick steps leading to the wide front porch laden with multicolored flowers growing in an array of stone, terracotta, and mosaic tiled pots. Dr. Hunter gestured to the menagerie of plants. "My wife loves flowers, too. You have a pretty place here, Mrs. Shepherd."

"Thank you." She led them into the kitchen and to the round wooden table covered with a floral print tablecloth she'd sewn before Steve became ill.

"Please sit down, I'll get the lemonade."

"Man. It smells wonderful in here." Dr. Hunter placed his hat in the empty chair beside him and combed through his thin hair with his fingers.

The fragrant scent of meat and onions combined with the shock and stress turned her stomach.

God, please help me not to throw up in front of these men, especially Payne.

She swallowed. "Thank you. I have a roast in the crock pot for my son, Scott. It's his favorite meal. He's coming home this afternoon for an allergy appointment."

Dr. Hunter chatted on about the house, the property, and its proximity to Raleigh.

Payne remained silent except for a few monosyllables addressed to Dr. Hunter. She tried to ignore the unbelievable fact that Payne sat in her kitchen as she prepared the glasses, but her fingers felt like weak twigs shaken by a summer storm. Only focused determination led her hands from the ice bin in the freezer to fill the glasses on the counter. She loaded a serving tray with the pitcher, glasses, and a plate of the chocolate chip cookies she'd made for Scott.

Bringing the crowded tray over to the table, she glanced at Payne, noticing he'd removed his cap and pushed sunglasses on top of his head. His eyes looked as cold as his mouth looked fore-boding. Her fingers tightened around the smooth handles of the tray, but she managed to set it down carefully without losing a drop of lemonade or a single chocolate crumb.

Dr. Hunter took his first sip and smiled. "Mmmm. Mrs. Shepherd, God bless you. This lemonade is the real deal. It's wonderful. My wife makes it with real lemons, too. It's delicious. Thank you."

"You're welcome. I'm glad you like it." After pouring her glass last, she sank into the chair across from Payne. A picture of another time they shared a table flashed in her mind, but she forced her attention to Dr. Hunter. Before they could begin talking about the farm, Ellen's cell phone, lying in the middle of the table where she'd left it earlier that morning, rang. Reaching for the phone, she turned it to silent.

She apologized, but the house phone began ringing. "I'll let the machine take a message." No sooner had the machine clicked on then off with no message, her cell phone vibrated with a text message for her.

"Someone is trying very hard to contact you, Mrs. Shepherd. Go ahead and read the message." Dr. Hunter encouraged her with a smile. "We don't mind."

Payne inspected the condensation droplets on the side of his glass.

The text was a message from Bonnie at the coffee shop pleading for help. "I'm sorry, but I need to make one quick phone call. Excuse me, please." Ellen stepped out into the hall so at least she could pretend she had some privacy.

ᔕᘎᔕᘎᏋᏋ

Payne watched Ellen disappear into the hall, but a mirror hanging on the opposite wall reflected her image and allowed him to observe her actions unnoticed. He realized she thought she was hidden. For the first time since he and Hank had arrived, she looked as if she were letting her guard down. Leaning her head against the wall, she gripped the phone in one hand and rubbed her temples with the other.

Hank chuckled, shaking his head. "Wow. I can't believe you two know each other. What are the chances? Small world indeed." He reached for another cookie and bit it.

Payne ignored his friend and closed his eyes. What had he been thinking to consider a job in Raleigh? At least he hadn't signed any papers yet. Not that he could. His contract with Maryland didn't end for eight months.

Still in the courting phase, he knew Hank expected him to take the job at NC State. It was a better position—more money, more in line with what he wanted to research, closer to Ellen. Until today when he'd seen that twerp pick her up, swing her around, and leave a big fat kiss on her cheek, being closer to Ellen had been the number one calling card for the job.

He drained his lemonade. The ice cold glass felt good in his hand.

Who was that guy anyway? Obviously, someone she liked a lot if he gauged her feelings by her 100-watt smile that followed him down the driveway. Had they known each other before Galway? Had they been dating even then? Was that guy the reason her emails seemed so stilted?

Yeah…those four measly emails. Each one shorter than the one before. He trailed the top of the glass with his middle finger and grimaced remembering when he'd discovered the messages. The excitement that rose in his chest when he'd opened his email account and recognized the emails from her knocked him for a loop. He'd enjoyed the rusty feeling as he waited on the tarmac for the return flight from Africa to take off.

The exhilaration soon subsided once he'd read what she'd written. Chatty and newsy, the emails looked fine on the surface, but he realized he'd been hoping for some heart sentiments. The closest he got was that she missed Galway. Was that code for "I miss you, Payne," or was it simply, "I miss Galway."

He rubbed his cold hand on the back of his neck, wishing he could loosen the tight cords that tied his shoulders into knots, too. He shook his head at the memory of his computer crashing. Right on the pull-down table of the airplane. Thank God for backup files or his entire project might have been sunk.

Hank dusted the crumbs from his hands, pulled out his phone, and punched a few keys.

Massaging the space between his eyebrows, Payne chastised himself again for not responding to her emails as soon as he'd landed, but he'd succumbed to exhaustion from the trans-Atlantic flight and spent most of his first two days back transferring his notes from his flash drive backup file.

Why did he think visiting Raleigh would be a good idea?

Hank's offer had sounded irresistible. He'd come to Raleigh to reconnect with his old friend, check out the campus, and get in touch with Ellen, of course.

He'd planned to call her first. Hearing her voice in his ear. Much better idea than writing three or four lines on a computer. Right?

He cringed remembering the fantasy that had replayed in his mind over the past week. He'd call her, she'd invite him to come to her house, and they'd continue where they left off in Galway. But after leaving several unanswered messages, Payne questioned the wisdom behind his plan.

He glanced toward the sound of her low-pitched voice and studied her reflection again. Even under stress, she was still a beautiful woman.

Who was that guy? Was he the reason she was too busy to answer her phone or return calls?

How he wished he'd said, "No, thanks," to Hank's invitation to ride with him to his afternoon appointment. At the time, it'd made sense to continue their lunchtime conversation in Hank's pickup, but now.

What a disaster.

He watched her end the call and cover her eyes with her hands. Her mouth moved silently, and he reasoned she prayed for whoever had called.

Payne wished she still prayed for him.

Chapter 27

Opening her eyes, Ellen found herself locked in Payne's piercing gaze via her grandmother's mirror. Had he observed her during the entire phone call? Any calmness she'd managed to scrape together shattered like a fallen Christmas ornament. She forced her feet back to the table, her spine straight, her mouth set in a determined line. Payne lowered his eyes, fascinated with his glass of ice.

She entered the kitchen again and grabbed a folder from the computer desk. "Sorry about that. We have a missing worker at the coffee shop downtown and a frantic manager who's about to be flooded with a horde of demanding teenagers." She ran her fingers through her hair.

Dr. Hunter raised his bushy eyebrows. "You own a coffee shop?"

"No. Our high school is renting a shop. It's a joint venture. The senior business class and the senior consumer science class are working together supplying the business plan, the workers, baking the goodies. The object is for the students to run the show. We've been open for only a few weeks, so we're still working out the problems." She offered a weak smile.

Dr. Hunter nodded his head toward her. "Are you one of the teachers?"

She shook her head. "I just helped out with the beginning phase, but the students like to call me for moral support."

"It was her idea." Surprise flitted across Payne's face before he shut it down again.

Had those words startled him as much as they had her?

She hadn't told him about the coffee shop idea in their Galway conversations, but she'd mentioned it in one of her emails. So—he had read them. Then why hadn't he responded? Evidently, based on his behavior today, he just wasn't interested enough to bother.

Sitting with his arms crossed and his jaw set in a stubborn clinch, he appeared closed off, unapproachable. Then why had he spoken up on her behalf?

"And it sounds like a great idea. Very interesting." Dr. Hunter clasped his hands on the table and leaned forward. "Now. Let's talk about your ideas for your farm. And Mrs. Shepherd, as I mentioned the first time we spoke, this meeting today is pretty unusual. State already has research farms, but you proposed some interesting ideas in your letter. I thought a lot of your husband when we served together on that agricultural committee a few years ago. He was a good man, and I'm sorry for your loss."

Ellen bit the inside of her cheek to fight the tears gathering in her eyes. Steve. Again. *God, thank you for Steve. Seems he's the only reason Dr. Hunter's here. Fine. Thank you for the opportunity.*

"Thank you, Dr. Hunter."

"Payne and I had a chance to discuss your idea, or what I know of it, on the way down here today."

A knot seized her chest. Payne? Talking about her idea? What did that mean?

"He had some good questions like, of course, budget requirements and man power, but we can get into that later. Talk to us." He clasped his hands together and smiled.

How could she talk now knowing that Payne's input had been more negative than positive? Tears stung behind her eyes.

Lord, Payne has nothing to do with my farm. Help me ignore him. Give me the right words, please.

She hoped her voice didn't betray the trembling inside her. She breathed in a steadying breath and launched into her proposal for the farm. "Steve's elderly cousin who has been farming our land for us suffered a stroke last April. Although he's recovered, his health has deteriorated and won't allow him to continue his work as he has in the past.

"My children love this farm, but they're pursuing their education right now and can't run the farm either. I don't have the expertise, but I don't want to sell the land for more subdivisions to sprout up. This land has been in my husband's family for generations, and my goal is to keep it that way."

Her fingers, splayed out in front of her, found a wrinkle in the tablecloth near the edge of the folder and worked to press it flat.

"Steve was passionate about education. He taught high school for many years before becoming a principal, all the while farming his family's land.

"Tobacco used to be king in Grafton County, but the federal bailout several years ago brought lots of changes to the farmers here, as I'm sure you know. Some have tried to move ahead with those changes, but a lot of them have struggled."

Dr. Hunter nodded, and Ellen smiled, grateful for his encouragement.

"Many farmers across the state saw the need for changes long before the bail out. We have North Carolina wineries producing award-winning wine. We have farmers that farm fresh water shrimp in their ponds. We have truck farms for the growing demand for locally grown food."

Willing her mind to remember her research, she opened the folder, then threaded her fingers together on top of the pages, determined to keep her grip loose. "All those are good ideas, but I have a few different ones. I'm hoping that NC State will join with me in making my land a study farm for the agricultural and environmental science departments. Bees are an important spoke in the agricultural wheel—our food supply depends on them, but they've been hard hit in the last few years with parasites and diseases. We need to study them more so that we can protect them and help them prosper again. State already has a good bee study established. We can provide more land for more research." She glanced at the first page of notes.

"I'm interested in wind farming, too. Some research indicates that wind farms are already producing two percent of the world's electricity, and that number has doubled already in the past three years. I know that most of the wind farms are located down at the coast, but I'd like to pursue wind farming here. Our farm comprises enough acreage to support at least a small study."

She heard the air conditioner click on, but her flushed body didn't register the refreshing breeze from the vents. She smoothed her clammy palms on her skirt and noticed Dr. Hunter leaned back in the chair, folding his arms across his rounded waist. Was she losing him?

She cleared her throat. "I'm also excited about bamboo, a new crop for this area. I've done some research. It's a versatile, earth-friendly plant, and it can be used to make everything from furniture, to flooring, to fabric that feels like silk. In fact, I carry several bamboo fibers in my yarn shop already, and…and we've already planted an acre down near the stream at the edge of our property just to experiment with it."

During the opening pitch, she'd focused only Dr. Hunter. She'd managed to ignore Payne in her peripheral vision, but at the mention of yarns, her traitorous eyes sought Payne's like a magnet slaps against metal. Big mistake. His gaze locked with hers, jumbling her thoughts for an instant. He grabbed a cookie and broke it in half before shoving a piece into his mouth.

She licked her lips, glanced at her notes again, and regrouped. "Ahmm. A plus for the earth is that bamboo absorbs four times the carbon dioxide as a forest of hardwood trees and emits thirty-five percent more oxygen. Bamboo grows about four feet a day. It's the most renewable resource on the planet.

"A few colleges have bamboo studies in place already. Georgia State is one of those schools. I mention other colleges not because State should want to copy them but only because that proves my point that bamboo is a viable agricultural option."

Distracted when she realized she'd been twirling her silver bracelet, she moved her hands to her lap. "One more quick idea. Sunflowers are beautiful, but they're also a food source with the seeds and the oil the seeds produce. I would love to see the old equipment used to harvest tobacco somehow refigured to harvest sunflowers.

"Grafton County is one of the largest agricultural counties

in the state, and it's located close to your campus. Farmers need to look to the future. This farm could be a great educational place to teach new skills to today's farmer as well as tomorrow's." Forcing up the corners of her mouth, she tossed her hair behind her shoulders and leaned back in her chair.

Rubbing the side of his nose, Dr. Hunter nodded. "You've obviously put a lot of thought into your proposal, Mrs. Shepherd. I've read your written application also, and I like how you've expanded those original ideas. I do have a few questions for you, if you don't mind?"

For the next ten minutes or so, Dr. Hunter asked pointed questions about how she envisioned the relationship between the university and her farm. She answered each question with as many details and with as much confidence as her waning energy allowed. Payne's brooding silence sapped a big majority of her composure, but she ignored the pink elephant at her table as best she could.

Just as Dr. Hunter reached for another cookie, the back door flew open, and Scott burst through carrying his overnight case in one hand and a duffle bag of what Ellen knew from past experience contained dirty laundry. "Scott!" Ellen leapt to her feet, almost knocking over her chair, and rushed to her son. "I'm so glad you're here before the meeting ended." She squashed him to her, offering a thank you prayer for safety and for his rejuvenating presence.

"Oh, Mom. It smells so good in here. I'm starving." He fixed his gaze on the stove.

After an hour of tension and stress, confusion and disappointment, the relief surging through her body—a welcome gift—wobbled her legs and arms. Clutching his arm for support, Ellen led him to the table. "Come sit down. These men are from State. We're going over the farm proposal, and I have cookies for you."

"Scott, this is Dr. Hank Hunter from State, and this is…" She met Scott's eyes, swallowed, and kept her voice even. "This is Payne Anderson."

Scott's head whipped toward her as he grabbed Payne's outstretched hand. He whirled his gaze back to Payne. "The Payne Anderson I spoke to in Galway?"

Payne nodded. "The very same."

Scott's face mirrored the confusion she'd felt earlier. "You didn't tell me he was coming, Mom." The statement sounded more like a question than a declaration.

"I didn't know he was coming." Ellen willed the words out of her mouth, thankful for her normal tone—successfully masking her churning insides.

Dr. Hunter chimed in, "Hey, he didn't know he was coming here either. I played on his sympathies after lunch today. I wanted a companion on the ride. We were already sailing along your road before I mentioned your name to him." He shrugged in a sorry-I-broke-the-window gesture. "I guess I'm the one who's responsible for the surprise."

Leaving the table to grab a glass for Scott, Ellen chanced a peek at Payne and met his inscrutable stare. Okay, so he didn't ambush her. It sounded as if he were an innocent player in this comedy of errors, too, but wait a minute…

What was he doing in Raleigh? Wouldn't that warrant a little email like, "Oh, by the way, I'll be in Raleigh for a few days? Maybe we could get together for dessert and talk about old times in Galway?"

She poured the lemonade and laid her hand on her son's forearm hoping to draw strength from him. Scott, nonplussed by the events that tilted his mother's world, grabbed four cookies and shoved them whole, one and the other, into his mouth, barely stopping to chew as Dr. Hunter resumed his questions about the farm.

ഇ൫ඁ

On the return trip to Raleigh, Payne pretended to listen to Hank's upbeat chatter. A few affirmative words from Payne sprinkled in every now and then kept the conversation flowing and, Payne hoped, kept Hank from noticing his preoccupation.

Ellen had mentioned her plans for her farm the last after-

210

noon they spent together. He'd even offered a few ideas of his own about wind farming. Who knew Hank referred to Ellen's farm when he'd asked for input?

She probably felt he'd thrown her under the bus with the questions he'd asked Hank. He wished he could have helped her plead her case instead of sitting at her table like a knot on a log. Not that she needed any help. She'd been great, recovering from her obvious shock like a trooper.

Frustrated with the day's events, he pulled at his shoulder strap and let the images from the afternoon roll through his mind.

How many times had he been jealous in the past few hours? When he saw that bozo twirling her around and kissing her cheek, when she jumped up to hug Scott, when she laid her hand on Scott's arm.

He'd imagined their reunion many times over. In his fantasy, he was the one picking her up, twirling her around, kissing her—but not on the cheek. No. He'd kiss her square on the mouth, just like in Galway.

Their reunion would have been—surprise turning into joy, and then what? Riding off into the sunset? What did that mean? Marriage? Whoa. Where did that thought come from? He'd vowed to himself years ago that marriage was a closed door in his life. He wasn't the marrying type.

Yet, he had found himself yearning for Ellen every single day he was in Africa. Before meeting her, he'd found everything he thought he needed in his work, a constant and reliable companion. But lately, his work fell short in keeping the memories of Ellen at bay.

In the few days they'd been together in Galway, she'd gently thawed his frozen heart. She'd shared her deep faith with him from the beginning. She'd made him laugh with her quirky humor. She hadn't pressed him but had simply waited for him to open up about his failure with Cindy and the loss of his son. She hadn't judged him but instead had continued to listen to him.

And most of all, she'd prayed for him.

Being with Ellen had been a balm to his cold, dry spirit.

His faith journey back to God that had sprouted tender shoots in Galway had continued to thrive and develop in Africa. After a particularly trying day on the project, Payne longed for Ellen, longed for her touch and her words. In Galway, he'd cried out to God and experienced His peace when he let go of all the bitterness, anger, and guilt he'd hoarded for years.

Out there in the rough country with millions of stars dotting the overwhelming darkness, he'd finally surrendered everything to God. He turned over his longing for Ellen, his frustration at being half way around the world from her, and his inability to change his immediate circumstances. He decided to let God have control of his life, reasoning that He could do a better job than Payne had for the last fifteen years.

But after today's events, the doubts crept back and whispered to him.

"Earth to Payne." Merging onto I-40 from Highway 70, Hank spared a quick sideways glance at Payne.

Payne jerked his head away from his miserable thoughts. "I'm sorry. I didn't hear that last thing you said."

Hank hooted and threw a teasing grin toward Payne. "I don't think you've heard anything I've said on the whole drive back, but no worries. I've got a pretty good guess where your thoughts have been. I may be nearing retirement, but I still have a few good years left in me. Something was going on back there, for sure. The tension was as thick as the kudzu on that ditch bank over there." He nodded toward the green vines running along the shoulder of the road and climbing up an electrical pole. "She the one you tried to call on the ride down here?" Hank pushed the cruise control button.

Payne gritted his teeth. "Yeah." When Hank had disclosed the name of his destination only five minutes or so before arriving, Payne had tried to call Ellen with a heads up. Awkward conversation, to be sure, but he hadn't wanted to ambush her. As the unanswered rings added up, he'd tried to come up with the best way to drop the news that he was minutes away from her farm.

Since she didn't answer, his clever words hadn't been necessary. He'd hung up on the recorded message. She must have been outside talking with Lover Boy.

Hank's voice splintered his musings. "So what happened in Galway? Care to fill me in?"

"Not really." Payne lifted his ball cap and scratched his scalp, wanting to focus on anything but Galway—and Ellen.

Repositioning his hand to the bottom of the steering wheel, Hank shifted in his seat. "That's fine. I won't press."

"I've just got a lot on my mind. Whether or not to take this job. If I do, I've got to start the whole moving process, looking for a place to live here. You know how it goes." Payne saw surprise and concern wrinkle the older man's face before turning back toward the passenger side window, his arm heavy on the armrest.

Hank turned off the sports talk radio show. "You're not seriously thinking about passing on this opportunity, are you? You'll head up the whole division, teach only if and when you want to, supervise a couple of grad students a year, and spend most of your time doing research. Plus, I helped put together the package you've been offered. I know how nice it is." Hank cocked his head toward Payne. "Your reluctance doesn't have anything to do with our charming Mrs. Shepherd, does it?"

"Hank." Payne clinched his jaw.

"Maybe that's why you weren't interested in Melanie, the gorgeous grad student who flirted with you—"

"Hank." Glancing at his old friend, Payne growled his name like a warning.

"Okay, okay. I'll be quiet. It's just that I've known you for a long time, and Mrs. Shepherd's smart and beautiful and—"

"Hank! That's it!" He pounded his thigh with his fist.

"Done. I'm done." Still gripping the wheel with his thumbs, Hank spread his fingers in surrender. He quit talking, but he whistled all the way back to the office.

ഇഇഇൽൽ

"Wow, Mom. Payne's really quiet, huh? I think he said more in that quick phone call from Galway than he spoke the whole time he was here today." Scott shoveled the roast and mashed potatoes into his mouth.

Ellen pushed her food from one side of her plate to the other. This afternoon's shock controlled all of her emotions and vanquished her desire for food. "Yes, he was quiet." Ellen hid baby carrots under clumps of mashed potatoes with her fork.

"So has he moved to Raleigh or what? I thought he taught at Maryland State." Scott scooped two more mounds of potatoes onto his plate, made a shallow well with the back of his spoon, and poured in the brown gravy until it ran over the sides.

"I'm not sure. Dr. Hunter mentioned something about it before you got here." More than ready to suspend the subject of Payne Anderson, Ellen turned her attention to the teenage girl sitting beside her. "Euri, you better take some potatoes before Scott eats them all."

The exchange student had discovered fast food in the few weeks since she arrived in the US. She already had her favorite, fried chicken in a country style biscuit, at a local diner. Ellen offered good choices at home to combat those unhealthy temptations elsewhere. Ducking her head to smile at her plate, Euri poked a lettuce leaf with her fork.

"How do you feel about that, Mom? I mean, hearing Olivia tell it, you saw a lot of him in Galway. She thought—"

"Scott." Ellen's voice, louder than normal and sharp, revealed the frustration tying her stomach in knots. "Olivia thought—and said—too much in Galway. Yes, we spent some time together, *and* I enjoyed it. But now I'm home, and I've got a lot of things to think about and a lot of things to do."

"It just seems really weird that he's in Ral—"

"Scott. Change the topic, okay?" She winced at the snappish tone in her voice. The control that had carried her through the bizarre afternoon was cracking. "Please."

Scott laid his fork down and looked at his plate. "Sorry, Mom."

Ellen rubbed her fingers over her forehead. "I'm sorry, too. I'm just so...I'm exhausted from giving my pitch this afternoon. It was tougher than I imagined, and I'm so glad you came before they left." She reached over and squeezed his arm. "It's good to have a lot of ears. I needed your input, too."

"It's a good proposal, Mom." Scott tapped her upper arm with his knuckles before grabbing another sourdough roll from the bread basket.

"I hope so. But I get the feeling the only reason Dr. Hunter showed up today is because of his acquaintance with your dad. He pretty much admitted it before you got here. It sounds like State has all of the study farms it needs. He probably just wanted a road trip today and took one to Grafton County." Plus, Payne's nosy questions had more than likely planted doubts in Dr. Hunter's mind. She needed constructive ideas, not negative ones.

Scott broke off a piece of the roll. "Mom, if Plan A doesn't work out, we'll move on to Plan B. That's what you've always told us, right?" He popped the bread into his mouth.

Ellen rested her head in her palms. "Whatever Plan B is."

Chapter 28

Payne headed to Ellen's farm with mixed emotions. On one hand, he wanted to see Ellen again. He was hoping to—what? To figure out her relationship with that other fellow. Every time he thought about that scene last week in her driveway, his emotions ran from anger to sick disappointment.

And he wanted to be near her again. Maybe they'd talk again. They had had such easy conversation in Galway. Over the past few days, he'd tried to call her several times, getting as far as punching in her number before hanging up. He couldn't think words to fix this mess he'd created.

On the other hand, a conversation with Ellen might be difficult because two graduate students accompanied him. Both interested in bamboo, they wanted to check out leads for possible thesis topics and study the acre growing on Ellen's farm. Kip Howard, a second year student who should be well into writing his thesis by now, had narrowed his topic choice down to two or three subjects. He wasn't much of a talker.

Or maybe Melanie Greene, the other student, never gave Kip an opportunity to speak. A first year student, Melanie seemed to be the kind of person to set a goal then work toward its completion like a river rushing downhill.

He'd met Melanie as soon as he'd come to town. Hank had invited Payne to the weekly gathering after Friday afternoon classes. A time for professors and grad students to share food, laughter, and war stories about the previous week, it was a fun time to let off steam.

Melanie had grabbed the seat beside him in the restaurant,

monopolizing his attention almost the entire time. He'd met few of the others that night and silently thanked Hank when he stood to leave.

On the way to Hank's car, he had teased him about robbing the cradle. When Payne protested, Hank shared some fatherly advice. "If you're not interested, that's fine. Hard to believe, though. She's got that jet black hair and those almond-shaped eyes. But I know Melanie from her undergraduate days. She sets her sights on something, and she marches toward it. It seemed like tonight she had her sights set on you."

During subsequent visits to Raleigh, Payne had avoided her until this morning when Hank, tied up with a doctorial candidate, asked him to drive her down to Ellen's for thesis research. Although her farm hadn't been approved as a research site yet, and Payne doubted that it would, Hank wanted to work with Ellen as much as possible to keep a relationship open.

Ready to refuse Hank's suggestion to chauffeur Melanie, he acquiesced when Hank mentioned Kip's needing a topic also.

Payne liked the gawky student from the first time they met. Although a grad student, in a lot of ways, Kip still seemed like a self-conscious fifteen-year-old. Payne had decided to take him under his wing and mentor him.

When he'd agreed to drive the two of them down to Ellen's farm, Hank explained that he'd already emailed Ellen, and she expected the students. Payne wondered but didn't ask if Ellen knew he'd be driving the students down to the farm. He sent up a quick prayer that this meeting would go well. Ever since his surrendering experience in Africa, he found himself praying throughout his day. It was a good change—brought about because of meeting Ellen Shepherd.

೫೦೫೦೮೪೮೪

Carrying one last load of boxes to her van, Ellen noticed the red pickup advancing toward her house, expecting it to be Dr. Hunter and his students based on the email he'd sent her earlier in the week.

Skeins of yarn peeked out of boxes crammed into the trunk and back seat. She planned to discount the yarn in the sidewalk sale during the annual Founder's Day Celebration on Saturday. Other boxes contained junk she and the children had purged for the community yard sale. She tried to find an open space in her van for the last boxes, and Taffy barked a furious hello to the truck gliding to a stop in the driveway.

The truck doors slammed, and she looked up to see Payne just as the top box started to slide off. Interesting. He'd remained in North Carolina. A male student ran toward her in an effort to catch the box. A female student velcroed herself to Payne's side, hindering his reach as he tried to help also.

"Looks like you're moving." Kip chuckled, setting a box on top of another one behind the passenger seat.

"No." Ellen smiled at the weak joke. "I'm taking these into town for our Founder's Day Celebration on Saturday." She noticed Payne's mouth stretched into a tight line as he took the last two boxes from her. "I'm Ellen Shepherd, by the way." She offered her hand toward Kip.

With a determined set to his jaw, Payne made the introductions. "This is Kip Howard and Melanie Greene from State. They're hunting for thesis topics this afternoon."

"Hello, Payne." She threw a half glance at Payne before giving her attention to Melanie. She congratulated herself for not gaping at the exotic vision standing in front of her. Beauty and brains. Of course, the whole package. "Nice to meet you, Melanie."

"Did you say Founder's Day? Doesn't that sound quaint and fun? We should come, Payne." She shook Ellen's hand, but she kept her almond eyes zeroed in on Payne.

He ignored her, focusing on Ellen instead. "I think Hank emailed you about this visit."

"Yes, he said that a couple of students wanted to see the farm sometime this week. He said they might have a few questions about bamboo and my input on what we've learned so far from our one acre." She shooed the curious Desi, her orange tabby cat with six toes on his front paws, out of the van and slid the side door shut. With a quick jump, Ellen's black and white cat, Lucy, abandoned her observation point on roof of the van.

"If we sit on the back porch, we can talk and see the field from there." She led them around the corner to the back of the house. Ellen invited them to sit in the wicker rockers, but Melanie chose the swing and pulled Payne to sit beside her.

Melanie pushed the painted floor-boards with her toe to set the swing in motion, but Payne left his feet flat, resisting the action. "I just love porch swings. I used to sit on my grandmother's and smell the Cape Jasmine bush growing at the corner. Your porch is beautiful with all these flower-pots. The mums look really fall-ish."

The corners of Ellen's mouth tipped upward, the strain of the tiny movement monumental to her, but she doubted the young woman noticed her effort. She had eyes only for her companion. Ellen hoped her voice kept secret the tension churning in her chest. "Thank you. I spend a lot of time out here when the weather's nice."

"No doubt." Kip nodded toward the field stretching from the back of the yard to the woods standing in the distance. "You got any deer back here?" He scanned the horizon as he rocked beside her.

"We see a few deer almost every morning along the edge of the woods."

"Yeah, I figured." He cracked his knuckles and pointed to the back corner. "So is that the field of bamboo Dr. Hunter told us about? How're you gonna harvest it?"

Ellen spent the next ten minutes explaining a condensed proposal for the graduate students. When the questions lagged, she peeked at her watch. "If you don't have any more questions, I really need to get to my shop. Dr. Hunter told me you could manage on your own, so stay as long as you need to."

She saw Payne open his mouth, but then seemed to change his mind and pressed it shut again. He simply nodded while holding her gaze. She hesitated, her heart hurting at his behavior since Galway. It felt like betrayal—with the farm questions, with this girl who clung to his side. She missed him. Breaking from the magnetic pull of his eyes, she pushed her legs to stand and carry her away from him to the van, leaving the trio to start their research.

ଔଔଔଔ

Ellen didn't breathe normally until she parked in front of her yarn shop. Another surprise from Payne. She'd thought Dr. Hunter was coming with the students. Maybe she'd misread the email. No matter.

An image of Payne and Melanie sitting together on the swing mocked her. She leaned her head against the steering wheel. Did they have a connection? Was she the reason for his stay in Raleigh? What a beauty. It was easy to believe that a man would move several states for her.

A tiny part of her had hoped that he'd come to Raleigh to be closer to her.

She considered the facts. A beautiful, smart, twenty-something with eyes a man might drown in and a widowed, but also smart, forty-something with three grown children. Not exactly a tough choice.

No wonder he hadn't returned her emails. Melanie looked exotic. Maybe they had met in Africa. Maybe they—

She groaned to stop the negative, unproductive thinking. Nothing was certain. All her thoughts were supposition. She must stop belittling herself. She was a strong, competent business woman with lots of friends who loved her, lots of projects that needed her help. She'd had a summer romance in a beautiful city. It was fun while it lasted.

But would God bring Payne back into her life just to rub her nose in the fact that he has a new relationship? No. Maybe God brought him here to show her that he is healthy and happy and moving on in his life. An email would have been less painful, however, than being blindsided with him in the flesh. Time to tuck Galway into her memories and move on herself.

Thank you, Father, for helping me to stop wallowing in a pity party for myself. Now, please take this ache I feel every time I see

221

Payne. I need to let it go and focus on what You need me to do here at home.

ဆာဆာ၏၏

After writing three pages of a new article in his long-term hotel room, Payne headed toward Bandon. Melanie didn't realize it, but she'd given him a great idea—attending the Founders' Day Celebration. Checking the town's website, he'd found the start time and the layout of the festivities. He saw exactly where *Knit One, Crochet, Too* sat in the heart of the town. Unfortunately, the three pages took longer to write than he wanted, making him leave Raleigh late in the morning.

He didn't care a bit about the celebration, but he hoped to see Ellen again. He sensed she wanted to say something maybe personal the last time he and Melanie and Kip were at her farm. Her hesitation just before she left gave him time to search her eyes. He hoped he wasn't making up the question he saw in her gaze.

True, his presence in her town would be another surprise for her, but maybe since he traveled solo today, he could talk with her alone. Maybe they could get back to where they'd been in Galway. He promised himself to do his best and see what happened.

ဆာဆာ၏၏

"Hey, thanks again for coming home to help with the sidewalk sale today, you guys. I don't think Agnes and I could have done it without you, even though Euri is a big help." Ellen watched Scott and Laurel struggling to get the tent poles to stand upright. Euri fought to keep the tag board signs indicating prices taped down in the correct places. The windy morning hampered their attempts.

"No problem, Mom. You know I couldn't miss Miss Myrtle's sweet potato biscuits." Scott had already visited the church's booth to get his first supply of those famous treats.

Miss Myrtle always baked one hundred biscuits for the church. She also donated scuppernong grapes packed into little plastic bags for two dollars each. She'd stopped making jelly several years ago, so now she gave away her grapes to anyone who'd come pick them and donated the rest to the church's sale on Founder's Day.

"Yeah, well, I want a funnel cake. I think that's all I'll have for lunch." Laurel held the corner post so that Scott could secure the bottom.

"You do realize that a funnel cake is just plain fried dough, right? Grease, sugar, and flour, right?" Although they were college aged, Ellen still prodded her children toward good nutritional choices, and they enjoyed healthy food usually. Sometimes junk food won out.

"Yes, I know exactly what a funnel cake is. Deeeeelicious! Euri, you have to try one." Laurel laughed, and Ellen couldn't help smiling.

A puff of wind blew one of her signs off the table stacked with the clearance yarns. As she rose from retrieving it from the sidewalk, she spotted Dr. Jim Meadows plowing toward her with a funnel cake in one hand. She cringed, thinking mid-morning was early to eat a funnel cake. But really, funnel cake or doughnut. Not a big difference when it came to calories or fat count.

He was still chewing when he stopped in front of her, so she acknowledged him first. "Good morning, Dr. Meadows. It looks like you're enjoying Founder's Day already." Trying to ignore the powdered sugar sprinkled on the front of his dark purple golf shirt, she concentrated instead on beaming a bright, platonic smile.

"Ellen." He drew her name out for several beats. "Please call me Jim. It's a beautiful day for the celebration, isn't it?" He broke off another piece of fried dough and wiggled it between his fingers. "You know, I dropped by your coffee shop yesterday. It's coming along quite nicely." He nodded to emphasize each word. "Those students are doing a fine job.

"I haven't seen the financial numbers, but I think it's safe to say that this project is a success. We might want to use this idea in other schools in the county. In fact, at least one school is already interested in trying something like it. I hope you'd consider being a consultant if this program takes off in the rest of our schools. I'm interested in being in on the next project, too." Holding her gaze, he popped the piece of funnel cake into his mouth and licked his fingers, waiting for her response.

She clutched the signs to her chest. Was Diane right? Was Dr. Meadows interested in her? Was this his clumsy way of asking her out? She had to end his fantasy before another second passed.

"I'm glad you're pleased with it, Dr. Meado—I mean, Jim. I'd be happy to consider consulting in a minor role, but my plate's completely full right now. Will you excuse me? I have to check on some yarn." Lame excuse, but she didn't have a customer to help. She had to think of an escape as fast as she could.

She closed the door behind her, relief surging through her. Wimp. Running away from a possible problem, but she wasn't interested in him. She didn't have time or energy for another major project either. After a minute or two, she peeked out the front window, saw that he had left, and carried a few more skeins of yarn outside to add with the others. Other vendors lining Railroad Street struggled to keep their tents standing and their merchandise in place, too. The wind had strengthened considerably since opening ceremonies earlier that morning.

ഔഔൾൾ

After lunch when all of the clearance yarn had sold, Ellen chose some slow-selling yarns to discount. She backed out of the store holding a hefty load of the marked-down skeins. Stepping sideways to let the door swing closed, she glanced down the street. Payne strolled toward her booth. An image of all those times in Ireland when she thought she saw him flashed in her mind.

Her mouth dropped open, but she gripped the box of yarn, crushing it against her chest. Feeling lightheaded, she sucked in a breath and held it. His eyes locked with hers, and he raised his

224

eyebrows.

As sudden as Payne's appearance, a gust of wind blew from down the street, ripping the iron awning away from the door of her shop. The left pole crashed onto Ellen's head and knocked her onto the sidewalk. Soft coils of yarn erupted from the box, spilling beautiful colors over the gray concrete. Laurel's screams cut through the piercing pain just before an all-encompassing black shut the door on her memory.

Chapter 29

When Payne arrived at the hospital, Scott and Laurel greeted him. Scott thanked him for coming, as Laurel moved toward the bed where her mother lay, sleeping peacefully.

"Like I told you on the phone, she's been out since that pole hit her. The doctor said nothing's broken, and all the tests look good. He doesn't know why she won't wake up. We're just waiting for her to open her eyes."

Scott jammed his hands in his pockets. "But every now and then, she'll start mumbling, thrashing about. We think she's gonna wake up, but it's like she's stuck in some bad dream."

He sighed. "The doctor told us to keep her calm and quiet, but we haven't been much good at it. We're hoping maybe you can."

"Me? That's why you wanted me to come?" Payne had jumped at the chance to come to the hospital when Scott called him, not asking for an explanation, simply grateful to be included.

Scott ducked his head and cleared his throat. "Yeah, well, sometimes she calls out your name, and we thought maybe having you here'd help."

A quick flash raced Payne's heart at those words. She called out his name? That sounded like a good thing.

When the young man met his eyes, Payne saw an unspoken question cloaked with vulnerability and pain. Willing his heart to calm its runaway beating at the implications of Scott's admission, Payne grabbed his shoulder. "Scott, I'm glad you called me. I'll help any way I can, but I don't have much experience with sick people." He crossed his arms and couldn't help himself from revisiting Scott's words. "Ah, so, she called my—"

Sounds from the bed interrupted Payne. Ellen mumbled, flailing her head back and forth. Scott nodded to Payne as if giving him permission to go to his mom.

Ignoring the awkward mantle that enveloped him with Scott and Laurel's eyes evaluating his every move, he grabbed Ellen's hand, bent close to her ear and whispered. "Ellen. It's me, Payne. I'm here. I'm here, Elly Girl, and you're fine. Can you relax for us? Can you wake up and talk to us? Shhh. You're fine. I'm here."

Flying by the seat of his pants, he repeated the phrases, brushing the hair back from Ellen's forehead with one hand and stroking her upper arm with the other. In less than thirty seconds, her knitted brow released, her frustration evaporated. Her body relaxed, quiet and sleeping.

Payne turned to Scott who glanced at his sister. "That's the quickest she's settled down all night. I told you it was a good idea to get Payne here." He ran his hand through his hair, traces of worry and fatigue evident on his young face.

"Look, if you two want to take a break, let me stay with your mom. She's settled now. I'll have you paged if anything changes." Payne offered, expecting them to refuse to leave. He hid his surprise when, after Scott's promise of leaving for only a few minutes, Laurel reluctantly agreed to leave the room.

Positioning a chair closer to the bed, he faced Ellen, grateful with time alone with her even if she didn't respond. Tracing her long fingers, he remembered sweet times in Galway with her hand in his. Sitting on the back porch the night of their scandalous sleepover. Walking through Eyre Square his last day in Ireland.

"Hey, Ellen, listen." He squeezed her hand. "I'm sorry about ambushing you the other day. I know it sounds lame, but that wasn't my plan. Please wake up. We need to talk. I miss you, sweet one. Wake up for me."

Silence, accompanied by soft breaths, answered his plea.

ℴℴℙℙ

Scott and Laurel returned within twenty minutes. Payne stretched from his chair to greet them. "She's been peaceful the whole time. No problems."

Intending to leave so that the two young people could rest, he clasped Scott's hand to say, "goodbye," but Ellen's muttering stopped him. This time he recognized his mumbled name as she twisted her head, eyes closed, from side to side. He returned to her and grabbed her rigid wrist, whispering the words that had calmed her earlier. She sighed, relaxed, and slept in peace.

Biting her lower lip, Laurel faced Payne at the bedside. She let out a breath. "Do you think you could stay here tonight? I know it's a lot to ask, but the doctor told us to keep her calm and quiet. You can do that, and we certainly haven't been able to. Will you stay? Please, Payne."

His heart flipped at Laurel's tender plea. His voice dropped husky with emotion. "I'll stay as long as you want me to."

Of course, he'd stay. He'd plant himself beside the bed until Ellen woke up and threw him out. Would she really do that? Maybe. Her reception of him in North Carolina had been on the cold end of the welcoming spectrum. Would he end up on the curb in front of the hospital if he stayed all night? He'd saunter over that shaky bridge when he came to it.

She'd called his name.

That's right. He'd heard her say his name, not that other guy's. That had to be a good sign. He'd stop worrying about her relationship with someone else for the time being and try to figure out that connection later. If he could help her children and her through this night, he'd gladly stay awake until morning.

※❀❀☾☾☞

Sometime after midnight, Payne succumbed to his fatigue. He pushed his legs underneath the bed and laid his head at her elbow. Scott and Laurel had slipped into fitful sleep earlier in uncomfortable looking chairs by the window. The dark and quiet beckoned him to join them, and he surrendered, still holding

Ellen's hand.

Fingers brushing through his hair coaxed him from his slumber. Raising his head to find Ellen studying him, he caught his breath. Recovering from his momentary surprise, he smiled at her. The corners of her mouth lifted in a weak return, a welcome encouragement as were her whispered words. "Payne, you're here."

"Yes, I'm here. How are you feeling?" He followed her lead and kept his voice low, not wanting to share her with Scott and Laurel yet.

"Happy. Very happy because you're here. Is this a dream?" Her eyes fluttered closed. "I can't figure out where we are, but I really don't care." She sighed, smiling broadly now.

Payne grinned. "I'm glad you're happy." He scooted nearer the bed. "You're in the hospital. I meant—how does your body feel? How does your head feel? Do you remember what happened?"

"Ow, my head is killing me." With her free hand she investigated the top of her skull. "I have a big bump on it. And I'm so sleepy." Her eyes closed again.

"Okay. Let me get the nurse. She'll want to know you're awake." He reached for the call box.

Her eyes flew open. She clutched his hand, still intertwined with hers. "No, please don't, Payne. Wait."

"Ellen, all I have to do is push the call button, and she'll come. I don't have to go get her." He smoothed back the soft, frizzy tendrils at her temples, trying to calm her.

Still agitated, she frowned. "Yes, but as soon as she comes, this sweet dream will end, and you'll leave again." She shook her head. "I don't want you to leave. You're the nice Payne. You're not the mean one. Please, please, don't end this dream yet."

He'd continued to caress her hair, careful to avoid the tender spots, but with those words, he froze. "What do you mean 'the nice Payne?'"

"I mean you're not mean. You have kind eyes." She stroked his eyebrow and scorched his cheekbone with a feather-light touch. "Your mouth is kind, too, and smiling." She trailed her fingertips to his lips, and he kissed them. "And see, you kissed me."

He couldn't resist asking the question pounding in his brain. "What does the mean Payne do?"

Ellen pouted. "I don't like him. His eyes are cold. His mouth never smiles. He's with that girl. He's mean. He makes Dr. Hunter doubt my plan." Her eyelids fell again.

Payne couldn't leave it alone. "But you like the nice Payne?"

She blinked. "Oh, yes. He's the Payne I fell in love with in Galway." Ellen smiled. "I miss Galway, and I miss the nice Payne." She closed her eyes.

Payne couldn't breathe. He'd clearly heard her say she'd fallen in love with him. Little bubbles of joy rose in his chest, but he tapped them down. He remained cautious. She thought she was dreaming. What if she were delirious? He leaned down and brushed kissed his lips against hers.

"Don't end this dream, okay?" She sighed again. "I'm so sleepy. My eyes won't stay open." Ellen drifted back to sleep before the nurse arrived, summoned with the call button. He answered her questions then waited by the window. Scott and Laurel slept while the nurse checked Ellen.

After the interruption, Payne resumed his position beside the bed holding Ellen's hand. There in the semi-darkness of the hospital room, listening to the deep breathing of Scott and Laurel and the muffled sounds of the night shift down the hall, he reviewed the conversation with her.

She'd called it a dream, and now he wondered if the encounter had been real or simply his dream.

He had to trust his own eyes and ears.

Remember whose name she'd called out during her delirium?

Remember who was able to calm her back to sleep?

Remember whose soft fingertips teased him out of his dozing?

Remember the coherent, sweet words she'd whispered before the blanket of sleep closed her off from him again?

The conversation, the playful exchange—all of it was real.

Yes, the last thirty minutes did have a dream-like quality

because of the midnight hour and the protective darkness and, of course, because of the things she'd admitted to him.

That part had definitely seemed like a dream.

His dream.

But the time with Ellen here in this hospital room was real, just like their time in Galway. Her admission gave him renewed hope, and he'd cling to that welcome feeling when she woke up and recovered.

Chapter 30

The doctor came by for rounds early the next morning. Payne caught Scott's eyes, nodding as he headed for the door to give the family some privacy. Stepping into the hall, he heard the doctor trying to wake Ellen.

Massaging a crick in his neck from his sleepover in the straight-back chair, he vacillated between staying and leaving. Of course, he wanted to stay, to resume and explore their conversation from the middle of the night.

But his mother had ingrained in him that hospitalized women who don't feel or look their best don't always welcome visitors. Would she feel that he was overstepping? Maybe this was family time.

As he continued to consider the pros and cons of staying or leaving, the elevator at the end of the hall pinged, the doors opening for the man who had ruined his homecoming with Ellen. That same person marched into the hallway dressed in a light blue, buttoned down shirt paired with a yellow and blue striped tie. Payne gritted his teeth, swallowing a groan. The man's carriage screamed, "I'm ready to tackle the world."

The young man strode straight for him. His eyes traveled to the door beside Payne. "I'm Blake Thompson." He held out his hand to shake Payne's. "I think Ellen Shepherd is in room 320."

Payne nodded. "Payne Anderson. The doctor's in with her right now."

"Oh, okay." Blake checked his watch. "Are Scott and Laurel in there, too?"

"Yeah."

"Oh, okay." He shuffled his feet and glanced at the door.

"You're close to Ellen?" Payne thought he might as well get a read on his competition.

He grinned. "Yeah. We go way back." He rubbed the side of his nose. "You know, I'm going to have to leave in a few minutes if I make it back to teach my Sunday School class. I'm ref-ing a soccer tournament this afternoon, so this is my only chance to see her. I think I'll just stick my head in."

He knocked on the door, opened it a few inches and peered inside the room. Laurel must have seen him right away. "Blake, come in. Come in. Mom just woke up."

Sporting a wide grin, Blake stepped inside.

The next voice Payne heard was Ellen's. "Oh, Blake. You're so sweet to come. You didn't have to." The door clicked shut.

As much as he wanted to join the group in Ellen's room, Payne conceded this round to Blake. He'd see Ellen when he wasn't sleep deprived, wearing rumpled clothes that had been on his back for almost twenty four hours, and tending a day's growth of stubble on his face.

Blake might have won the first game, but Payne planned to win the match.

₿₿₿₿

"Mrs. Shepherd, I'm glad you're feeling better this morning." Her doctor scribbled notes onto her chart.

"I feel fine except for the lump on my head. I'm still tired a little."

"Yes, and because of that bump, I want to keep you here today just for observation. If all goes well, and I don't see why it shouldn't, I can release you tomorrow morning. With a follow-up visit, of course."

"But my children could observe me at home, couldn't they?"

The doctor shook his head. "I'd feel more comfortable with you here."

She'd be more comfortable at home. Working her arms behind her back, she wiggled her pillow higher on the bed. "All right. If I have to, I have to." She closed her eyes.

"You have to," Scott and Laurel chimed together in true twin fashion.

ೋೋೲೲ

Exhaustion seeped through to Ellen's bones. The doctor's visit along with Blake's abbreviated one depleted most of her energy. Her brief phone call with Olivia to reassure her to stay in Galway and finish her semester had zapped the remainder of her energy.

Happy to have two of her children with her, she yearned at the same time for solitude so that she could go back to sleep. She also wanted to relive that delicious dream from last night. Payne showed up beside her bed as sweet and kind to her as he had ever been before he left Galway.

What a terrific dream. He'd kissed her fingers and caressed her hair.

And he'd smiled at her.

She'd longed to see that smile for months, and it had shown up in her dreams. She wanted to drift off to sleep remembering that dream. Her eyelids, heavy with the promise of slumber, fluttered closed for one second before stretching wide open again. "Oh, no. What about Euri? Where's she?"

Laurel stood near her bed. "Don't worry, Mom. Robin spent the night at our house with her. She's fine." She patted her mom's shoulder. "Do you need anything?"

"Sleep. But first, I'm really thirsty." Struggling to sit up against her pillows, she winced at a throbbing in her head. "Ow. And I think I need some ibuprophen."

"Sure thing, Mom." Ellen's eyes followed her daughter's movements to her bedside table. She drew in a sharp breath. She blinked hard, grappling to understand the image before her.

"What's wrong, Mom?" Scott jumped forward from his lounging position in his chair.

"That pitcher. How did you get that pitcher?" Sitting beside her bed was the piece of pottery she'd deliberated over in Galway.

235

A testimony to her time with Payne, its vibrant colors of blue, purple, and scarlet contrasted with the hospital's plastic pitcher and cup. She remembered deliberating over it, replacing it on the table just before turning into his chest.

Would she be tortured by those bittersweet memories forever?

Laurel poured the water. "I don't know where it came from." She handed the cup along with the ibuprophen tablets to Ellen.

"Payne brought that in and set it on the table when he got here last night. I forgot about it till right now." Scott leaned back in the chair when he realized his mother was fine.

"Payne was here?" Ellen could barely speak for the thudding in her chest.

"Yeah. Sorry, Mom. He went out into the hall this morning when the doctor came. I figured he'd come back in after the doctor left, but he must have decided to go ahead and leave. I forgot to mention it to you." He crumpled his face, trying for the contrite look he always went for when he thought he might be yelled at.

Ellen pushed her muddled brain to work out the details of this unbelievable scenario. "Payne was here, and he left this morning? How long did he stay?"

"I don't know. He got here sometime in the early evening last night. We weren't really paying attention to the clock." Scott moved to the bed and grabbed his mother's hand.

"He came last night and left this morning? He stayed the whole time?"

Easing onto the coverlet, Laurel spoke in low tones. "Yes, Mom. We slept on these two chairs, and he sat in that little chair by the bed."

"Why?" Ellen balled up a section of the top sheet with her free hand, clinging to it for support or in frustration. She didn't know which.

She watched a silent power struggle between her twins. Scott must have lost because he squared his shoulders, heaved his chest, and tried to explain. "Mom, you ah, you weren't exactly having an easy night of it. The doctor had given you some medicines. I don't know what to be honest, and you still weren't settling down. You...you kept calling for Payne."

Ellen closed her eyes and cringed.

Scott continued. "At first, the nurse thought you wanted more pain medication, but then Laurel figured it out. You were calling for Payne, so we called him." He glanced at his mother. She wiggled toward the foot of the bed.

"He was in town yesterday for Founder's Day, which is kind of hard to believe come to think about it, and he saw the awning knock you to the sidewalk. He helped keep people back away from you while Dr. Meadows called for the ambulance. He handed me his phone number before I ran to my car. Laurel rode with you in the ambulance.

"When Miss Agnes called to check on you, she told me he stayed and helped her and Euri pack up the sidewalk sale." He rubbed the back of his neck. "He's a pretty good guy, Mom." He ducked his head as if he didn't know how she'd take that statement.

"He's staying in a hotel, one of those long-term deals, not far from here. You know the kind executives stay in when they travel..."

"Scott. Finish the main story, please." Ellen wanted the details, however embarrassing they might be.

"Right. Sorry. Anyway, when we called him, he came right away. Mom," he licked his lips, "I hope you're not upset about that. He really helped out a lot. You settled down fast once he started talking to you, and you slept through the whole night."

Suppressing a groan, she pulled the sheet up to her chin. So it wasn't a dream. Payne had really been here last night. She could see his smile but couldn't hear their words. Why couldn't she remember what she said to him? Her brain wouldn't work. At least he was smiling in her foggy mind. Smiling is good.

"No, Sweetie, I'm not upset. I must have woken up during the night because I remember his being here." She summoned a weak, half-hearted laugh. "I just thought it was a dream." She smiled to reassure Scott, but what could ease her anxiety over this new wrinkle in her life? She had questions that only Payne could answer. She wanted to talk with him, but at the same time, the hairs standing on the back of her neck warned her it might be an awkward conversation. What had she said to Payne to make him smile again?

Chapter 31

Ellen dozed on and off for most of the rest of Sunday. The doctor released her early Monday morning. Agnes and Euri welcomed her home, and Scott and Laurel helped settle her in. She worked hard to convince them to go back to their respective colleges. The tipping point had been Euri and Agnes. The twins' reluctant confidence in the women's ability as care givers and watchdogs had helped Ellen win her argument. They left late in the day, shouting last minute commands from their open car windows.

She'd promised to take it easy for a few days, intending to keep that promise when she made it. But on Tuesday morning, an idea dropped into her mind and set down roots.

After hearing of Payne's nighttime visit to her hospital room, she'd secretly hoped he'd call or come by the farm to see her. Every time the phone rang, she held her breath, bracing herself for that familiar, teasing voice. He hadn't called or visited either, but his ignoring her didn't stop her wanting to see him. She needed to talk with him.

Raleigh beckoned her like a forty percent off sale at her favorite shoe store.

Contemplating visiting Payne prompted hot and cold flashes to zing through her body. Fighting her physical reactions, she analyzed the bold idea from every angle. It pushed her out of her comfort zone and required offering herself up for possible humiliation if that beautiful grad student lurked nearby or if he decided to tease her about losing the fight between the awning pole, but she knew she had to go.

What if she combined seeing Payne with other errands in Raleigh? She needed to drop off more forms about the farm to Dr. Hunter. She could also plan a lunch with her friend, Margie.

Have lunch, deliver the forms, and drop by to see Payne during her campus visit. Although he was the magnet drawing her to Raleigh, seeing him was simply one item on her to-do list. This plan resembled more of a by-the-way-while-I'm-here-I-thought-I'd-drop-by kind of tactic that she might be able to pull off.

But her brain had a difficult time picturing herself going to Payne. Could she actually knock on his office door and walk right in?

Wait. Does he have an office at State? He's staying in a long-term hotel. He hasn't moved here. What's he doing?

Maybe Dr. Hunter knew the scoop about Payne. She'd have to call him for details. Great. She didn't like dragging other people into her plans, but this time she conceded she had to if she wanted to hear the answers to her questions.

She located Dr. Hunter's business card and punched in his numbers before she could talk herself out of it.

Her patience stretched to breaking with the volleying of pleasant greetings, Ellen zeroed in on her real objective. "Dr. Hunter, I'm hoping that you can help me with something."

"I'll do my best if I can."

"Thank you. I'm trying to get in touch with Payne Anderson. I believe he's staying in Raleigh, but I'm not sure when he's on campus."

"Sure. I can give you his cell number."

"No. No, that's okay. I already have his number." Words tripped over each other. "Ahmm. I really just wanted to drop by the department. I've completed the forms you've asked for."

"Ah ha."

She could hear a smile in the professor's voice.

"You want to give him a little bit of his own medicine, huh? Surprise him like he surprised you the other week?"

She didn't answer. She wasn't ready to admit out loud the real reason behind her call.

"I'd be happy to help you, Mrs. Shepherd. He's been busy writing up articles for professional journals based on his Africa notes. He uses an empty office next to mine when he's in town. He's been going back and forth between here and Maryland. His chairperson's counter offered since his contract there is up next summer." He chuckled. "You probably know this already. Anyhow, he writes in the morning, and lately he's made himself available to help some grad students in the early afternoon. He really likes mentoring those young folks."

Sure. If they look like the Queen of Sheba. She thumped her forehead for the mean thought.

"You should be able to catch him this week. And I won't spoil your surprise."

After thanking Dr. Hunter, she hung up and considered her original idea. Could she actually go to Raleigh to see Payne? Surprise him without an invitation?

Payne Anderson was the king of surprises—in the pottery shop, in Eyre Square, in her own driveway.

Maybe surprising him was the best tactic. Catch him off guard. Let him see what it feels like to be blindsided. She should be proactive. Quit waiting for Payne to email or call. Get answers to every single question, starting with explaining that hospital visit and then why he never emailed. She grabbed her phone to make a lunch date with Margie before she changed her mind.

ഇഇ⟩ഇ⟩ఴ⟩ఴ

Walking into the paletas shop right across from campus, Ellen admitted to herself that she was stalling for time, trying to gather her courage. Her lunch date with Margie had been fun, a balm to her spirit, but much too short. Their lunch concluded within an hour because she'd had to pick up one of her children from her babysitting coop for a braces check-up.

Ten years Ellen's junior, Margie was a high-spirited mother of four who always sparked their lunches with animated stories about life in the "diaper dugout," as she called it. They'd met several years ago in a Bible study, remaining close ever since. El-

241

len wished they could see each other more often, and she always looked forward to their next lunch.

Waiting in line, she perused the list of flavors as she anticipated enjoying the gourmet Mexican ice pop. Since her lunch date had been cut short, she decided to give Payne some extra time to return to his office if he'd taken a lunch break from writing. She planned to savor the frozen treat while she mulled the words she wanted to say to him.

She greeted the cashier who wore a Meredith College T-shirt and requested her favorite flavor, Mango Chili. "Mexican Chocolate is better," tickled her right ear. She gasped and dropped her two dollars.

Her heartbeat thundering in her ears, she turned to see Payne scooping up her money and grinning.

"For crying out loud. You really do enjoy surprising people, don't you? Do you ever think about announcing your presence?" She paid with shaking fingers and took the paleta, stepping aside so that Payne could order.

This was not the way it was supposed to go. She was supposed to surprise him. She wanted to stomp her feet and hit something or at least pout.

His grin faded, a look of remorse washing over his face. "Hey, I'm really sorry about surprising you in your driveway with Hank that time. It must have seemed like an ambush or something. I've wanted to apologize ever since." After receiving his Mexican Chocolate popsicle, he guided her to an empty bench next to a wall covered in children's colored drawings.

She arched her eyebrow. Again Ellen fought the urge to pout and opted for cool nonchalance. "Don't worry about it. Dr. Hunter explained it, remember?" She nibbled on the corner of the frozen mango puree and swallowed the delicious ice. The chili part of the duo flavor kicked in, the hot, spicy essence leaving its mark all the way down her throat.

"So what are you doing in Raleigh? Scott said you're better, but I'm surprised to see you up here by yourself." Payne stuck half of his popsicle into his mouth.

Her breath caught, her pulse accelerating. Another surprise.

"You talked to Scott?"

"I called him on Monday. It sounded like you had a lot of visitors. I figured you were still recovering and tired, so I just talked with him. I'm glad you're feeling better."

She fiddled with her napkin but faced his gaze square on. "Thank you. To answer your question, I had lunch with a friend, and Dr. Hunter needed some more information about the farm. I'm dropping off more forms for him." She made a face. "I'm not sure having more information is going to help, though."

"Hey. Hank really wants to work something out with you. He's trying, but with budget cuts…" He crossed his legs, grabbing his ankle that rested on his knee. "Which reminds me. I apologize for throwing in my two cents' worth about financial requirements and manpower. I didn't realize Hank was talking about your situation when he asked for my opinion."

Warmth permeated her insides. An apology. Payne hadn't sabotaged her idea. He'd asked logical questions.

"Thank you. He's been great. If a relationship doesn't work out with State, we've talked about other options. Grafton Community College is opening an agriculture department, so there's a lead." She bit her lip. "There's one more reason I'm in Raleigh." She swallowed. "I came to see you."

She'd noticed a subtle change in his countenance when she mentioned, "a friend," and she caught the flash of surprise that winged over his face now.

Both eyebrows stretched over gray eyes. "You came to see me?"

She nodded. "I wanted to thank you for coming to the hospital and helping Scott and Laurel. They sang your praises when I woke up." She drew in a breath. "And I wanted to thank you for the pitcher you left on the night stand for me."

He took a bite of the frozen chocolate, and it was his turn to nod.

"So—thank you, Payne. You can imagine how shocked I was when I saw that pitcher. I'd admired it in Galway and gone back to buy it, in fact, but it was already gone."

"You'd set it back down on the display right before you

bumped into me the second day we met." A whisper of a smile played around his mouth.

"Yes, right before *you* ran into *me*. I remember." She didn't realize he did.

The tiny smile grew into a full blown grin, and he paired it with a chuckle. "I remember this whole conversation, too. Who bumped into whom?"

"Seeing that pitcher beside my bed with my brain foggy with sleep and medication threw me into major confusion. I'd remembered your being in the hospital room, but I thought it was a dream." She laughed, licking the last taste of mango from her popsicle stick.

His eyes narrowed. "You thought it was a dream?"

"Yes, a sort of cloudy dream." She bit the empty stick.

Cocking his head, he rubbed his chin. "What do you mean, 'cloudy'?"

His eyes, the color of an overcast Galway morning, pinned her to the back of the bench. Dragging her gaze away from his, she glanced at her watch. "Hey, aren't you supposed to be in your borrowed office now helping floundering grad students?" Glad for a distraction, she wrapped her napkin around the naked stick.

"Yeah, I am." He narrowed his eyes. "How'd you know that?"

"Dr. Hunter mentioned something about it that last time we talked." Payne didn't need to know he'd been the topic of that conversation.

"I see. So you've discussed me with Hank, huh?"

"I said, 'mentioned.' not 'discussed.'" *Discussed* might have been the better word choice in this instance, but Payne didn't need to know that either.

"Whatever. And you decided to 'drop by' instead of calling or emailing."

She crossed her arms in front of her. "We haven't had much luck with computers or phones."

If Ellen were a betting person, she would have wagered a whole dollar that Payne's check colored. A tiny flicker of satisfaction soothed her at his discomfort.

If he had any sheepish feelings, he covered them quickly.

"And you stopped by here first for some frozen courage, huh?" He wiggled the wooden stick, one last bit of Mexican Chocolate clinging to it, in front of her.

"Frozen courage? You think I need courage before I see you?" Ellen remembered his uncanny way of striking close to her truth during their conversations in Galway.

"Just teasing. I know you're a force to be reckoned with. I've seen you in action, remember?" He stood, offering his hand to help her. "Let's walk to the office, okay? It's just across the street." He guided her to the door holding it open for her. "We'll drop your papers off in the main office, and then we can go up to mine...well, the one I'm using anyway. And while we walk," he grinned again, "You can explain about your 'cloudy dream.'"

Wonderful. He wasn't going to let that subject drop. "Fine." First, she had a question of her own. "So it's not your office. You haven't taken the job here?"

He held her gaze before answering. "No. I'm back and forth. Responsibilities up in College Park. Figuring out stuff down here."

She nodded. Figuring out what kind of stuff?

They moved to the crosswalk and waited for the light to change. "You wanted to know about the dream. I suppose we should stop calling it that. I know now you really were in my hospital room, but it still seems like a dream to me. I don't remember much about it."

Did he look disappointed?

"What do you remember about it?"

A Wolf-line bus carrying State students zipped through the intersection, and Payne pulled her back from the curb. She wished he'd grab her hand, but he seemed more interested in asking questions than holding hands. He released her arm.

"Not any real specifics. I don't remember anything we said. Just sort of general feelings, I guess."

He leaned in closer to her, his voice dropping with an urgent edge to it. "What kind of feelings?"

Why was he so determined to wring out the details of his hospital visit? He was there, for Heaven's sake. Had she said something really stupid?

She refused to say, 'warm, good, happy,' feelings. No telling what he'd make of those adjectives. "Well, really just kind of…of positive feelings." That description sounded weak even to herself.

They crossed Hillsborough Street, his hand planted at the small of her back. As they neared his building, he caught her elbow, stopping her on the walkway. "Ellen, wait. I have to ask you something first." He licked his lips and swallowed. A muscle worked in his cheek. "Are you seeing someone?"

Her jaw dropped. The air whooshed out of her lungs as though she had been punched in the stomach. Where did that question come from? After Galway, how could he think that? How could he ask her that? Quick tears burned behind her eyelids.

Before she could gather words to respond to his question, shouts from down the sidewalk shattered her attention.

"Payne! Payne!" Melanie, the graduate assistant, galloped toward them. "I stopped by your office, but you weren't there. I'm so glad I found you. I really need to talk with you about my thesis." She flipped her glossy hair over her shoulder and glanced toward Ellen. "Oh, hello, Mrs. Shepherd. I didn't realize it was you talking with Payne."

Ellen fought with the jealousy working overtime in her heart. Melanie, a poster child for everything that she was not— young, tall, perky—stood so close to him that it looked odd. Ellen stepped backward to give them all more room.

Keeping his focus on Ellen, he didn't seem to notice Melanie's close proximity.

The grad student persisted with her quest. "Payne. I've got some questions about my thesis topic. Can you help me now?"

Payne glanced quickly at the younger girl and snapped, "Call Vera in the office, and she'll set up an appointment for you tomorrow. I'm busy right now." His gaze settled back on Ellen.

Melanie winced at the sharp words but recovered with a weak smile.

As much as she resented the interruption, especially since it was Melanie's doing, she realized Payne had a job to do. Plus, having a break to process his last question appealed to her. Where in the world did he get a crazy idea that she was seeing someone? Fatigue crept into her bones as well, reminding her that she'd promised her children to take it easy.

Ellen counted Melanie's disruption as a gift so that she could escape from Payne's piercing gaze. "Oh, you don't have to wait till tomorrow, Melanie." She glanced at Payne. "Dr. Hunter said you help students in the afternoon, and she needs help. We're finished talking anyway. Good luck with your thesis, Melanie. Bye, Payne. We can talk again soon." She stepped away from him, but he grabbed her arm.

"Wait a minute, Ellen. We're not finished." Payne ran his hand through his hair twice.

Ellen perceived his controlled frustration but refused to be intimidated. "Payne, it sounds like students have come to expect you to help, and here's a student who needs your help now. You should go." Ellen peeked around his shoulder at Melanie who stared at them with curiosity and a bit of hurt.

"They're not even...I don't have..." A fierce determination set Payne's face like flint, but his grip slackened on her arm. He capitulated. "You're right." He rubbed the top of her arm with his thumb. "I don't like it, but you're right." His voice, a notch above a whisper was firm and didn't invite opposition. "Okay, I'll let you off the hook now. I'll go mollycoddle Melanie, but we will finish this conversation. I know where you live now, remember?"

She straightened her spine and met his glare with unblinking eyes. "That almost sounds like a threat."

"Call it whatever you want—threat, warning, omen even. I'm saying it to you as a promise, however. We're going to finish this conversation." His smile softened the resolve behind the words. "Count on it." He winked, turned away from her, and plodded back to Melanie.

Chapter 32

Ellen delivered her forms to the secretary in Payne's building and thankfully didn't see him or his student again.

Their sidewalk conversation strong armed the one or two other thoughts she needed to contemplate and demanded attention for the whole drive back to Grafton County. Payne's last question had been so astonishing it bordered on the ridiculous. How had he come up with the notion that she was seeing someone? Is that why he had been so different from the man she'd met in Galway? How could he believe that she would be seeing someone after the memories they'd made last summer?

Deciding to drive into Bandon instead of going straight home, she stopped to visit the student coffee shop, Wheat 'n Beans, before dropping in on the yarn shop. She halfway expected Payne to make good on his threat or warning or omen to continue their conversation, waiting for her at her front door. Surely, he would wait until another day to press her for an answer to his unbelievable question since it was late in the afternoon already.

The inviting aroma of coffee and chocolate wafted through the open door as she entered the shop. Bonnie placed two clean mugs back on a shelf and turned toward her. "Hey, Ms. Ellen."

She waved, closing the door. "Hey, Bonnie. How are you?"

"Worn out." Bonnie turned another mug upside down to join the others, covering a quick yawn with her free hand. "Can I get you something? I don't have a lot to offer, though. We're pretty much wiped out of the baked goods except for a few muffins."

Ellen leaned against one of the stools in front of the counter. "The after-school crowd was hungry today?

"Yes ma'am. Ravenous. Enormous, too. We were crammed packed in here for a half hour or so. The soccer team lost in the playoffs last night, and those guys were in here blowing their training diets together. They put away a ton of goodies."

"No problem. I just stopped by to see how you're doing, but…" She considered the three forlorn muffins left in the display case. "I'll take those three ginger lemon muffins. Will you separate them with one in a bag and two in another, please? I'll take one to Ms. Agnes at the shop, and the other two will be for breakfast for Euri and me."

While Bonnie took care of her order, Ellen studied the shop. She'd purposefully avoided coming in here since the first few weeks because it evoked bittersweet memories of all the time she and Payne had spent in cafes in Galway. She noticed the artwork on the walls and recognized the artist of a beach scene as one of the seniors from her church's youth group. "Bonnie, all this artwork is from Mr. Pope's students, right?"

The coffee shop committee had suggested to Jonas Pope that his top art students might want to display their artwork in the shop in hopes of selling their pieces. Jonas had been excited about the idea, but Ellen had never heard whether the idea had panned out or not. Evidently, it had.

Bonnie handed her the two bags. "Yeah. We just got them in last week. Two have already sold. I think they make the place look kinda cool."

Ellen agreed. The new wall paint had done wonders for sprucing up the building, but the eclectic tastes of the different students added a fresh feeling to the old store front. She loved that, along with the business and consumer sciences students, art students joined the coffee shop venture.

"Thanks, Bonnie. See you soon." Ellen left Bonnie to another load of mugs and strolled down the street for *Knit One, Crochet, Too*. She wanted to high five someone. She'd had a good idea, and now the dream was a reality. Students could run a successful business. She'd love to give Tamra Creech the sales figures. Giggling, she patted her own back. She enjoyed the satisfaction for a few short moments before the antsy feeling she'd had since

Raleigh returned.

Agnes greeted her with an open-hearted smile as she stepped through the doorway. "Hey, Honey. It's always good to see my boss."

Ellen wiggled the bag in front of her. "Especially when she comes bearing gifts? I hope you like lemon ginger muffins."

"Oh, yummy. My favorite." She opened the bag and sniffed the tangy aroma. "I'll have it for breakfast if I can wait that long. Thanks a bunch, honey. Did you have a good day?"

Her sunny disposition helped to soothe Ellen. She was glad that Agnes' managing the shop had worked out so well. Ellen liked having more time for other pursuits, and Agnes liked interacting with the customers, sorting new yarn, and having a new purpose to combat her loneliness without her beloved Henry. A win-win situation for both women.

Ellen sank into the floral wingchair near the window. "It was a pretty good day, I guess. How was yours?"

"Oh, it was a good day for my quiet time, meditation, twiddling my thumbs."

Ellen raised her eyebrows.

With an exaggerated sad countenance, Agnes exhaled a long, slow sigh. "Only three customers—maybe—crossed our threshold all day, and one was just browsing." She rested her hand on her hip. "Either everyone's finished with Christmas projects, or everyone's procrastinating."

Ellen chuckled. "I'm thinking it's the procrastination theory."

"Heeeey, what are you doing here anyway? I thought you were supposed to stay home taking it easy for a few days." She folded her arms against her chest and twisted her face into a mock frown.

Ellen swiveled the chair. "I'm not on complete bed rest. I can do what I feel up to."

"And what have you felt up to today? You look exhausted."

"I ran a few errands and had lunch with a friend." Ellen didn't want to talk about Payne yet. She hoped the vague answer would satisfy Agnes' curiosity. "Why not call it a day? I'll keep the shop open for a while just in case someone comes in. I'll go over receipts and work on our next yarn order."

"Are you sure, dear? I think you ought to go on home."

"I'm fine. I promise I won't stay long. Go ahead. Really."

Agnes shook her head and tut tutted as she grabbed her belongings. Closing the front door, she sang out, "Toodles."

Ellen spent the next half hour staring at paper-work and fiddling with the yarn baskets on the floor. Her attempts at tidying were really unnecessary because Agnes kept the store in tiptop shape, but the activity helped release some of her nervous energy. She jumped every time she heard a noise from the street expecting to see Payne walk through her front door.

Why was she anxious about finishing their conversation? Hadn't she wanted to hear his answers to all of her questions? True, but she hadn't anticipated that he might have questions, too, especially that last question. Was she seeing someone? How crazy was that?

Her instincts told her Payne wouldn't let the day end without hearing the answer to his question. Since he hadn't shown up at the shop, she expected him to call at least or to show up at her house.

As much as she dreaded the possibility of finding Payne there, she longed for her bed or at least her couch. The extra physical as well as emotional exertion of her day had taken a toll on her. She grabbed her purse and muffins, squared her shoulders, and headed for home.

Chapter 33

The soothing melodies of a favorite James Taylor CD couldn't help her shake the feeling of apprehension as she drove home. The hair on the back of her neck stood at attention. Her shallow breathing and quick pulse warned her that something important might be just around the corner.

As she turned down her driveway, her intuition proved correct. Payne leaned against a silver hybrid mini SUV, arms folded in front of him and one leg crossed on top of the other. Her heart beat revved into high gear. Although the time change back to standard time had taken place the previous weekend, the light outside still allowed the determined set to Payne's jaw to show.

God, please help me do this. I don't have any energy. I'm really not up to sparing with him right now. I need your strength. Please give me the right words to say.

ഇ൞൞ൈ൞

Payne watched Ellen's van turn onto the driveway and mentally readied himself for the confrontation he expected. He rubbed his sweaty hands over his khaki pants and tried to calm his erratic heart with a prayer. *God, I need some help here. You're the One who can give it. Please.*

Besides the crazy nervousness robbing his breath, he was a little bit annoyed, too. He'd floored it down here from Raleigh, thankful for the seventy mile per hour stretch on the 70 by-pass, only to find an empty, open garage. He'd dismissed the notion to go into town to look for her because he thought she'd be too exhausted to do anything but come home. He didn't want to miss her, so he camped out on her driveway. He'd been waiting for over an hour, and now was the time to get everything straightened out.

Was she seeing someone—and that thought made his stomach churn—he wanted to know? If she wasn't, he wanted… What did he want? He wanted to be with her. He was actually thinking about switching jobs and moving to Raleigh to be nearer her. He knew deep down what that meant. He loved her, and he had a hunch… No, he had more than a hunch if she had been speaking from her heart in the hospital room that she loved him, too. Get the feelings figured out first. Then see what comes next.

ဆာဆာလလ

"Payne, I wish you'd called first before you drove all the way from Raleigh." She closed the van door and walked over to him. "I'm really wiped out." She pulled the edges of her cotton sweater together to settle her nerves. Taffy stood wagging his tail at her heels, and Desi and Lucy wanted attention, too.

He scuffed his boot-covered foot against the concrete. "I hate talking on the phone."

"Yeah. I know that, for sure. You hate emailing, too, apparently." Weariness softened her pointed words. She gripped the bakery bag with shaking fingers.

Payne narrowed his eyes as an expression resembling embarrassment moved over his face. Clinching his jaw, he stretched his back to his full height and cleared his throat, resolve winning the battle of emotions. "I need to explain all about that, and I'm sorry you're tired. You're probably doing too much too soon. But I need to know the answer to my question. Are you seeing someone?"

Exhaustion fled as anger took its place. "I can't believe you're asking me that." She could hear the frustration rise in her voice.

Realizing her muffins were in danger of becoming crumbs in her death grip, she crammed the bag in her pocketbook. The fading light twinkled in the tears gathering in her eyes.

254

"I know you think it's none of my business—"

"It's not that it's none of your business. It's just that, that—" She broke off and stamped her foot. Her throat constricted. Her last words sounded thick and unnatural. How could she back away from the edge of complete breakdown?

Payne reached his hand toward her, but suddenly headlights zigzagged down the driveway. A car horn blared. Taffy added his bark to the cacophony. As the vehicle screeched onto the concrete pad, Ellen recognized the jeep.

"Blake!" Out of the corner of her eye, she caught Payne dropping his arm, slamming his hands in his pockets.

Blake burst out the door shouting, "We're having twins! We're having twins!" He bolted to Ellen, and grabbed her, swinging her around and around, exactly as when he'd told her about Callie's pregnancy. Ellen couldn't stop the tears now, letting them flow freely. The men could think she cried for happiness, and she did, but she cried for other reasons, too—for Payne's thinking that she could be involved with someone else and from sheer exhaustion.

"Oh, Blake. Thank God." She dropped her head onto his shoulder, her tears soaking his madras plaid shirt.

"From whom all blessings flow!" He laughed as he set her on the ground and startled as if seeing Payne for the first time. "Oh, hey, man. You were at the hospital."

"Uh-huh. You're… having twins." Payne's brows knitted, a stunned expression marking his face.

"Yeah. Isn't that the greatest news? We still can't believe it." He turned his gaze back to Ellen. "Come on now. Stop crying. We've made it to the happy time. The doc says everything's good. You'll have to give us pointers, Ellen. You're a pro."

"Uh, I don't know about that." She wiped her face with her hands, wishing for a tissue.

Blake glanced at his watch. "Hey, I need to get on home. Callie's probably there by now. We drove separately to the sonogram appointment. That's how we found out. Two babies showed up on the picture. Is that huge or what?" He pumped the air with both fists.

Ellen laughed. "That's huge, Blake. I'll call Callie soon, okay?"

He jogged back to his jeep and blew his horn all the way down the driveway. Ellen grinned at him and understood he'd be flying high in his joy for a long time to come.

"He's having twins...with somebody else."

She skewered him with a "well, duh" face. "Yeah. He's having twins with his wife, Callie."

Darkness settled down for the night, but the full moon peeking over the trees illuminated the parking pad in front of the garage. The soft glow didn't help her discern the puzzling look on Payne's face.

He scratched the side of his head. "I talked with him outside your hospital room. He said you and he went way back."

Ellen nodded, smiling at the thought of babies that might resemble an infant Blake. "Yes, we do. All the way back to my babysitting days."

He blinked twice, his eyes widening. "Babysitting days?"

"I used to baby sit Blake and his brothers. All of them are wonderful boys, but Blake's always been special."

"So Blake's married to someone else?"

Her brow furrowed. She shrugged her shoulders. "Of course. What is so difficult about that concept?" Her fatigue and Payne's silly questions summoned irritation, frustration. She rubbed her temples.

He rose on his toes and rocked back down on his heels. "The hospital wasn't the first time I'd seen him."

She shook her head. Where was he going with this talk about Blake? "Okay. So you'd seen him before."

"So the first time I ever saw him was the first time I came to your house with Hank." He paused and shifted his stance. "Do you remember what you were doing when we drove up?" He stopped, biting his lip.

Wrapping her hair behind her ear, she thought back to that horrible afternoon. She remembered how shocked she'd been, how angry and cold Payne had looked. Then a picture of Blake popped into her mind's eye. Blake had been there before Payne arrived. "I was talking to Blake."

Payne nodded, flexed his hands and stuffed them in his pockets.

That was the day he'd told her Callie was pregnant. He'd swung her around, hugged her, kissed her on her cheek... Her mouth dropped open. She stared wide-eyed at Payne.

He nodded again. "We arrived in the middle of it."

"You thought that... No, you didn't think that Blake and I, that we..." She couldn't finish the question. The idea was too ludicrous to say out loud.

"He hugged you. He kissed you. He made a date with you. I heard him." Payne pulled his hands from his pockets and settled them on his hips.

"For Pete's sake, Payne, he invited me to a family dinner to celebrate their pregnancy. It wasn't a date. I used to babysit him." In her frustration, she'd put her hands on her hips, too. They faced each other like opponents in a duel. They remained in this standoff for several moments—no one blinking, no one moving—until Payne chucked, and a sheepish smile curled the corners of his mouth.

He rubbed his chin. "I'm sorry I jumped to the wrong conclusion, but can you understand with those pictures in your mind how I might leap to that assumption?" His voice trembled with an emotion Ellen hesitated to name.

His explanation—crazy as it was—and his apology—as tender as it was—melted away her anger and frustration, but the fact that he could have forgotten how she felt in Galway still hurt.

"It's just hard to believe you'd think I could be interested in someone else after..." She clamped her mouth shut, saving herself just in time. She wasn't ready to profess anything or admit to anything either.

He leaned toward her. An urgent tone couched his words. "After what?"

Seething blood cells pulsed in her veins. She held her breath. If he wanted her to spell it out for him, he'd have to wait a long time. She pressed her lips together and set her jaw.

He hesitated and then took a deep breath. "Okay, Ellen. I

thought we had something special in Galway. That's one of the reasons I'm even in Raleigh talking with Hank, for Heaven's sake. But we hadn't communicated in weeks."

"And whose fault is that? I emailed you, but you never responded." The bottled-up hurt rose in her chest, threatening to spill out in newly-minted teardrops.

"Yes. Right. Let's don't forget those four measly emails."

Anger at his supercilious tone curled her hands into fists. "I told you I don't like to email. But measly or not, they were more than what you sent me."

Payne stepped one step toward her and searched her face. She remained in her spot, refusing to back down. He took another, only inches away from her. She shivered.

"Are you cold?"

"That's part of it." She opened her mouth to continue, but his arms wrapped around her before she could utter another word.

His left hand cupped the back of her head, and the other one pulled her closer. Arms encircling his waist, she leaned into him. Despite the long, hard wait, despite the confusion, disappointment, and misunderstandings, she was where she wanted to be. Fresh tears dampened the front of his navy Henley.

Leaning back, he brought his hand around and pushed her chin up with his thumb to receive his kiss, the one she'd been waiting for since Galway, full of tenderness, passion, promise, and hope.

She returned his kiss with all the pent up emotion she'd carried for over three months. Payne broke away but still held her crushed to him. "Ellen." He rested his forehead against her own. "I've wanted to kiss you since before I left Galway. It's been too long." He moved his chin on top of her head, stroking her hair. "I know you're exhausted. Let's go inside so that you can sit down. You probably need something to eat, too."

She nodded into his chest and let him guide her through the garage to the door leading into the mud-room. She squinted when he flipped on the bright lights. She ignored the chairs at the table and continued on into the family room. Bypassing the wall switches and lamps, she preferred the kitchen fixtures to fill the room with a muted warmth.

As she collapsed on the couch, fatigue descended on her shoulders like a warm shawl. She leaned her head against the full cushion and gazed at Payne with half closed, happy eyes, waiting for him to speak.

Chapter 34

"I can't believe we're finally alone." He faced her with his arm along the top of the couch, smiling. "You're always surrounded by people."

"Me? What about you? I'm surprised you could tear yourself away from that moonstruck grad student." She heard the jealousy coated on those words and watched Payne's tender smile turn into a satisfied grin. He leaned in toward her to cover her mouth with his.

He kissed her until she relaxed against him, leaving tiny kisses on her cheek, on her eyes, on her temple, near her ear. "I'd forgotten your jealous streak."

She attempted to object, but his mouth found hers again for a quick kiss. "She doesn't interest me, and I never led her on. You're the only one I want." He cupped her cheek in his hand.

She closed her eyes as his lips settled on hers for a third time.

Savoring the feel of his arms around her, she wanted to let the several months' worth of disappointment, confusion, and hurt dissolve in his smile, but she remembered she had questions—a whole lot of questions. If she could stop him from kissing her, maybe she could hear some answers.

Even as her arms wanted to remain holding him close to her, she forced them to push against his shoulders. He scowled and loosened his hold.

She pulled her hair back from her face. "Payne, I can't keep kissing you like this. I've got some questions. You've got to clear up some things. And Euri's going to be home in a little while."

"Oh, Euri. Your exchange student." He traced a finger down the length of her arm, stopping at her wrist to play with her gold bangle bracelet. "We met when we were breaking down your booth after your accident. And that proves my original statement—you're never alone."

Ellen grimaced. "I don't understand why you keep saying that. I'm alone plenty. Believe me."

"All right. Let me describe one day to you. Think about Founders' Day just before your accident."

"Okay." She let him take her hand in his.

"You saw me just before that pole crashed down on top of your head, didn't you?"

She nodded. "I thought I was seeing things." The picture of him walking toward her popped in her mind, but the circles he drew in her palm wrecked her concentration.

"Well, until our eyes met, I was almost ready to turn and go back home. Your tent crawled with people. Scott and Laurel, of course. A couple of women digging through the yarns. Blake lounged by the back corner. And another man was there, too, wearing a bracelet and eating a hot dog."

"You noticed his bracelet?"

He wrinkled his nose. "Not a fan."

She laughed. "That was Dr. Meadows. You know, I wondered why he was there when I caught a glance of him. We'd talked earlier in the morning. I don't know why he came back."

He snorted. "I have a pretty good idea why judging by his actions after you were hurt. He pretty much took over for Scott and Laurel. He was the one who called 911 and kept people back away from you… He seemed very protective of you." He frowned. "Not a happy memory."

"Now who sounds jealous?" She teased.

Payne growled and leaned toward her again, but she pushed against his hard chest. "No, Payne. No more kisses until you explain some things."

"I thought you liked my kisses." He tried to pout, but his eyes sparkled with an inner light.

Ellen grabbed a throw pillow to hold onto. She wanted

to kiss him as much as he seemed to want to kiss her, but she couldn't let him until he explained what happened between Galway and showing up in her driveway. "Payne, you are just too handsome for your own good. Now—"

He grabbed her, pulling her toward him. "You think I'm handsome?" His grin teased her and tugged at her heart.

"Payne, I'm serious. Stop it. I mean it. You have to talk to me and not about silly stuff." She straightened on the couch and smoothed her skirt. "Why didn't you return my emails? Why didn't you pick up the phone and say, 'Oh, by the way, I'm coming down to Raleigh? Want to meet for dinner while I'm in your neck of the woods?'" Jutting her chin, she folded her arms in front of her, determined to hear answers.

"I did call. I left three messages." He moved the pillow from her lap. "You're a hard one to get up with." He leaned toward her, but her hand against his chest stopped him.

At her tilted head and raised eyebrow, he sighed. "You're right. I do owe you an explanation, but some of my reasons seem silly now even to me." He rubbed his eyes with his hand, leaned back into the cushions, stretching out his long legs.

"Just talk to me, Payne." Uncrossing her arms, she claimed his hand, remembering another time they sat like this on a back porch in Galway.

He squeezed her hand. "I ended up staying in Africa two weeks into September. We experienced a few problems right at the end of the project. I finally rolled up at the airport with only minutes to spare before my flight out of the country left. So the first time I got to look at my emails was while I was sitting in the plane out on the tarmac.

"Your first email was great. Long and chatty. I felt like we were back in Galway, and you were flirting with me over a cup of tea. But then each one got shorter…and shorter…and shorter. The last one was what, three sentences maybe?"

She threaded her fingers through his, thinking about how she'd struggled with every sentence.

"I sat waiting for takeoff trying to figure out what the problem might be. I remembered you wondering if what we shared was just a flirtation or a distraction. I started to wonder a little bit, too. Our time together seemed like a dream. I hadn't seen you in over a month and a half, and your messages dwindled every time you wrote."

He dragged his hand through his hair. "So here's the funny part. I'm sitting in my seat, right? Trying to decide how to respond because it's my first email to you, you know? I'm staring at the screen when all of a sudden the toddler who's in the seat next to me drops her sippy cup right on top of my keyboard."

Ellen gasped and laid her free hand on his knee.

"The top that's supposed to be toddler-proof, or spill-proof, or whatever? Somehow it was loose and let about four ounces of apple juice drench my lap top." He dragged his top lip between his teeth.

"Oh no, Payne. What happened?" Ellen's eyes widened with shock.

"The mother grabbed the cup, of course, but she didn't have anything to mop up the juice, not that it would have made any difference. I thought she might burst into tears. Her daughter did cry, wailing actually because she'd lost all of her juice."

"So what happened to your laptop?" Ellen hated to imagine the damage.

"It was pretty much done. The screen went immediately blank, and actual smoke started rising up out of the keys. It kind of sounded like a bowl of rice krispies dancing in milk. I was so frustrated it was all I could do not to break something, but I tried to be cool so that the mother could calm down. You can probably guess we had a miserable flight." He swiped his face with his hands.

"Anyway, it took me two days to get home, then I just crashed for two more. By the time I got to my department to use the computers there, I was even more gun shy about writing you. You hadn't sent another email, and it had been over two weeks since your last one. It was easy to question all my sweet memories from Galway."

"Sweet memories?"

His warm smile tingled all the way to her toes. "They're

sweet to me. How about you?"

"Uh-huh."

He studied her face as he pushed a tendril of hair behind her ear. "I have an email to you in my drafts box, but I've been too chicken to send it. Writing unless it's for work is not my strong suit. I don't enjoy writing for pleasure, and I don't pick up the phone to chat either. I'll talk to people who call me, but I usually don't initiate conversations, especially over the phone."

A loud, strong laugh burst out of Ellen's mouth, defying her fatigue. She jabbed his shoulder. "Payne, you were the one who started talking with me that first time, remember?"

"I remember. That should tell you something, don't you think? You were the one who said it might be a divine appointment that day."

Surprise that he remembered her words from their first meeting brought her up short. "Are you saying you might agree with me now?" Suddenly serious once more, she studied his face, hoping to see... To see what? Hoping to see seriousness reflected in his eyes, too. Hoping he wouldn't tease her about something so important to her.

"I know that the whole time I was in Africa, I thought about you. I couldn't get you out of my mind. Your gentle words about God and blessings and truth and prayer kept replaying in my mind." He stroked her cheek.

"I told you that I asked for God's peace on your back porch glider in Galway, and He graciously gave it to me right then. It took me a while to process all my feelings from that night and from the church service with Charlie and Kate." He hesitated and brought his gaze to hers. "That night was really special to me. I hadn't opened up to anyone in decades, and it felt good. It felt good to talk with God, too... And in the mix of all those emotions were my feelings for you." He pressed his palm against hers.

"I had a lot of time to think in Africa. God helped me get everything sorted out. You gave me a glimpse of what I'd been missing, and I don't mean the stuff between us, although that's true." His tiny smile tugged at her heart, reminding her of his playful side.

"I mean you helped me remember what it feels like to be close to God. I knew I wanted that again, so I surrendered everything to him in Uganda. Just me, God, and a million stars one beautiful night in Africa.

"I want to follow His will for me, whatever that is." He shrugged. "So while I was still struggling to write you a stupid email and finish up my articles from my project, Hank called with his proposition to come to NC State. At that time, I didn't know exactly where you were in North Carolina, but I figured being in Carolina would be closer than being in Maryland.

"I googled your address right after he hung up. Finding out you live less than an hour from Raleigh brightened my day. I should have planned a strategy to let you in on all of this, but I didn't."

"You think?"

He pulled her to his chest and closed his eyes. "The first day I visited his office was the day we drove to your farm. Hank told you that I didn't know we were driving to your house until we were about a mile away. I couldn't believe it. I couldn't believe I found you in the arms of another man either."

She squirmed out of his embrace to tease him, but a close look in his face revealed that the memory still pained him. "Payne, you know Blake's hug was just a friendly, share-my-joyous news kind of hug." She grabbed his hand again and kissed it.

"I do now, but I didn't for—how many weeks? It was hard. I started to second guess everything about us. Thank goodness for your little concussion."

She stopped stroking his fingers. "What do you mean?"

"I'd still be second guessing if you hadn't shared your real feelings with me in the hospital."

"I don't know what you're talking about." Ellen's heart beat pummeled as if she had just run a cross country meet in record time. So, she *had* said something during their night together in the hospital. But, what? Confusion and apprehension knitted her brow.

Payne cocked his head, revealing a slow grin. "That's when you told me that you had fallen in love with me." He finished those words with a full-fledged grin, his eyes pinned on her open mouth. "But that's good because I fell in love with you, too."

She caught her breath. "You fell in love with me?"

"Uh, huh."

She waited for him to continue, but he remained silent. She acknowledged this as a pivotal point in her life. She could either keep waiting, or she could forge ahead toward something she wanted. She could steer her life onto the path God cleared for her. "So where do we go from here?"

"Where do you want to go?" His eyes seemed to be searching her soul.

She didn't flinch from his intense gaze and decided on truth. "Anywhere you are."

She welcomed his embrace this time and didn't push him away as he leaned over and reached for her.

ဆာဆာလလ

Euri came home a half hour later, and sang out, "Hello, Momma Ellen. I am home now." She jumped when Payne, standing at the island, shushed her. "Oh, Mista Payne. You scared me so bad."

"Sorry, Euri. Ellen is taking a little nap on the couch, and I'm cooking up some omelets. What would you like in yours?" Payne pushed the chopped onions onto a plate with the sliced mushrooms.

"I'm awake now," Ellen called from the family room. "Euri, did you have a good day?" She joined them in the kitchen.

"Yes. Cuisine Club ate at Jack's Burger Palace for supper, and Robin brought me home. Mista Jack make the best burgers. I had bacon and cheese on mine, and I so full." She patted her mid-drift. "Thank you, Mista Payne, but no more food now. I get so fat. I need new jeans." She tugged at her snug waistband.

Ellen laughed and climbed onto the stool at the bar. "It's all those French fries and cheeseburgers. Are you going to start on your homework now?" Ellen watched Euri pad in her socks toward the stairs.

"Yeah. See ya."

Ellen swiveled back to Payne. "She's learning some of the teen slang. I'm not sure that's good." Leaning her head in her hand, she watched Payne crack the eggs into a glass bowl. "I can't believe you're cooking your first meal in my house."

First meal. He lightened at the sound of those words. "It's the least I can do. You're still recovering. Anyway, you're cooking for me at Thanksgiving, right?" His eyes focused on scrambling the eggs, he wanted to kick himself for allowing that question out of his mouth. He'd wanted her to bring up Thanksgiving first.

"I am if you're still coming."

He grinned, relieved. "Just wanted to make sure the invitation was still on the table. What can I bring?"

"How about your banjo?"

Payne raised his eyebrows then laughed. "No problem."

Chapter 35

The next few weeks before Thanksgiving disappeared as quickly as the falling leaves on her crape myrtles. She saw Payne almost every day. During the week, she either traveled to Raleigh for lunch with him, or he drove to Bandon for dinner. Weekends were gifts because they spent whole days together. Their time together passed with lightning speed while the time apart dragged like a frazzled teacher's last few days before summer break.

Still, every day was new with him. Charming, attentive, funny, and kind, he never visited without bringing some kind of gift—a potted lavender mum or a perfect red maple leaf. Once he surprised her with a small basket of Winesap apples, her favorite variety. Another cool gift was an arrowhead he'd found on her farm when he and Kip had conducted soil samples. She laughed out loud the day he brought a small cooler full of still-frozen paletas, mango chili and Mexican chocolate with a couple of new flavors to try.

When she'd protested that he didn't have to bring a gift every time he came to see her, he cocked his head, smiling. "I'm courting you." And he pulled her to him.

"Courting me?" She chuckled with arched eyebrows and slid her hands up his arms.

"Hmm mmm." His lips grazed the sensitive spot near her ear. "I thought you'd like that word."

"I do like it, but I like you better." She threaded her fingers behind his neck. "So this is how you court women?"

He shrugged. "I don't know. I've never courted a woman before." He bent his head and whispered beside her ear. "This is

269

how I'm courting you."

Tingles from his warm breath rendered her speechless for a moment. Before she could think of a reply, Payne's head swooped down, his mouth covering hers.

Ellen's happiness with Payne magnified as her children warmed to him. Payne's positive presence during the night spent in the hospital helped Scott and especially Laurel accept his closeness with their mother. Their genuine affection for him grew as they shared a few weekend dinners together.

Olivia kept tabs through phone calls and chatted with Payne a few times. Ellen enjoyed the light banter between the two of them. The tiny seed of grudging acceptance of Payne in her mother's life that had begun in Galway was growing into true affection. Olivia admitted to Ellen that she was happy to hear joy and excitement in her voice again.

Ellen did feel joy and excitement with Payne. The only time she felt unsure or even a little apprehensive was if she allowed herself to think about the future. Whenever a question about what might happen popped into her mind, she forced it out. If anyone in town or at church wondered out loud about her relationship with her "handsome beau," as Miss Myrtle called him, she made a droll remark and quickly changed the subject.

She didn't want to borrow trouble by what might or might not happen. She thanked God for every minute with Payne and tried to live in the present, not in the what-ifs.

ഇൻഇൻൽൽ

At 7:00 on Thanksgiving morning, Ellen slid the turkey in the oven as she heard a rap on the back door. She turned to see Payne smiling at her through the window. She ran to open the door.

"I can't believe you're here this early, but I'm so glad you are." She maneuvered around his banjo case and leaned close to kiss him.

"I wanted to be the first one to wish you Happy Thanksgiving. So Happy Thanksgiving, Ellen." He pulled her to him with his free hand and added a kiss to his greeting. "You wouldn't let me bring anything besides this," gesturing toward the banjo case, "so I'm here early to help. What do you need me to do?"

∞∞೧೩೩

With his leftovers carefully packed into recycled sour cream cups and placed in a cardboard box, Uncle Joe left late in the afternoon, the last of the guests to go. Scott pulled the Tupperware rectangle with the sliced turkey out of the refrigerator to make a sandwich.

"How can you even think about eating again, Scott? I'm still stuffed." Ellen could never quite believe how much food her son consumed.

"I've been waiting all week for a leftover turkey sandwich. Can't a man eat in his own house? Help me out here, Payne. Don't you want one, too?" Scott spread a glob of light mayonnaise over a slice of whole wheat bread.

"As good as that turkey is, I still can't take another bite yet. Maybe later. Hey." He glanced at Ellen. "You want to go outside and get some fresh air?"

"I might have just enough energy left to breathe in some fresh air. That sounds good."

"Don't stay out too long. We have to watch *It's a Wonderful Life*, remember?" Laurel searched the book shelves for the DVD that always began their holiday season.

Ellen hid a yawn behind her hand. "Don't worry. I call the couch. I can't wait to stretch out on it and vegetate for a while. We'll be back in a few minutes."

Payne grabbed her barn jacket from the hall coat tree and wrapped it around her shoulders. As they descended the front steps, Taffy bounded up the walkway for some attention. Payne stopped to scratch behind the dogs ears. "I enjoyed today. Thanks for inviting me."

"It was a good day. Thanks for coming." She pulled the collar together at the base of her throat. The day had been more than good. It had been special. Payne had lived true to his offer to help. He'd peeled potatoes, helped set the tables, and stirred the gravy.

When her usual panic arrived a few minutes before the first guests, he caught her in the middle of double and triple checking the pots and casseroles, hugging her with a whisper of "everything's fine" beside her ear. Then he smiled at her, and she believed him.

She clutched his coat sleeve. "You were such a help today. Thank you for keeping me sane. And you were a trooper fielding all those questions about us." She plucked at his sleeve. "Everyone loved your banjo playing, too. Banjos and pianos don't sound too bad together, do they?" She laughed as she remembered Laurel and Payne's duet during the sing-a-long. "*Peace Like a River* was the favorite, I think."

"Yeah, ahmm, Laurel's a good sport." He licked his lips and rubbed his jaw, glancing back at the house.

Suddenly, a light in her foggy brain switched on. She realized Payne had looked at the dog, at the house, in the front yard—everywhere but at her. Something was wrong, but before she could form the question stuck in her chest, he cleared his throat.

"Ellen." He pushed his hands into his pockets and let out a long, hard breath as he dragged his eyes to hers.

Something was going on, and Ellen couldn't quite figure it out. She dropped her hand from his arm. Old, familiar doubts struggled against the pictures of him in her kitchen, standing at the stove, laughing with Uncle Joe. He'd been a perfect guest today. Was that all? Was he making good on his Thanksgiving promise and now he was ready to say bye?

That couldn't be right. That wouldn't make sense. But why did he look so desperate? Something fluttered in the front window, but she kept her attention on Payne.

He squared his shoulders and zeroed in on her face. "Ah, Ellen. These past few weeks and the time we spent in Galway have probably been...have probably been the best time I've ever had." He shook his head. "No...they've been the best."

Everything sounded good so far, but what was making him

stammer like a school boy?

"It sounds like a 'but' is coming up." Ellen forced a laugh out of her constricting throat, but the sound had more of a shaky quality than a lighthearted lilt.

Payne cupped her face in his hands and shook his head, eyes blazing steel sparks. "No! No 'but.' 'And.' This has been the best time, *and* I want it to continue. But I want more, Ellen. I hate when we have to say 'goodbye' every day. Either I leave you here with Euri, or you leave me by myself in Raleigh or College Park." He released her cheek and grabbed her left hand, freeing her coat of her vice-like grip.

Her breath stopped in her throat as he kneeled in front of her when she realized what he planned to do. "Ellen, you make me happy. I love being with you. I love you. I want to marry you. Will you marry me?" He held a beautiful silver diamond ring in his free hand. Three diamonds, surrounded by delicate filigree work, reminded her of antique rings she'd always admired at estate sales.

"It was my grandmother's engagement ring. My mother gave it to me two weeks ago when I went up to Virginia for the day. I told you I wanted to check on my parents which is true, but I also wanted to get this." He wiggled the ring, sparkling in the light from the windows. "They're looking forward to meeting you, by the way." His solemn face showed hope and a little apprehension at the same time.

She tried to speak, but again something flittered in the edge of her peripheral vision. This time she turned her gaze toward it. Scott, Euri, and Laurel crowded together in the living room window. Laurel held her cell phone against her ear.

Payne followed her gaze. "It's looks like we have an audience."

Ellen looked back at him, and he saw the question in her eyes. "I've talked with all three of them. Yes." He nodded. "Even Olivia. They gave me permission to ask you. I think they're really okay with the idea."

Ellen glanced back at the window. Scott and Euri grinned at her and waved. Laurel blew a kiss to her.

"Hey." He shifted his position. "I don't mean to be pushy, but this concrete is killing my knee. You're kind of leaving me hanging here." He tugged her hand gently. "Ellen, will you marry me? Please say 'yes' and save my aching knee—and me, too."

Payne's humor was all she needed to come out of the fog that had kept her silent for the past few moments. Ellen giggled, pulling him to his feet. "Oh, Payne. Yes. Yes, yes, yes! I want to marry you, too." Payne slipped the ring on her third finger, yelled, "She said, 'yes!'" toward the window, and scooped her up into a massive bear hug. Ellen could hear the shouts and claps from inside the window, but she had eyes only for Payne. He set her on the sidewalk keeping his arms around her waist as he finished his proposal. "I know we have a lot of details to work out—before and after the wedding too, but I think I know the perfect place for our honeymoon."

She looked into his crinkling, gray eyes, immediately realizing the location he had in mind. "I'm thinking Galway City might be the perfect place. Is that what you're thinking?"

He grinned at her, "Always," and sealed their agreement with a tender kiss.